Other books in the Saddleworth Vampire Series

Sticky Valves

SILVER BANNED

BOOK TWO OF THE SADDLEWORTH VAMPIRE SERIES

Silver Banned by Angela Blythe
Book 2 of the Saddleworth Vampire Series.

First Edition.

Please contact me for details of future books at
http://www.angelablythe.com

Published by Willow Publishers.

Cover Illustration and Design Copyright © 2017 by Dark Grail
https://www.etsy.com/uk/shop/DarkGrail

Contents

Prologue _____ *8*

1 – Ripe _____ *11*

2 – May _____ *30*

3 – Owl _____ *32*

4 – June _____ *40*

5 – Beehive _____ *44*

6 – Blueish-Grey _____ *62*

7 – July _____ *74*

8 – Marbles _____ *76*

9 – August _____ *84*

10 – Camera _____ *90*

11 – September _____ *103*

12 – Metal Mickey _____ *106*

14 – Hogwash _____ *124*

15 – Kebab _____ *130*

16 – Wrong 'Un _____ *141*

17 – Succulent _____ *157*

18 – Shopping Bag _____ *168*

19 – Dentist _____ *176*

20 – Fang _____ *189*

21 – Antibiotic _____ *194*

22 – Snowmobile _____ 202

23 – Poison _____ 212

24 – Swede _____ 221

25 – Message _____ 236

26 – Trap _____ 243

27 – Flugelhorn _____ 249

28 – Parkin _____ 258

29 – Virgins _____ 267

30 – Meat _____ 285

31 – Chunk _____ 299

32 – Carol _____ 314

33 – The Return _____ 327

34 – Cowboy Boots _____ 355

35 – Masculine _____ 371

36 – Tracks _____ 399

Silver Banned

Prologue

Friday 18th November

I have decided to throw another *secret* blood party. This time for the scourge that call themselves The Villagers. I have not had very much success in turning their Council Workers. But enough have *come round to my way of thinking*, to be useful. By hook or by crook, shall we say? Better luck with the villagers, I hope. If not, it is their loss and my delectable gain. I will destroy and then remake this village before I am finished, or my name isn't Morgan! My invasion has not had enough impact for my liking. Where's the chaos? The screaming? The rivers of blood? Heck, where's the love? Off for my dinner of raw ribs and a bowl of steamy gore. Got to keep my strength up.

Saturday 19th November

I had the luscious party. It was a success. I had a good time myself (strange in the presence of so many that are not worthy!) and think I made some friends. I found a particularly good acolyte named Sarah, who I turned immediately after blood preparation. As I was lonely without my brothers and other little playmates. She will prove very useful to me. I toyed with keeping her a day-walker as she is influential in the community. But I have a few of those already don't I? Haha! As her wound that I made was very deep, I ran her a lovely bath of blood, for rejuvenation. She is sleeping peacefully now. I am off to lick the bath of its remaining drops of blood. Yummy!

Wednesday 23rd November.

I instructed my children to block off the mountain roads with their trucks. The snow will do the rest. If they haven't got out before now, they are mine. From previous experiences (bad ones), I have decided to ban all forms of silver metal in Melden. I have sent my children and a day-walker out to each and every shop to buy anything that could be used against us. Of course, there will be many pieces of jewellery in houses, but it is a start.

If people don't have it at the beginning, they won't get it now! There are a few plants to be wary of, wolfsbane being the main one. Of course there are others, but I don't expect anyone to be intelligent enough to work it out! If they can't work out what I am, they will never find rare plants in the snow. I think I might be safe. A cheery happening today! I found a lovely skull inside one of my failed turnings. It always pays me to look inside afterwards and see what I can find. Tonight I will clean, bleach and mount it in my room. I like a craft project better than most people. This will look so pretty.

1 – Ripe

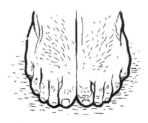

Freddie was shocked at what Brenda had just shouted from the kitchen. Surely Melden wasn't in the same state as Friarmere?

'Brenda can you hurry up with that brew!' Shouted Freddie.

The rest of the party looked around at each other. They were worried, anxious and in disbelief. Brenda continued to clatter about in the kitchen but remained silent. As they were all intrigued by her comments and wanted to learn more, Laura and Sue took it upon themselves to help her. The other guests heard Brenda protest, but Sue explained to her that they needed to talk urgently, so they had to prepare the tea quickly.

Wee Renee started to wander around Our Doris's living room. She rubbed the fabric of the heavy lined curtains between her finger and thumb.

'These curtains are worth a few bob,' she remarked.

'She has some beautiful figurines as well,' Pat added, and sniffed in appreciation.

Our Doris's living room was a large rectangle shape with an enormous bay window at one end and double glass doors to the kitchen at the other. There was the entrance to the hall to one side. Above the fireplace, a picture of Our Doris and her husband obviously taken some time ago from the fashion of the clothes, dominated the room. She had two large comfortable four-seater and three-seater matching sofas and two upholstered pouffes to compliment the set.

Freddie sat down at the end of one of the sofas, chuckled and said 'Ere, watch this.' He reclined his seat back, and the foot area of the sofa rose as well. Freddie raised his eyebrows, put his hands behind his head and closed his eyes.

There was still plenty of noise coming from the kitchen. Brenda was getting all the cups out, and Our Doris's dog seemed to have chosen that time to ask for his dinner. Pat said she would like to use the toilet and Freddie told her that there was one downstairs next to where you could hang your coat. Pat went out of the room and Wee Renee walked over to the hall door and watched Pat.

'What's wrong?' asked Gary.

'Shhhh!' she replied abruptly. She put a finger up into the air and they watched her with interest. 'Bide a wee.......bide a wee. Okay.'

Wee Renee watched her shut the toilet door. She turned to the group.

'Oi, listen you lot.' She was interrupted by Brenda, Laura and Sue returning with two trays containing teapots, various cups and saucers, and plates with sandwiches and cakes on them. They were all very happy to see the feast. Brenda announced, as she entered, that there was plenty more where that came from.

'What were you going to say, Wee Renee? Shouldn't we wait for Pat?' Asked Gary.

'No,' she said, 'it is about her.'

They were quite perplexed knowing that Wee Renee was Pats best friend.

'Listen,' she spoke quietly and glanced towards the door all the time as she addressed them. 'When Pat takes off her boots, there will be an almighty smell. You wouldn't give it credence. No one say anything. She doesn't look like she gets offended, but she does. I know. I made the mistake of bringing it up one time. Just be prepared that that's what's going to happen.'

Bob laughed and Tony grabbed a sandwich stuffing it into his mouth.

'I'd better eat these up then before they start to curl,' he said through a mouthful of mushed up bread and ham.

'Right, and she wouldn't take kindly to jokes about it either. Let's just say that.' Wee Renee looked around for a moment in silence. Freddie was already wrinkling his nose as if he could smell her feet.

'Be thankful it isn't summer, when she is wearing no tights and plastic shoes.' She shook her head at the thought of it.

'I am going to sit down on the carpet over here with Bob then,' Tony said, moving to the opposite side of the room. No one else said anything, but gazed at the tea and cakes, waiting for the horror that would soon envelop them.

'I just wish she would hurry up. Smelly feet or not. I want to know what's been going on here,' muttered Freddie.

'Come on. Have this tea, cakes and sandwiches everybody, whilst we are waiting,' Brenda said, frowning at them.

'I think I'll hang my coat up, so I can enjoy it better,' Sue said.

'Oh yes,' Liz agreed. Some of them took off their coats and went into the hall, just to come back with them in their hands.

'Yes, yes. There won't be enough pegs for everyone will there.' Brenda commented, she looked to one side thinking. 'I tell you what, put them in a pile in the corner with your boots and bags.

Pat returned and sat down coughing and puffing. She flopped herself down on the sofa next to Wee Renee and then seemed to have a thought, as she watched the others discarding their outer garments in the corner. She bent over, grasping one of her boots by the foot and started to tug at it. She then dropped the foot and looked at the men.

'Is no one going to give a lady a hand?' she asked.

All the men looked around at each other. No one seemed to want to move. Then, when it was just getting awkward, Gary threw his shoulders back as if to gain courage and nudged Danny. 'Come on Danny, let's grab one each.'

Approaching Pat slowly, they both grasped a boot, each pulling hard in the opposite direction and yanked as quickly as they could. Pat slipped halfway down the sofa, but didn't say a word. The smell was indeed very ripe and instantly found all their noses. Pat adjusted herself on the sofa, smiled down at her feet and wriggled her toes.

'That's a blessed relief. Thanks chucks.' Pat said. Danny and Gary took each boot and pushed it down at the back of the pile of outdoor clothes, underneath everything else.

'Are you going to put some of those boots in the garage to keep the carpet clean?' Brenda asked knowingly. Everyone agreed very enthusiastically and Wee Renee looked down into her tea for a long time, before taking a sip of it. Pat had no idea that they were on about her boots in particular.

They drank tea, ate sandwiches and feasted upon cake hungrily, as their stories unfolded.

'Well then, what has been going on Freddie?' Brenda asked.

'Sorry love, I was just having a minute to catch my breath and have a tiny bit of comfort,' replied Freddie.

'There have been physical violations in Friarmere. That is what's been happening!' Exclaimed Wee Renee putting her hand on Brenda's knee.

'What! Sexual assault? Rape?' Brenda was horrified.

'No, not that kind of physical violation. A violation of their physicality, their blood. They have been violated by an evil host.'

'I don't understand,' said Brenda. 'Whose body? What evil host?'

'Bloody Nora.' said Pat. 'Rene, start from the beginning or she'll never get it. We have to tell how it started. That is just as important as how it ended.'

'Okay,' said Freddie, 'it started with a party at The Grange on Bonfire Night and the band were booked to play.'

'It sounds like a party Our Doris went to.' Brenda muttered.

'There was food and drink and fireworks and all that, but it seems from what we can gather, that the food and wine was infected somehow.'

'There was this man named Norman.' Liz continued. 'I was infected. The entire band there was infected. After that party, he came to them one by one and made them into what we now know…… as vampires.'

Brenda was going quite grey. She held her cup in front of her mid-way between the saucer and her mouth. Her eyes went from one to another as if to say it was a joke, waiting for the first person to break the tension by laughing.

Liz's voice broke with the promise of tears.

'I was really sick and I didn't want to eat normal food. I also wanted to eat meat, which I don't do, as I'm a vegetarian. I am still. I made sure people were with me the whole time, so that he couldn't get to me. It was a few days until we realised what was going on.' Liz lost her battle with her tears and they started to fall. Andy put his arm around her. Freddie passed over a box of tissues that had been on the table next to him.

'A ten piece band originally went, with one committee member.' Freddie met Brenda's eyes. 'I was lucky that wasn't me. One by one they stopped coming to Band as they were turned into vampires.' He gave a little chuckle. 'Once they were undead, they seemed to feel healthier. For instance, Maurice is one.'

'No!' Brenda gasped.

'Yes. He was one of the ten-piece. The following week he could not stand the smell of garlic in the band room.'

'Is that all?' laughed Brenda. 'I think it takes a bit more than that to be considered a Vampire, Freddie.'

'Oh, right, I'll throw in that he doesn't need his glasses anymore and he doesn't need his bloody stick. He stopped coming to Band and he stopped coming to the pub. But as far as we know he isn't on the offensive, so it seems. One by one people disappeared or showed weird symptoms. All the people who had been there on Bonfire Night, ended up getting infected like this. After a few of them, we started working it out because obviously it is a little farfetched. It isn't the first thing that comes to mind.'

'No, it isn't the obvious choice,' Laura added.

'Me and Bob knew it first,' said Wee Renee. 'We are both very open-minded. But it didn't take long before we all started putting two and two together. They were dropping like flies at Band. But the day it really hit home was when we found Ian.'

'Butcher Ian?' asked Brenda.

'Yes. Sadly he has expired, Brenda. We found him one Saturday afternoon in his own shop, hung up like a piece of meat on a hook. All his entrails were hanging out and someone had been biting them.' Wee Renee replied.

"Ewww...No!' screeched Brenda.

'Don't forget the pool of blood at the bottom.' said Andy.

'Oh, yes, a pool of blood had leaked out and you could see where someone had been lapping at it. Like a cat drinking cream.' Freddie waited to see Brenda's expression, before he gave the next titbit. He was rewarded with a combined look of terror and revulsion.

'And blow me who was behind him dead as a dodo! Aidy!'

Brenda gasped. Wee Renee took up the story as Freddie drank his tea.

'Adrian who had obviously been turned into one previously, was green inside. Green!'

'And when I poked him with a metal rod he felt weird,' said Bob.

'Yes the texture of them certainly changes, Brenda,' Freddie explained. 'They are quite soft. The thing is, we couldn't get help because the landlines and Mobile networks are down because of the snow. Incessant snow came, cutting us off. We were on our own Brenda. We had few choices. We decided that we would make a stand at the Christmas Concert, as we knew they were planning something. But their plans amounted to a bit more than we could cope with. We lost some people.'

Several people were looking at the plates in their laps. This telling of the facts was very hard for them. Andy was chewing a cuticle. Laura stood up and wandered over to the window, clutching the hem of her sweater tightly. She opened one of the curtains, looked out, then turned her back to the window, crossed her arms tightly in defence across her body. Laura looked at the fire. In her mind she returned to the battle. All the heartache, the fear, the futility of that night, was with her in the room.

'We haven't had to kill anyone that we loved,' said Sue, 'it would be terrible if you had to do that.'

'You have to do what you have to do. We have had to work at the base level, a primordial state. You never know what you are capable of until you have to fight for your life and do things that no human being should have to do to another. But that is what we have done. It is the sole reason why we are still sitting here and I am not one of them.' Said Wee Renee

'I don't know how any of us got out alive, Brenda. There were kids that were already vampires in the choir. Kids! When we actually saw them eating and killing right before us, we couldn't believe our eyes. Their parents too. The infection was much more widespread that we had anticipated by then. He had obviously been branching out into the village. Ruining Friarmere Band wasn't good enough. We had to kill some of our friends. Even the Coopers have been turned!' Freddie stated.

'No!' cried Brenda.

20

'Yes. This is all we think is left of the band. We had to hide out overnight in the bandroom. The next day we tried to make it out over towards Manchester but they had put a bus in the way and the drifts had made it impossible to get either side of it. We walked over to the viaduct. Guess what, they had done the same there. When we walked back to the centre of the village, Michael Thompson was standing there in broad daylight obviously not one of them. Git!' Freddie shook his head. The thought was still very bitter to him.

'I think he is infected like me.' Liz said. 'You see, he was the committee member that went with the ten-piece on Bonfire Night.'

'He told us in no uncertain terms that they were going to kill us off that night, so we had a quick bite in the pub and decided to try and make it over here. We picked up some camping stuff, so to speak, and hiked up onto the tops. It was dark by then but luckily we had a bolt hole. We went into a little den that Bob uses and camped there for the night.' Freddie took another sip of his tea.

'A whole night and day in the Melden Triangle! We were protected though, I made sure of that.' Wee Renee said, looking towards the heavens. Gary cleared his throat.

'I will let you all into our secret now. Me and Wee Renee heard the wolves in the middle of the night.' Gary said quietly. 'I didn't want to tell you before in case we needed to spend another night there.'

'So what's this about these wolves then?' Asked Brenda. 'What to do *you* know about them?'

'Well between either them or the vampires they destroyed a whole flock of sheep at the farm on the tops, because the farmer heard the wolves howling from his bedroom at night. The next day, they were just bits and pieces of blood and wool. He had his head in his hands when we saw him in the pub. Devastated. The police won't do anything about it, because the two policemen are now vampires too! We needed to come here to find help. The last thing we thought was that we would be walking into more trouble.' Gary laughed at the end. 'Oh the irony.'

Brenda held her cup in the same position still, her mouth open. She turned to Liz.

'So you are in fact infected with vampire blood?' She asked her.

'Yes, I have been poorly but don't worry about me biting you or anything. It's not like that. I feel slightly better each day. I have had to come most of the way here on the sledge,' Liz answered. Brenda now turned her head to Freddie.

'And Maurice and the Cooper's and the rest of the band are vampires and are roaming around our village killing people?' She asked Freddie.

'Yes.' he said. 'I can't be sure that Maurice is a killer though. But other people and loads of kids were. Which is very scary indeed, when you clap eyes on them.'

'We don't know who is dead and who is alive. in the village. Or who is living on human blood, because some have been eating dog's and cat's as well.' Wee Renee said.

'I was really scared for my three kitty's.' Sue said, taking hold of Tony's hand.

Brenda put her cup down finally, placing both hands on her knees and looked around the group waiting to see what reaction she would get with her next question.

'Tell me this doesn't mean, what I think it means. That my sister Doris, is a vampire lying in her bed upstairs?'

'From what you have said,' said Gary, 'it sounds like she could be, I am sorry to say. Or something like it. As much as Liz is anyway. But we can't be sure until we hear her story and know all the facts. We need to know what happened at, and after the party she went to. Tell us about her.'

'She's fast asleep right now and I am glad that she is. Yes, she certainly has been unwell and does not want the curtains open.' Brenda gave a half-shrug, 'which I suppose is a bad sign. But definitely she has had no other visitors, only family. And we are all wandering around in the daytime, so none of the family can be one. Her windows are shut because it is so cold, so one of them hasn't floated in and got to her. Or would that be a bat? Plus she hasn't tried to bite me, which is a good sign.'

The others nodded as they ate and drank. For a while they sat in reflection of the past, and uncertainty of the future.

Norman had asked Michael to attend to a couple of the vampire's injuries from the previous night's battle. Kate, Keith, Norman and a few of the other vampires looked on. After all, it was something to do of an evening.

Colin wandered droopily up to him. He seemed very unhappy about the drumstick that was protruding out of his chest. None of the vampires would help him out by giving a yank.

'Why can't you do this yourself?' Michael asked.

'It burns me when I touch it!'

'Hmm.....it burns but it hasn't killed you! Very interesting.' Michael grasped hold of it, giving it a gentle tug. The stick came out, with barely any resistance. It reminded Michael of taking the teaspoon out of a sugar bowl.

'If you had jiggled yourself forward, this baby would have dropped out on its own!' Michael looked at the stick. Three-quarters of it was a stained dark green now. He examined where the stick had been. He blew the residual powder off Colin's chest and out of the hole, like blowing chalk off a snooker cue. 'Looks clear now. You're done,' he advised him. 'You were lucky Colin. If this hadn't been cheap muck, you would be dead by now.'

Colin didn't seem that cheered by the notion. He got up and proceeded to meander round the room, trying to look in the hole that the stick had left.

Next on Michael's list was Vincent, who wasn't feeling unwell but was looking very unsightly. A tuba mouthpiece had become firmly wedged in his eye socket and out of the wide end, a black fluid ran lazily out and down his face.

'Does it hurt?' Asked Michael, wrinkling his nose in obvious disgust.

'No. But I don't like the look of it. I want it out.'

'Yeah, I get that. This reminds of when I stood on a plug. I fell backwards once and my mother had just unplugged the iron and it was on the floor. One of the prongs went straight in through one side and out the other. But you know I have very soft feet, Kate. Maybe if I had grown layers of hard skin, I would have been alright.' The rest of the room said nothing, so he thought he might as well get on with it. He rolled his sleeves up, turning to The Master.

'What tools have you got?'

'Nothing!'

'You must have something. A screwdriver, pliers, a block and tackle?'

'I don't have common tools here. I always pay someone to do my work.'

'Great. What am I supposed to use then?' Michael glanced over to Kate who was sitting on a table, swinging her legs. He raised his eyebrows at her. She sighed getting off the table to go and look for something useful.

'Something metal.' Michael shouted. He turned back to Vincent.

'The problem is mate that since last night, it looks like the skin has puffed up around it. It's become a bit absorbed into your face. I can hardly see any of the lip part anymore. It looks pretty deep set as well.'

'I don't like it.'

'Yeah, you've said that before. What if I get it out and it is the only thing keeping your brain in. You won't thank me then, will you.'

Vincent said nothing and continued to sit there. Michael heard Kate's footsteps getting closer and she appeared, holding something in her hands. She slapped the object into his hands, walked off and sat back on the table, to continue to watch the fun.

Michael looked down at his operating tools. Kate had bought him a silver ladle, which was still in the house from Bonfire Night.

'Are you serious?' He asked.

'It's that or nothing.' She replied flatly.

He examined the ladle and decided that the flat handle would be better than the bowl end.

'Brace yourself.' He advised Vincent, who grasped hold of the arms of the wooden dining chair, firmly. Michael put the end of the ladle by the mouthpiece edge. He wiggled it under the soft white skin around Vincent's eye. It smelled like soil or mushrooms. Probably best not to bring that up, as they all smelled the same in that room, apart from him.

'Alright, tell me if it hurts.' He started to angle the handle so that it would prise out the mouthpiece. He increased the pressure and could feel the suction of Vincent's eye socket resisting him. It seemed to like this mouthpiece in it. He decided to really go for it and pushed back even further. The waxy skin above the mouthpiece split, opening Vincent's eyebrow a little. However, it did not bleed. Michael thought it looked infected or dead. He applied a little more pressure. Just when he thought it was coming, the ladle flipped back, away from the mouthpiece. Vincent's eye socket seemed to gently suck it back in place. Michael looked at the ladle. The handle end was now firmly bent at the tip.

'It's not happening mate.'

'What am I going to do? I don't like it.' Vincent said again. Michael stroked his chin weighing up his options.

'You could wear black sunglasses. No one would be able to tell.'

'Well what about the issue from it?'

'Ah yes. That would run out from under the lens. You could shove a rubber bung in it.'

'Do you have one?'

'No…… Oooh, I know. Stuff a load of toilet paper in it and wear an eyepatch. Jobs a good 'un. Next!'

Stephen walked up and sat in the *doctor's chair*.

'You have been burnt Stephen.' Michael said.

'Tell me something I don't know. How can you help?'

'You know before you were turned, do you remember that?'

'Yeah.'

'Do you ever remember me being a Doctor or even a Vet?'

'No.'

'So why do you think I can do something about burns, especially on a vampire.'

'I don't know.' Stephen looked downhearted. 'But you've helped the others.'

'Not much,' Michael said under his breath.

He looked at him for a long time. Half his face was black dry and puckered. It looked like he must have closed his eye as he burned. It stared out at Michael. Red and sore out of an ashy, baked slit, that used to be an eyelid.

'I don't suppose you have any salve for burns, Master?'

'No.'

'Butter?'

'No.'

'Well I am at a loss, what do you suggest.'

'I think fresh blood, drunk and applied to the area.' Norman said.

'Fair enough.' Michael said. 'There. Rise, you are now healed.'

'Just as I start to get women, this happens. Now they will never look at me long enough for me to hypnotise them.'

'Maybe you could learn to do it with one eye, keep this side of you away from them. Anyway, The Master's solution may work. Luckily you can only go out in the dark, so they won't see much of you as it is. Next!'

2 – May

Excerpt from Anne's Diary

31st May

I loved living in Lutry. Our beautiful Vineyard's –
feasting on migrant workers, whenever we liked.
Tastes from all over the world. How many years have
we had the perfect set-up? I cannot truly remember.
Len says we have been rumbled and blames me for
not cleaning up after my last meal. Why me? He
doesn't know for sure!
He has a plan now to move to England and we will
have to scorch this place before the locals find out
what had really been going on.
I liked Switzerland. Sleepy. Everything shut at night
gave me plenty of space to roam. It was right that in
the spirit of neutrality, everyone kept themselves to
themselves, so we had no visitors disturbing us.

For a place with such money the illegal migrant workforce was in abundance. All of them amazingly different in taste and texture! They were so eager to keep themselves off the official radar, which was right up our alley. We only had to hire two foremen to cover the work whilst we slept. Very economical! And now it's going to be bloody England. What's worse *Manchester*! Wet, wet and wet! All because Len likes to play on the canals, with his many boyfriends. I think I would rather go back to the peat bogs of Ireland. He has been coming to this northern area, on and off since the 1980's. In fact that is where he found his three best friends. So I have a feeling they are behind all this. They want to get home. To watch over their kin. To be in their natural lands. Len is constantly waxing lyrical about the North of England. I don't get it. Everyone tastes the same. Or they did when I was last there, about two hundred years ago. Boring!

So much to do, so little time. Especially important is to find somewhere for my furry babies to stay, until it is safe for them to come live with me.

3 – Owl

It was at this time that Our Doris's dog wandered in. After finishing his dinner, he looked like he had had a big drink of water, from the dripping fur around his mouth. He burped loudly and Brenda turned to him.

'Here he is. The Lord and Master. This everyone is Haggis. He is a messy little hound, but he is the apple of Our Doris's eye, so don't moan about him.'

'Come here lad,' said Bob and rubbed his two hands together towards the dog. Haggis bounded towards him and Bob hugged him. 'You are a good boy aren't you.' He rubbed him vigorously. Haggis burped again.

'Better out than in.' Gary remarked.

'So it's about time I got you lot settled in,' said Brenda. She thought for a moment then said 'Our Doris is in one room. Me and Freddie will take the box room, if that's alright. That leaves the two other big bedrooms. One for the girls and one for the boys. If that is okay with everyone. That is probably the best we can do for the moment. Our Doris has plenty of pillows and blankets so we should all be sorted with that, at least.'

Wee Renee and Pat offered to help. Sue and Laura automatically got up too. They followed Brenda upstairs and into one of the rooms. This was the box room where Brenda and Freddie would be staying. Inside the wardrobe were blankets, quilts and pillows. They were lovely and smelled fresh. The women shared them out equally between the two bedrooms for males and females. With the pillows that were already in the rooms, and the ones they added, there was at least one for everyone.

Freddie was downstairs chatting with the other men. They could hear him through the floorboards. The voices were muffled, but they could hear the odd word through Our Doris's plush carpet.

'What did he say? A dido?' Pat asked.

'Probably,' said Brenda.

From the living room, there were sudden bursts of laughter, which was reassuring. After they had sorted out the bedrooms, the ladies went downstairs to get their bags.

There would be five of them in the ladies' room. Pat, Wee Renee, Laura, Liz and Sue. The bed was a king size and two or three of them could go in there if they went top to tail. Maybe all five could fit in one bed. Although, it was left unsaid, that none of the women would want to lie all night next to Pat's feet. There were also a couple of quilts and pillows on the floor, for some that wanted extra room. In the boy's room, there would be Danny, Gary, Andy, Tony and Bob.

Brenda went back downstairs, telling the men that the bedrooms were sorted. The ladies collected their bags saying they were going to unpack. After diving deep in the mounds of coats boots and backpacks, they returned upstairs each with their own bag.

Wee Renee put her backpack on the chair in the girl's room and began to get everything out. She had packed everything very tightly and there were surprisingly, a lot of items coming out. Like rabbits out of a magician's hat. As usual, with Wee Renee some very unusual items were being revealed.

'I have got tons of stuff in my bag, you are welcome to any of it, ladies. I know we only called at a couple of houses.' Wee Renee stated.

Laura said that she hadn't got a nightdress and would need a change of clothes for the nighttime. Wee Renee winked, looked in her bag, and started to pull items out. She pulled out something that looked like a nightdress with patterned splodges on it.

'This is for you then?'

She shook it out towards Laura. Wee Renee looked at it then appeared crestfallen. Laura realized it wasn't a nightdress as it had a totally open back.

'What's that?' Laura asked.

'Damn it,' Wee Renee laughed, 'I thought it was a nightie but it is my wee painting smock. Just shows you how much of a rush we were in.'

'What are you doing with a painting smock?' Sue asked.

'Well you know, I dabbled a bit. I must have picked it up by accident. I thought they were flowers. I was wondering where it had got to. It must have been folded up in my nightie and underwear drawer. I guess that means I don't have a nightie. But I do have some leggings, quite a few pairs, and T-shirts, Laura. So if you would like to wear some of those, because that's what I will be wearing too, it's cold. I have one dinky nightie and pantie set, but I'm not wearing it tonight.' Laura wondered when she had been planning to wear it. The mind boggled.

Wee Renee turned to Pat. 'I am going to wash some of my clothes through in the sink and put them on the radiator,' she said, 'I only bought one pair of pants, can you believe that? I am going to wash them through.'

'I have only bought one pair too, never mind.' Uttered Pat. 'Maybe Our Doris has some fabric freshener. I might see if I can spruce them up a bit.'

Liz's, Laura's and Sue's eyes met. All were wide-eyed. Wee Renee never batted an eyelid however, still intent on taking out the contents of her backpack.

'I would rinse them through just to be safe, Pat. We've been camping. There are lots of weird bugs flying about up there. And also I would rinse through the feet and crotch of your tights, especially rubbing hard at the reinforced toe, you know. I don't mind doing that for you if you like whilst I am doing mine,' she said.

'Thanks Rene. I'll flip them off for you later.' she said.

'No problem Pat. I'll ask Brenda if she has a wee bit of washing detergent going spare for us.'

Brenda had stood at the door watching them unpack. After they had finished their conversation, she coughed and they all looked at the door.

'I will go and look through Our Doris's stuff. She is quite a small build, you will see but I'll see what she has in nightwear and underwear.' Brenda said this with a smile and turned.

She disappeared through another door that was obviously Our Doris's room. All of a sudden out of the quiet they heard a howl. Then what might have been a scream. There was silence again and they all looked shocked.

'Was that a scream?' Laura asked.

'It was definitely a scream,' whispered Liz.

'I don't know.' Said Wee Renee. 'It could have been an owl screech. You know some owls screech and don't go twit-twoo.'

They relaxed with Wee Renee's reassuring comments and continued to unpack. Then they heard it again.

'That is a scream. Definitely a scream.' Liz said, a little hysterically. They were quiet for a while listening. They could hear the men talking downstairs and their ears strained and ached for a confirmation.

'I know what you mean though it did sound like an owl screech again. But I think it was a scream really far away and distorted by the snow. Someone could be getting attacked,' Liz said looking at the others.

'Let's go back down to the men, see what they think.' said Wee Renee.

They started to walk out of the door and Pat stopped Wee Renee by putting her hand on her arm. The others walked down the stairs. Pat waited until they had got to the bottom, then whispered to her friend.

'I've got a problem.'

'What?'

'I'll tell you what! I don't know where I'm going to put my teeth tonight Rene. I can't see a denture bath anywhere'

When they all got downstairs some of the men were having a bit of a look through Our Doris's drinks cabinet. They hadn't heard the scream because they were talking quite loudly, so dismissed it as an owl screech, unless they heard it for themselves. This annoyed Liz because she felt like all the men were calling the ladies liars. She sat on the sofa and folded her arms, frowning at Andy. Freddie said Our Doris wouldn't mind them having a nip out of her drinks cabinet at all or anything else in the house. That is how Our Doris was. He said they would all like her.

'Who is for whisky?' Asked Freddie.

Most people said that they would have a small whisky. Pat said that she would prefer a brandy if there was a bottle, and Freddie poured her a generous one in a brandy glass. They all agreed that they were only having it for the shock and didn't really fancy drinking it. Pat said she felt the same but would choke it down. She then proceeded to choke it down in one, asking Freddie to pour her another for the shock, which he did.

Brenda appeared and told them that she had put some of Our Doris's clothes in the ladies bedroom for them. She had even found some men's clothes and had put them in the men's bedroom. She announced that Our Doris was awake and she had briefly told her their story. Our Doris was excited to meet them all, had asked for a drink of Ovaltine, and was just getting herself together. Brenda asked who else wanted Ovaltine and they all said they did without exception. Pat said she might have a brandy in hers.

Norman was still angry about not being able to find the group of bandsmen. He had visited nearly all their houses now in turn with his children. There had been a brief scent at a couple of houses, but this was now a day old. The bandroom's smell was even weaker. He had checked back at the Civic Hall too. There was a possibility that they could have gone to see if they could still save anyone, or to retrieve items that they had left in haste. But alas, definitely no scent there. He had sent out Stephen, Keith and Stuart to bring him a couple of fresh unsullied humans as he needed to eviscerate something quite badly that night. That always helped.

Surely they hadn't got out of the village. He had everywhere covered and they would have needed to pass The Grange. To have walked right under his nose to reach the top roads, which would have been treacherous. Even if they had done that, they were definitely in for a surprise whichever way they went. His sister was in Melden and his brother was in Moorston. So whichever way they had taken when they got past The Grange, they were going to be in for a big shock. He heard the return of his children, along with the sounds of screaming, crying and pleading humans. He would be having fun tonight. Everything would be better tomorrow. He would catch up with the lost little sheep soon enough and then, oh what plans he had for them.

4 – June

Excerpt from Anne's Diary.

30th June
I am in a hotel in Manchester. Although luxurious, it isn't a place you can relax and be yourself. I won't last long here. What about my special beauty regime? I am managing to keep my face beautiful at least. I go out and pick up a dizzy person. There are lots lying in shop doorways at night, basically waiting for me.
I then take him back. No questions are asked here in the foyer – not with how much Len is paying for these three suites! I can then fill the sink with the blood and wash my face, finally! The man is usually too sleepy to realize what is going on. I have to work with such precision and a small blade – no teeth, that would be too obvious.

After I have finished, I take him back to where I have found him. So he stays alive – until I find him again, haha. Len and Norman have forbidden the killing of anyone, until we have a disposal method. So off he goes, returned to his pavement with fifty English Pounds in his pocket and living to fight another day. Or sleep in his case. I have to do this every night. It is ESSENTIAL! Then guess what Len has told me to do? After I have drunk from my face washing basin, I have to wipe it out with the hotel towels, before I undo the plug. Then he takes the towels and throws them into the canals before one of his *'dates'*. Usually, in the rain. What a fuss! I am sure they are being *too* careful. Silly boys. Please let me find a home soon! It is all too exhausting.

Of course, Len is in his element here. Boy after boy, and he doesn't even drink their blood, well not all of them. He just wants to surround himself with young men and his three friends, who pander to his every whim. He sometimes has no interest in his younger siblings. Len should be looking after us! He makes me want to rip something open, which I do. Afterwards, on occasion, I am vexed with myself, but I don't blame him. Who am I kidding? Of course I do!

For me and Norman this is hell. No freedom, no grass, no hills. We can't be ourselves in the city. He does not tell me, but I know.

We have started to look for a new home but this time I have managed to convince Len that it would be best for us to have a home each rather than a communal living arrangement. I don't like his friends and they don't like me. So, I sacrificed living with Norman, so I could have seclusion and get on with THE PLAN!

How does Len feel? I think he was glad to get rid of us too. He quite likes the idea of being free to practice his every indulgence without the risk of his sister or brother walking in on him, mid coitus. Eventually, it will dawn on him that it was a bad idea, but by then I will have established a community, which won't be moved on every time some little thing goes wrong. That will teach him to think using the shrivelled thing between his legs rather than the shrivelled thing between his ears!

I think Norman has a similar plan but its hard to tell with him at the moment. Ever since arriving here he has started thinking he is a musical impresario and spends his evenings travelling to Brass Band concerts. He should be with me! Always sitting with me, and then hunting. Walking keeps us fit!

Norman arranged for a lovely *'family'* night out. He dragged us to a festival in one of the places we are planning to live. A Brass Band festival where bands marched up and down and played tunes for the drunken masses. I was forbidden to taste any of the meat on offer.

I think we could be in the right place however, because there seems to be one thing these people can't get enough of – alcohol. And that is something we have coming out of our ears….quite literally! It is a wonderful thing isn't it? It disguises all kinds of tastes and makes humans very susceptible to intoxication, infection, transformation and seduction (Len tells me). Anyway, Norman was so enamoured with the place that had the bands that he said he would look for a house there. Of course, it has to be *right* for Norman. He was always a particular boy. Each to their own!

5 – Beehive

As they walked up the stairs with their Ovaltine's, all twelve of them, they were excited to meet the fabled Our Doris. Freddie motioned for Brenda to stop.

'I don't know how Our Doris will take all this? With her being ill and everything.'

'Don't worry,' Brenda reassured him, 'she will be more receptive than you think. She takes everything in her stride.'

'I know. But nevertheless, this will be a hard pill to swallow.'

Our Doris's room was warm and well lit. She had a king size bed with pink flowery bedding. On the bedside table there was a bottle of Sanatogen tonic wine. There was also a bottle of Lucozade, a large romantic novel, and a box of tissues.

She had two double wardrobes in there, a set of drawers and a dressing table. On the dressing table was a large jewellery box and a half-used bottle of Estee Lauder Youth Dew. She had a flat screen television mounted on the wall and this was on, but the sound was turned off. She was watching a shopping channel and they were demonstrating a motorised Santa Claus that they had for sale.

The carpet was deep and pink and the room smelled of ripe peaches. Beside her bed were a few chairs, used by Our Doris's sisters. Some of the group sat in these chairs and some on the bottom of the bed, as Brenda had gestured. The final couple sat on the floor, underneath the flat screen television.

Sitting in the bed was a lady who was in very good spirits, with twinkling blue eyes. She was very small. They could tell how tall she was by how much bed she was taking up. Even though she was tiny her presence filled the room. She was blonde and had a bouffant kind of hairstyle that had obviously been coiffed recently.

'She has a wee beehive hairstyle.' whispered Wee Renee to Bob.

'I like it,' Bob whispered back, 'but I thought it was supposed to look like an Easter Egg!'

Our Doris laughed as they come in she had a very loud and hearty laugh for such a small lady.

'Oh you like my hair-do, do you? I had the mobile hairdresser in today, I'm not going to let myself go, am I? Even if I *have* been at death's door.'

'Sorry about that,' Wee Renee said, a little embarrassed.

'It's fine, I'm glad you noticed it. I just seem to have extremely good hearing at the moment which is unusual for me.'

Freddie glanced at Gary. They both gave each other a knowing look.

'How are you, Our Doris?' asked Freddie. He walked over to her and gave her a kiss on the cheek.

'Not too bad. Actually, better than I was yesterday and that's better than I was the day before. Improving slightly all the time and getting my Mojo back.'

'I have told them that I have explained *their* story, and they would like to hear yours.' said Brenda.

'Yes, I would love to tell you. I will get it out as quick as I can, as even though I feel better, I soon get tired. And I have some questions for you, of course. Did you bring me my Ovaltine, Brenda?'

'Yes love, here you are.' Brenda passed her the cup.

'Thank you.' Our Doris said, taking the cup in both hands. She drank, closing her eyes, obviously savouring the moment.

'That's a lovely bed jacket you have on.' Wee Renee remarked.

'Thank you. I have a few, because you know at my age we are in and out of hospital quite a bit, with various ailments or the odd nip and tuck.' She winked. 'I have some other ones besides this pink one, if you would like one for tonight.'

'Thank you, Our Doris. I do get a bit cold, and would appreciate it.'

'Brenda will sort one out for you, we look about the same size.'

'Bless you. My name is Wee Renee anyway, nice to meet you and thank you for your hospitality in our hour of need. This is my best friend Pat.' Pat nodded at her.

'Nice to meet you, Our Doris.' Pat said, a little too loudly.

'I am Tony. This is my wife Sue and this lad here is Bob, our son.'

'Hello, Our Doris!' He laughed cheekily.

'Hello, young Bob.' Our Doris laughed back.

'I am Gary, pleased to meet you.

'And I'm Danny.'

'Andy and Liz. I think we might have more in common than you think but we will get to that later.' Liz said.

'And I am Laura. I have got a lot of family here in Melden. You might know some of them. My Uncle Terry and his daughter's, Sally and Kathy from Melden Silver Band. He is the dentist as well. I don't know if you are one of his patients.'

'Oh yes, I know them. Terry sorts me out something grand, you can't even tell when he is in your mouth.'

'Steady on Our Doris!' Exclaimed Freddie. Pat bellowed with laughter and then everyone got what Pat was laughing about.

'I meant he is such a gentle dentist. Freddie, get your brain out if the gutter.' She laughed back heartily. For a moment they all felt normal.

She took another drink of Ovaltine and then set it down on the bedside table.

'Well let's get to it then.' Our Doris took a big breath. 'So I believe some of you went to a party and that is where it all started. I think this is how it started here too. There is a house just outside of Melden. It is very large and the people who lived there before had quite a few horses and livestock. It has quite a bit of land attached. Anyway, it has been for sale for a while because it is quite a target for burglars you know. The insurance companies tell them, I believe, that they won't insure it. It was on the house market for three million quid.'

'Three million quid!' exclaimed Bob.

'Yes really. It's a biggun. So it got sold this year, and a lady moved in. There were tales that she was quite an animal lover. She had workmen coming putting different animal pens in the grounds. I heard it was for some llamas and some peacocks.

I don't know if she has them now. I haven't seen them, but that is the gossip that was going round the village. It was said she had a private zoo licence, from the council. She sounded a very interesting addition to the village. Some people hoped she would have open days for the kiddies. Like a petting zoo.'

Our Doris took another drink of her Ovaltine and placed it back down. The others were fascinated with her story and she was very engaging.

'So she decided to have a party as a form of housewarming. Everyone obviously wanted an invite so that they could have a nosy round this three million pound house, and a goosey gander at her little zoo. She didn't invite anyone that was likely to be boisterous. Just decent folk. She invited the band as well, which I thought was really nice to use local talent, you know. So we all got dolled up in our finery and I went along. She certainly had put on a good spread and invited us to look around the house. She told us she hadn't had time to do much with it, because she had only just got there but the previous owners had certainly made it very nice and comfortable.'

'Did you see the animals?' Asked Bob.
'No.'
'What was she like?' Gary enquired.
'Well she is probably about my age, I would say and she had an accent.'
'Was it European. Like Swiss or something?' Liz wanted to know.

'I am rubbish at accents. I thought it was Irish. Ah well. She is about a foot taller than me and very gaunt. She has quite a big hooked nose, hawk like and a bit of wispy grey hair. Squinty red-rimmed eyes, and a receding chin. Big teeth. A very dramatic dresser. I didn't look at her much, you know.'

'She sounds a beaut! We'll know her, if we bump into her, I bet!' Tony said.

'The strange thing is, I think that she imagines that she is a lot more attractive then she is. She is very full of herself. Very confident. It was weird though,' Our Doris stopped for a moment, going back to that night. 'The whole evening she kept on laughing quite maniacally over nothing, every so often. I thought she had had a bit too much of her own hospitality.'

'How many people were there?' Gary asked.

'Er....about sixty to eighty, I would say. Plus the band.'

'Oh crap. Over a hundred then. For the love of Mike,' Gary said. His shoulders sagged. He put his head back and looked at the ceiling.

'That's more than there were at the start, in Friarmere. He only did the ten-piece,' Laura sighed. Gary sat forward, his hands on his knees. Talk about out of the *frying pan and into the fire*, he thought. Collectively the group began to feel beaten before they had begun. Freddie thought he would change the subject.

'What did she lay on for you then?' He asked.

'Let me think.....Okay, there was a lovely beef casserole, crusty rolls, butterfly cakes, homemade Eccles cakes. It was really nice, you know.'

'Did the band have separate food?' Asked Wee Renee.

After thinking for a few seconds Our Doris replied. 'I don't know.'

'We had chocolate fudge cake and cream at our party, did you?' Liz said.

'I bet there was blood in that fudge cake!' Pat blurted out. Andy dry swallowed. 'And you know what, you have to soak the raisins for homemade Eccles cakes. She could have soaked them in blood, or some of her other juices!'

'Er, can we change the subject from cakes?' Andy asked, putting down his cup of Ovaltine. 'And juices.'

'Was there any wine?' Liz knew the answer, even though she had asked the question.

'Yes, there were copious amounts of red wine. Only red though. And I thought that there was plenty of wine in the beef casserole as well. It was very delicious though, I had two helpings.'

'Oh Bloody Nora.' Pat said under her breath and Freddie shook his head looking down.

'Anyway as the night when on we were all getting a bit giddy with the amount of wine. The band was playing and I ended up dancing with this lovely young fella. I don't think I was his cup of tea though, or even the right sex,' she winked, 'but we didn't half have a good old boogie that night. They were playing plenty of Tom Jones hits and you know how much I like Tom Jones.' She directed this comment at Freddie, with her eyebrows.

'Yes you do, Our Doris. Who was this fella?

'Haven't the foggiest. I have never seen him before, and I probably wouldn't recognize him if he came to my door. I was quite sozzled, Freddie! So, it wasn't a bad night. Probably about midnight we called a taxi and came back to the village, as I had my heels on and there was no way I was walking at that time of night. Four of us shared the taxi and came back. We were all the worse for wear by then. When I got in, I dropped straight off to sleep, still in my clothes and make-up. I even forgot to take Haggis out for his walkies. But that following morning I woke up and I felt absolutely terrible, so I stopped in bed all morning. I was due to meet my other two sisters Rose and Jennifer at lunchtime for a spot of lunch, but I called them and cancelled.'

Wee Renee was nodding at this and taking every detail in.

'Jennifer called round to the deli and picked me up a lovely sandwich. Her and Rose brought it over after their lunch, with a vanilla slice. Jennifer knows it is one of my favourite's and always tempts me to eat, even if I have been off food for ages, doesn't it Brenda?'

'Yes, she could never turn one down, ever.' Brenda said matter-of-factly.

'But I couldn't manage any of it. Not a crumb. I'd not realised, that I hadn't changed from the previous night, and when they came in, Rose said I looked like a half dead drag queen.'

Brenda pursed her lips at this. She was holding something in.

'I didn't eat on that day. The next day I felt the same. At that point I rang Brenda, and she came to look after me.'

'Who looked after Haggis?' Asked Bob.

'My sister Jennifer and her daughter Beverly took it in turns, Bob. They are good girls and he likes them,' said Our Doris.

'She was very weak when I got here, I am so glad she called me, especially after what we know now, with the visitations.' Brenda confided in them.

'But you know, since that night, I have had the weirdest dreams. In them, I am running through the forest and killing animals. Horrible, horrible dreams.' She shivered thinking about them. 'And I sweat don't I?' She said to Brenda.

'You do.'

'I was just so glad that Brenda was here because since my husband died, I would have been very scared in the night on my own, waking up like that. They are so vivid. Over the last couple of nights we have heard wolves and Brenda has told me that this Anne, that is her name, who had the party, has been walking around the streets. And in them pens she hasn't got llamas or peacocks. She has a load of bloody wolves! Can you imagine that? Who would want them? But she seems to be able to parade them round the village, with no collars and leads. No one is saying anything! I expected more from Melden. If I wasn't bedridden, I would have said something.'

This was a new development to the situation that the others did not know about and they shifted in their seats, wondering what to make of this new aspect of horror in Melden.

'Brenda says that there are a couple of people from Melden walking around with her, so now so she has got some mates. I have been sitting here thinking….. what is a woman of her age doing, walking the streets with wolves? But now you have come along and I know that Friarmere is in so much trouble all bets are off! Brenda has told me that there are vampires there. That they seem to have taken over the village and that there was another party a while back over there.'

'That's right,' said Liz, 'I am the only one here who went to that party and there was not a lady named Anne there. The man there is named Norman. Norman Morgan. And he seems to be the boss of them.'

'Anne Morgan! That's her name!' Doris exclaimed.

'Hmm...Wife? Sister? Mother maybe? Very interesting,' Gary interrupted.

'So Norman bought the old Grange on the hill.' Liz continued. 'He had a party there on Bonfire Night. A ten-piece band went because it was short notice, and we couldn't get a full band to go. We were given separate lots of food and drink. In time, we realised that this contained his blood, which had infected us. I can only imagine that this is what happened at your party and that this Anne is another one of them.'

'Are you saying,' said Our Doris loudly, 'that some dirty devil has put their blood in my food and drink?'

'Yes,' said Freddie 'that is what we are saying and this is why you are having those dreams. Your body is getting ready to be transformed.'

Our Doris was visibly shocked and upset. Liz moved up the bed from where she was sitting and put her arm around Our Doris.

'I have been infected too, Our Doris. It can be fought and it is not easy but I feel a little better every day and you seem a very strong lady. It sounds like you are through the worst of it, but I did not have any nightmares about running through the forest. I just wanted to kill people, that's all.'

'That's nice,' said Andy.

'Yes. Particularly you, I am sorry to say,' said Liz. She faced Our Doris. 'I think you are very lucky to still be human Our Doris. I am the only one left. Norman got to each and every one of the ten people that were there and it was only for the fact that Andy was with me all the time, that he didn't get me too. I think with Brenda being here, and your sisters visiting at other times it prevented her from coming in. But I have no doubt that she knows that you are infected with the virus. *They just seem to sense it*.'

'So what happened with the others, how does he do it? What is his next step?' Our Doris asked Liz.

'From what we can gather Norman, or another vampire, visits them and basically bites them or kills them. We don't know that bit for sure as none of us have experienced a one to one attack. But whatever they do directly causes them to return as vampires. Then they seem to go and live with him at The Grange, dropping out of circulation. Losing touch with normality completely.'

'Do you mean like the government?' Our Doris asked. Freddie laughed and Liz continued.

'There seems to be a way that you can resist it slightly, because there were a couple that did not fight against us at the Christmas concert. Once you are a vampire, you mainly do his bidding, unless you are very strong willed. So I think that *what you were* before he got to you, carries through into vampirism.'

'I have to say,' said our Doris, 'that I am really scared about all this now. Especially knowing that I am in so much danger and a target for her or this Norman.'

'Don't worry,' Gary said gently, 'we are here now. We have looked after each other. We know how to protect you, how to fight and we know more about him, than he thinks. You are safe now.'

They heard another howl in the distance as if to make a mockery of Gary's words. Now they needed to fight the wolves, as well as the vampires. How would they do that?

'You had better get some rest, Our Doris,' Brenda said. 'We'll see you in the morning.'

Brenda gave her a kiss and they all processed out of the room one by one. Brenda shut the door behind them. Sighing, she walked down the stairs.

Pat beckoned Wee Renee into the ladies bedroom.

'Rene, what do you think about that?'

'Yes, she has a beautiful headboard, there's no denying it. I'm just off to the little room, Pat.'

Pat shook her head in disbelief. That was Rene for you.

Excerpt from Anne's Diary

Friday, 9 December
It has been three weeks since my party for the villagers. I have been able to mark some people but still some people remain hidden. I have discovered older people sometimes do not take to the change willingly or easily but there are some exceptions. However, this area still seems to have a better success rate with older subjects that other areas. They build them strong and made to last in the north. I have to call on more infected today. I will find them all. I aren't worried. Nothing worries me. After all, I am wonderful. There is a very strange smell in Melden. Very cheesy.

Tonight I will bathe in more blood. I feel that it does me the world of good. It enriches my skin, I have a lovely blush afterwards and it is a comfort to me. Earlier I went out with my wolves on the hunt. They were howling a lot more than usual. Norman thinks sometimes they object to the wonderful changes in their bodies. I think not. How I wish I could have been infected the same way as them. Have their wonderful changes! They are so lucky! Alas, I am limited to my human abilities.

My faithful servant Sarah told me of a strange tale tonight. Sarah, and a group of my beloveds went into a kebab shop. They and the wolves were drawn there by the raw meat smell. But of course, the person inside, who cooks the meat, also drew my children. His door was wide open, inviting them in. He sent them away with a flea in their ear, but to be honest, it was not an attack from them in earnest. Just a bit of fun. That is what this new life is about. Fun! I am angry about this. He will pay for spoiling my children's evening. Filth! We will get round to him another night. I love hunting with my wolves. The exercise keeps me fit as well as aiding digestion. There are many playthings to be found on the jaunts too. Tonight I walked past a wonderful house with walls around it. A newer house than mine. Unfortunately, this house was not on the market when I was looking for my abode. I would have chosen this instead. It is so wonderful and secure. I see that they have a camera over the front entrance. I have shouted in it for them to come outside and that I have an amazing deal for them. A fantastic opportunity! I would offer them lots of money for their abode. After a while, this deal will be done. I have told them again in the camera about this. I always get my way. I will talk to them again, in their camera. Tonight my children took two dogs and three cats from the village. From the moors we found a wild fox and two rabbits. I have taken the rabbit and the cat, for my experiments, proceeding to mix their blood this evening. I am wondering what creature this will make. I injected it into one of the people I have in my cellar. He was unwilling but never mind about that. They always scream when I come towards them with my syringe. I find it really funny. I walk even slower than I normally would, syringe in the air, listening. It prolongs my amusement. A good idea from me, again! Now I have close to twenty people for my experiments. They see what I am doing. I think they are in awe of me. Norman has kept someone down there before. I was not allowed to touch him. Norman does experiments too. This is why we are alike and I love him so much. His experiments are different than mine. He thinks that when a person is afraid for a long time, the blood tastes sweeter. Even though a bus had hit him, Norman said the blood was tastier. That is up to him. Many years ago, I took a whole pincushion full of pins and stuck them in a small child. They tasted the same before and after (which was delicious, I might add). I have TOLD him this. It's pointless. Little brother's eh? Len never experiments's. He is too busy having pleasures of the flesh in other ways. Mister popular. I am fully in the middle of my testing's and mixings. A true scientific pioneer. They are a combination of animals from the moors and people out of my houses. I constantly think about my brother Len finding out about this and what he would think of it. I know he would object. But he is WRONG! I begged Norman to not tell him. I said I am close to a breakthrough, but I am not. I would be compelled to stop if Len forbid it. I know he would too! It is all right for him to have his fun, but I cannot? I am sick of him and his domineering ways. Sometimes I wish he was human and I could rip him apart, make him into food for my wolves. I still think that would not be enough revenge for me. Not enough to make me truly happy.

6 – Blueish-Grey

It was just before six in the morning. Maurice sat in his living room alone, within the deathly silence of Friarmere. There was no comfort from the sound of even his own breath. He might as well have been at the end of the world, alone on an island of snow. His curtains were shut and behind them, there was newspaper stuck to the windows. He could hear the snow creaking outside, the weight on the roof, sometimes slowly slipping. The snow had bought down so many telephone lines now. Not as they were working before. It really didn't matter, did it?

It had been a couple of days since he had heard any news of Freddie or the rest of the band. He was still hoping that they had escaped. As he hadn't seen any of them walking around, either alive or dead and having not heard a word from The Master to say that he had caught up with any of them, he still lived in hope.

Maurice was so lonely. He thought that even though he could never change his situation, maybe he could change their fate in a positive way. That is if they ever came back to Friarmere. He was determined to help them in whatever way he could, whether they liked it or not.

It would probably mean the end for Maurice. But, what the hell, he would go down fighting. Helping his friends was not up for debate, especially Freddie. Norman, even though he was part of him now, meant nothing to him. Neither did the others. What Norman called *his brothers and sisters*. What tosh.

Maurice knew that Freddie would die for him, and he certainly would for Freddie. That had not changed since he had become one of the undead. He sat and got to work on a plan of action. How he could help his friends. If he ever gave in to the urges to feed on human flesh, then he would be lost. Maurice was still eating his liver and would be able to do this for an awful long time. He wandered over to his bureau and took out a writing pad and pen. Now to work.

By the time it was light that morning, there were already a few people up and about in Our Doris's house. Our Doris wasn't one of them and neither were Liz or Bob, but the others were wandering around quietly, taking turns in the toilet. They all thanked their lucky stars that they had made it successfully through another night of known, or unknown threat.

Each had enjoyed a good nights sleep, even though some of them were on the floor. But after spending the last two nights either in the band room or outside under a tarpaulin, it was no surprise. Compared to the last few nights they felt that they were in the lap of luxury. Besides that, they were mentally and physically exhausted, plus they ached all over. They were quickly depleting Our Doris's stores of paracetamol and ibuprofen.

Brenda had told them the previous night that Our Doris had unlimited amounts of hot water, so they all started to have showers and baths. They changed into some of their own fresh clothes or some of the ones provided by Our Doris. For the first time in days, they felt normal.

Soon everyone was awake and Brenda had toast and coffee for everyone. She said she would go to the shops later so that they could have a more substantial meal. As it was, Our Doris had a few loaves of sliced bread in the freezer, which Brenda had got out the previous night to defrost. She just kept filling the four-slice toaster over and over again.

Liz came into the kitchen and Brenda looked over to see who it was.

'Ahh, the very person I wanted to speak to.'

'Ohh really, how exciting,' said Liz.

'Not really. It's just an admission of ignorance. I have never met a vegetarian and I don't know what to feed you.' Brenda looked guilty and Liz laughed.

'Don't worry about it. I will have some of what you have without the meat. If I really can't avoid the meat, I usually have a tin of tomato soup, or something. As long as we have them in, I will be fine. I will sort myself out. You have enough to worry about.'

'That is a relief actually, Liz. Thanks. Can you round everyone up to come and get their breakfast? I will give them a shout too.'

'I am buttering up the toast for you, but there is jam, peanut butter, lemon curd, marmalade and other stuff on the kitchen table. I've got a big saucepan full of porridge too,' Brenda shouted above the increasing noise in the house. Pat had already eaten a bowl of porridge topped with golden syrup. There was a moment of pure and utter joy from Wee Renee when she noticed that there was Marmite on the table. She advised them that is was food of the Gods and insisted everyone try a bit. Everyone refused apart from Pat. She had tried hers on top of a heavily laden slice of toast. Now it had butter, peanut butter and marmite on it.

'Oh Pat, I think you might start a trend with that. What does it taste like?' Wee Renee asked. Pat tried to tell her but her dentures seemed to be stuck up with the peanut butter. She gestured towards her mug of tea and Wee Renee passed it over. She took a large gulp, swilling it around her teeth like a mouthwash.

She tried to talk, then lifted her top dentures up a little with her tongue. She took another swig of tea, tilting her head this way and that.

'Oh Rene. I thought I'd never get out of that. The bloody thing had got me. I thought I was a goner,' she said breathlessly.

'What was it like?'

'Chicken Satay. Lovely. I might have a couple more slices of that mixture,' Pat said smiling. She then took an even bigger bite of the first piece of toast and began to try and masticate that.

'I'd better make you a fresh mug of tea then,' Wee Renee said. Bob was watching all of this. He took a small piece of each of the *chicken satay* ingredients and put them on his empty side plate. He stirred them together with his fingers then had a taste.

'Pretty good,' he said.

Brenda continued piling up the toast and nearly went through all of the loaves as people had five or six slices of the hot buttery comfort. The kettle went on, over and over again as coffees and teas were consumed. The rest of the women helped by either making drinks, buttering toast or washing up the dishes afterwards.

Brenda said that Our Doris was feeling right out of the loop upstairs. She still wasn't strong enough to come down and sit there with them. However, she said there was an open door policy of visiting. And please would they use it.

Bob said he would go up because he was a little bit bored and thought Our Doris was quite funny.

When he got to her door, he gently knocked. Our Doris shouted for him to come in. When Our Doris saw who it was, she fluffed up her hair with her hands and beamed at him.

'How is my Easter egg this morning, Bob?' He laughed. It wasn't what he thought her first words would be. He surveyed her hair from his position at the door, with one eye open and one closed, cocking his head from one side to the next.

'It is very oval,' he announced.

'That's just the look I was going for.' She patted the chair next to the bed and he went and sat on it. Liz entered the room and Brenda was just behind her, coming up with a small amount of porridge for her sister.

Our Doris started to eat her porridge. She had only asked for a small portion, so it did not take long. Wee Renee came into the room, kissed Our Doris on the cheek and said she looked a little better. Brenda took the bowl off Our Doris and set it down then she then passed her a cup of coffee.

'I've got the best sister ever, haven't I?' she asked her visitors, obviously commenting about the devoted attention of Brenda.

'It's a good job I am, considering the others,' she said under her breath. Brenda then pursed her lips.

'You're not wrong there, Brenda, particularly one,' Our Doris said with certainty and the others didn't discuss it further.

'You know as soon as I got to Our Doris, she said to me that there was something very strange going on with her. An unnatural state. Even though she didn't know all the details of this infection and attack, as we know now. But she was adamant. You never guess how she knew.'

'I bet I know,' said Wee Renee, 'I bet it was her wee!'

Our Doris spat out a small mouthful of coffee she had just taken. 'How did you know?' Our Doris asked aghast.

'You can tell everything about your health from your wee. It's well known in our family. What was wrong with yours?'

'Well…… it was grey!'

'Grey!' Exclaimed Wee Renee. She made an O with her mouth for a long time. Then looked at the others.

'Mmmm….actually Bob, I think you should go downstairs. I think Pat would like to know that Our Doris is feeling better. Alright?' Wee Renee announced.

Bob got up hastily and walked out of the door shutting it behind him. He was happy to go, as he didn't really want to hear the ins and outs of Our Doris's wee, and what Wee Renee would make of it.

They waited until the door had shut. Then Wee Renee turned to Our Doris again.

'Grey! Oh, Our Doris.'

'Yes. Blueish-grey.'

Wee Renee put her hand over her mouth.

'Our Doris knew it was wrong there and then, because she puts a lot of store in the colour of it,' Brenda said quietly.

'Wow. I am sorry to say, it shows something very foreign in you. Weird and strange. Your system isn't producing the right coloured waste, lets face it. I have never heard of blueish-grey wee, in all my days. I used to eat coal and suck pennies when I was pregnant, but it was still a natural colour!' Wee Renee stated.

Our Doris looked crestfallen. Then seemed to have a thought.

'What colour's yours Liz?'

'Er...normal.' Liz said, with a little bit of regret. She would have loved to put Our Doris's mind to rest.

'Very, very interesting.' Wee Renee said slowly, thinking aloud. 'It sounds like even though you are presenting similar symptoms, and have been infected in the same way, that it is not the exact same infection.'

'It's vexed me, because I was working on it and had seen improvements.' Our Doris confided.

'You've been working on your wee? You need to get a better hobby, Our Doris,' Liz laughed.

'There's nothing wrong in that Liz. It is very important. I have got mine now where is it is as clear as a bell. I don't have any doubt, that you could wash your face and hands in it. Even drink it maybe!'

'Right,' chuckled Liz, 'Wee Renee's Wee Water. Does that sound like a good name for the next brand of mineral water?' They all burst out laughing.

'You know what, it would be cheap to produce anyway,' said Wee Renee. 'I'd have my face on the label doing a thumb's up. Saying Aye its good.' The others were in hysterics.

When Bob got downstairs Freddie was fiddling with the radio. He put on BBC Radio 4 the time was five minutes to ten. He said he was putting it on for the news on the hour, to see if it was a mass epidemic. Or whether they were coming on to tell lies about it being a biohazard situation or something like that. Generally being treated as a mushroom, in his words.

Bob said he had to come downstairs because all the ladies were talking about ladies toilet stuff. Pat patted the sofa, next to her.

'Eee lad. You sit down here with me then. I don't want to talk about that either. I'll stop down here as well. Is Our Doris all right this morning?'

'Yeah good, apart from the grey wee,' he replied.

'I thought I had grey wee one time,' said Tony.

'What!' Everyone gasped.

'Are you infected, Tony?' Gary asked crossly.

'No, no. this was years ago.' Tony replied. 'It was when Sue had put one of those toilet blocks in the cistern and not told me. I had a bit of shock for half an hour. Then I made the decision to call the doctor about my waterworks and she cottoned on. What a morning that was!' Pat sniffed at him and shook her head.

'It gets worse, doesn't it Bob. Sometimes I think we have entered an asylum and no one has told us. Moving on, I think I have spied a game of Scrabble somewhere. How do you fancy taking on your old Pat?' She asked Bob. 'Mind though, I will beat you hands down, so I hope you are prepared.' He nodded.

Pat puffed and huffed and got out of her seat. She opened the sideboard and next to some of the glasses there were a few games. She pulled out the Scrabble box and put it down on the coffee table. She then pulled the coffee table towards them and started to assemble the letters.

On the news, the headlines mostly seemed to be about politics, a starlet who had mysteriously had a baby and the weather that was going to turn increasingly bad again. Especially in the north of the country. No mention whatsoever about biohazard's, vampires or the end of the world. Freddie thought *they are covering it up. Swines!*

'You know, when I was in the army, years ago and stationed abroad, you could find out a lot more about your own country, from their news, than you could if you were living in it. The headlines there, about England, you would never believe it. You wouldn't want to live here. Then I would go home and start talking to my mother about it and she didn't have an inkling what I was talking about! You're right Freddie, we aren't told *'owt* in England about what's going on. Especially up north!'

'Yes, we're right at the bottom of the scrapheap, Gary. Anything north of Watford Gap and they aren't interested.'

'I wish I'd have emigrated to Australia years ago,' Tony said. 'I bet they get told stuff. Honest, straight to the point people. As well as beer, sunshine and Christmas on the beach. Imagine all those tanned girls in bikini's serving up your stuffing and sprouts, Danny.'

'I don't think they have Christmas Dinner on the beach, Tony!' Danny said confused.

'No?'

'No. How would they roast the potatoes? They have barbeque and prawns. You'd have to miss your dinner for that year, if you wanted the beach babes.'

'Not prawns again. They spoil everything. Bloody prawns. The bane of my life. I'm glad I stayed here then. I'll enjoy being treated like a mushroom instead. I'll not go without my Christmas Dinner for that! Prawns!'

Bob laughed as Pat spelled out the word *'Fart'* out on the scrabble board.

He added *'urnip'* on to the *t*, to make *'turnip'*.

'What's ironic Bob, is that it is the very thing that *does* make me fart. Turnip. And porridge of course.' Pat said happily.

Freddie put one of Our Doris's magazines over his face.

7 – July

Excerpt from Anne's Diary

26th July
It is done, I have bought a selection of terraces in Yorkshire (with cash haha). A village in a valley. They call it Melden, but it is hardly my beautiful Lutry. Damp, wet, cold and barren are the main features of this old mill town, even in summer!! However, on the plus side, I have moorland for my fur babies and plenty of space for them to play in.

The terraces will be made into Special Housing for the more unfortunate souls in the community. The ones who are most vulnerable. Lonely ones, drunks and some lovely prostitutes. Maybe former prisoners. Those that used to prey on the weak themselves. They live such a nomadic lifestyle. Who would notice or care if they go missing? Lambs to the slaughter and all the time I am a shining light of the community offering to help.

I should have thought of this before. I win every way. Surely no one would expect me to do it for nothing. I won't take them all. Well, not all at once. I need lots. Lots and lots. I use them for food, for bathing and for experiments. They are very useful. Essential you might say. Mind you, these terraces didn't come cheap, or the labour to quickly turn them into the habitable food traps they will become. I am sure Len and Norman won't notice the missing funds. Now, on to my accommodation. I have my eyes on a few places but need to arrange some evening viewings to check the cellars and stables. It has to be very, very private. Somewhere that Len can't just breeze in as well, with his friends. Its so hard being a vampire sometimes. Haha. No its not! But soon I will have everything I need for my success. I will!

8 – Marbles

After the discussion about Our Doris's grey water, maybe because she was in high spirits, Our Doris told Brenda that she was feeling quite a lot better. They had given her hope, not to mention a distraction. Today, another day further away from the initial infection, there was a slight improvement. After her porridge and coffee, she wanted to get out of bed. She said that if Brenda helped her to get dressed, and if then Brenda and Freddie would be good enough to help her down the stairs, she would prefer to come and sit with everyone else. She felt isolated and useless in bed. If they put plenty of cushions around her and brought the pouffe for her feet, she would manage. This was a big step for Our Doris. For Brenda, it was a very encouraging sign. Brenda dressed her in a loose leisure suit and pop socks.

Our Doris sat on the bed whilst Brenda fetched Freddie from downstairs. She was indeed weak, but they all kept laughing when her knees were buckling. Freddie kept shouting *more water with it Our Doris*, which he knew made her laugh, so they made quite the rowdy group on their way down.

When they got Our Doris down the stairs, the rest of the group could see she was indeed less than five feet tall.

'It's a good job you have stuck a large Easter Egg on your head Our Doris, or else you would be tiny,' Bob laughed.

'Never forget young Bob, that good things come in small packages.' Our Doris winked at him. Brenda tutted.

'That is not good news for me then.' Brenda said dismally. She was the tallest of the four sisters at about five feet nine and very slender.

'You'll do for me.' Freddie said and gave her a hug.

At about eleven o'clock Our Doris's two other sisters arrived together. They knew Brenda was there, but were quite surprised at the other eleven people in Our Doris's house.

Jennifer was the youngest and had inherited all of the family's good looks. It was plain to see that she was well to do. Her clothes and hair were immaculate and she obviously had manicures and facials on a regular basis. She was slim and toned. Being the youngest sister she was quite spoilt and feisty.

Rose being one of the middle sisters was a little bit more in the background. In fact, you would probably describe her as boring and certainly plain looking. Quite a large build, she had Brenda's height and was overweight. She didn't take to looking like this very well, so always seemed a little bit bitter about everything.

When Rose saw the collection of new people, as well as their brother-in-law Freddie, she seemed cross and put out about it all.

'Don't you think Our Doris has got enough on her plate without having to look after eleven other people?' She snapped.

'Don't talk about me like I'm not here. Besides that, they are looking after me, not me after them. I've only been out of bed about ten minutes,' Our Doris said.

'This is an emergency situation,' said Freddie. 'We cannot live in our village anymore. There are nightwalkers. Vampires. And now from what we hear in Melden, wild wolves roaming free in the night. Don't tell me you haven't noticed.'

'We've certainly seen the lady with the wolves,' said Rose, 'but I think everything else you are saying is pure fantasy. Yes, she is eccentric. But no one is more open-minded than me about accepting a diverse mix to the village.'

'Haha, open minded? Are you kidding? You are singularly the most closed minded person I have ever had the misfortune to meet. If you like her that much, why don't you go and embrace her then, Rose, see what happens.' Freddie said sarcastically. Rose ignored him.

'They're not exactly bosom buddies, are they,' Pat said to Our Doris quietly.

'They hate one another. We've had over forty years of these arguments. Neither will back down. Most of the time me and Brenda ignore them. Let them get on with it, Pat. She pokes him with a stick and he rises to the bait every time.'

'Right you are, Our Doris,' Pat sniffed. As the other people in were not privy to this historical information, they all started to feel a little awkward.

'No, it is not very nice to think that there are wolves,' Rose continued, 'but she seems to have them under control. I thought you said wild creatures, not tame ones, roaming around the streets of Melden plus a load of fantastical dark creatures. Vampires, whatever next? I think you are testing our sanity. What are you getting out of it? Are you trying to turn Our Doris mad so she leaves you everything in her will?' Rose asked.

'Rose!' snapped Jennifer. 'Don't say that. You know Freddie's not that kind of person or Brenda! And Our Doris certainly has all her marbles.'

'Am I invisible?' Our Doris asked the others.

'I am just saying, stranger things have happened.' Rose said quietly.

'Yes,' said Freddie, 'THIS is happening. This is strange and it's happening right now under your fat nose and if you don't listen you are going to end up dead or turned into a vampire.'

'Don't you threaten me, Freddie,' She shouted.

'I aren't threatening you, I am promising you. If you don't wake up, you will end up in one of those states, and it won't be my doing. Since when have I been a vampire? I can't carry out the threat, as you call it. Anyway I have got no time for you, Rose. I am here trying to tell you everything and so is everyone else. We all have the same story and you're too ignorant to work it out.'

'Hello, Rose.' said Wee Renee gently. 'My name is Wee Renee. I will just say that we were all resistant to this. We are all sensible people but there isn't one person here that will tell you any different from what Freddie is telling you. There are supernatural beings walking round and we are going to be done for. Certainly, if we don't wake up pretty quick and fight back. That is what we had to do in Friarmere. Freddie, me and the other's here. That is why we are here. Able to tell you all about it, Rose.' Rose shut up. Pat was staring at Rose angrily, which might have had something to do it.

Jennifer cleared her throat and stood up to address the others.

'I have certainly seen the people with the wolves so please tell me what you know and let's discuss it.'

80

They spent the next half an hour telling their tale of Friarmere from beginning to end again to Brenda's two sisters. Our Doris would interject every so often to say how that was similar to her situation here in Melden.

When Bob and the others gave witness as to what happened in Ian's butcher shop and the texture of the vampire, all that Rose did was fiddle in her handbag, as if she wasn't listening. Pat kept flaring her nostrils at her, but Rose was definitely not looking in her direction.

'Well, that certainly is a hard story to swallow.' Jennifer said when they had finished. 'And I don't want to believe it is true. I don't know how I will cope with all this. I think that is part of it.'

'These are the facts plain and simple.' Pat said. 'We cannot tell you any more or less. This is what has happened to us and it is up to you whether you walk away from the facts blindly, run out and get eaten, or fight back. What is it going to hurt if you give us the benefit of the doubt? None of us want to believe this or do what we are doing. Do you really think that we wanted to walk from Friarmere in the snow? That was out of desperation for our lives. This whole thing has taken this boy's innocence, don't you realise that. If he can cope,.. and believe it,... and fight,... then so can you. Your sister Our Doris is ready to fight back. She is ill, currently an invalid. But she is with us.'

'One hundred percent!' Our Doris said.

Michael Thompson sat alone. He was the only one in the house with a beating heart. Last night there were four others in there but now their hearts were no longer beating. They were brought either for food or for the Master's pleasure. To make another child for him.

From what Michael had been told by Stephen, three ended up as food, and he really did break them apart. Just scraps of skin were left. The Master had decided to make one of them his own. Another freshly made child of The Master's blood. Michael still wished to become one, now he had gone this far and was living here with The Master, his brother and the others. He should have been turned by now but The Master had other ideas. He had no more power now that he had a month ago. Really he was in a worse position not better. At least Stephen had physical strength. Could make people do what he wanted. Stephen was part of something. *He belonged.*

Michael still wondered sometimes whether he had picked the right side, but it was way too late now. He had shown his hand to the others from Friarmere band. They thought he was a Judas. And to them, he supposed he was one.

Michael was neither one thing or another. He didn't belong to any side. He was on his own. Unwanted and rejected once again. He was living a half-life in The Grange. Not undead, but a living shadow amongst the walking corpses.

He sat in the rocking chair with the curtains open. He would have to shut them in about three hours. Michael looked out at the snow and rocked and waited. Waited and rocked. He missed the Brass Band.

9 – August

Excerpts from Anne's Diary.

1st August

I have found my nest, tucked away from prying eyes with a gated drive, stables and trees on all sides. It has lots of rooms upstairs for entertaining and lots of cellar space for entertaining me too! There is a so much work to do in the house before I can move in. Once the stables have been converted into pens, I will be reunited with my babies.

The Special Housing has gone well. It seems that here, there is a dire need for this type of dwelling. Every room is going to be full. It has been such a success that I might actually buy some more if the incentives are right (mmm...more humans!). A big pat on the back there for Anne!!

With that in mind, I have offered to meet members of the local council to see what they can offer me. Usually, most humans can be swayed by promises of money or power or even both. Sometimes when the carrot doesn't work there is always the stick. Norman thinks he may have to move in with me for a while. I am torn now. I love Norman, but he wants his independence too much, so that makes me cross. He can stay here with me if he wants. It's only Len I have a problem with. Norman's new house is even more derelict than we thought, so his will take a little more time. We can't stay in the hotel much longer. Questions are starting to be asked. It isn't my fault either. I am sure I wasn't the only one feeding on the dizzy people. Norman will be with me for a while. He is admitting he needs his big sister. We are still young after all and as our parents are gone, we are orphans! Yes, orphans!

10th August

On my own at last. It must be nearly two hundred years since I have had this luxury. It is so refreshing to rise and go about one's business without having to step over someone else leftovers, or even worse catch sight of someone in the middle of some business they should be ashamed of (again) (Len I am talking about now, of course) Yes, its time to move onwards and upwards before he works out what I am really up to.

The meeting with the council went well. Small-minded bureaucrats with their minds on power, suit me. They are so easily manipulated. None of them have any backbone and would sell their souls to rise a few more rungs up the ladder. Ironic really as that is what they are practically doing – selling their souls I mean. There will be no ladder for them.

I have promised them more housing in return for a few favours and the first of them is giving me access to council workers to finish the work on my animal pens. They even rushed through the permit for me to have my fur babies. Sadly I couldn't do anything about the quarantine regulations, but I am only going to declare five of them for this, the others will be arriving by a different route. What they don't know won't hurt them, as they say - funny how most old wives tales don't always tell the truth.

I have also decided to turn to the oldest profession in the world again. Not that I will be doing anything myself (just the picture of innocence, aren't I?), but I think it might turn out to be lucrative in this environment. Judging by some of the conversations I am picking up from the council members it seems that a few of them have some interests that would make even my older brother blush. I could make use of this weakness in case I need a stick to beat them with.

29th August.

My babies are back! Apart from the ones I have had to officially put into quarantine, which are not my primary pack. (I would never do that to Sophia) They only have to be in there for thirty-one days anyway. All of my babies made it safely into the country. Their couriers were adequately compensated and now help to feed them - as part of their daily meat intake. Waste not, want not. I have learnt long ago to never leave any loose ends

All is quiet from Norman and Len. Len was last seen dressed in a frock and ostrich feathers somewhere in Manchester, getting in touch with his inner diva. He attends the 'Proud' Festival, he tells me. Norman seems to be still set on living in Saddleworth, but has heeded my warnings to respect my personal space and seems to believe that a hill between us should suffice.

My brothel business is booming and like a spiders web, I have caught many a juicy fly. To be exact, I have caught me some naughty Councillors. This has increased my power base significantly. Sadly I had to arrange an accident for one of the Councillor's, who chose the wrong moment to grow a backbone. When they found his body on the moors without it, I think it ensured that the others kept their jelly ones.

It also started a nice retelling of the old rumour of the beast of the moors. As I officially have no animals on the premises (yet) I take every opportunity to feed the fire, so that when my flock and my pets are feeding, we can refer them back to this moment – when I had no wolves at all! Haha! Anyway, I have mounted the Councillor's backbone on the wall of my cellar. I like it. I find it quite interesting, but that is no news to anyone that really knows me!

The moors are certainly interesting from my point of view, and such a rich source of material. It seems that the humans use the moors for all kinds of things. One of them is walking alone across bleak, windswept areas. Hidden are small caves, streams and other hazards. Many humans have gone missing in this area. I imagine many more will soon. The moors provide natural little traps for me. With a reduced mobile phone signal there as well, someone could lie there for weeks, with a broken leg. I am stopping the pain for them, they are providing me with a hot bath. It works for both of us!

There is another hobby going on around here too, called dogging. It seems to involve rutting like animals in car parks, with other people watching. Romantic couples grabbing a brief moment of passion before returning to their husbands or wives, and the monotony of their futile existence. This never went on in Switzerland, I am sure! Maybe it was the clean Swiss air. Or the fact, that they consume their own body weight in cheese every week. I don't know. This place is in the industrial north. Who knows what these fellows are taking in! It doesn't change their taste of spa benefits and that is all I am bothered about. The beautiful thing about all these activities is that they usually take place at night, with very few other people knowing the exact location of where they are. I mean would you tell your friends that you are going to spend the evening on all-fours in a car park? Exactly. And for some reason that I haven't found out yet, it seems that mysterious disappearances were going on long before I decided to pluck at the natural resources of my new home. It's haunted. Oh, I know that. But there are other creatures at large here. Even stuff I wouldn't tackle. But that is for another time, isn't it? It's hard to laugh off – and when I say that, it means a lot. The area even has a name. The locals call it *'The Melden Triangle'*. This triangle does not only encompass Melden, but a village called Moorston and the top part of Friarmere. If I believed in a higher power I would say that it was providence that brought me here.

10 – Camera

Jennifer all of a sudden had an idea. 'Wait a minute. I have got two security cameras. One on the front of the house and one above my conservatory at the back. Maybe they have picked something up and we can see what is going on in Melden.'

They all thought this was a wonderful idea. Laura wanted to call and check on her Uncle Terry and cousin's, as she had been very worried about them. She could do this on the way. Our Doris was too poorly to go but Wee Renee, Pat, Brenda, Laura and Sue said they would go over to Jennifer's house. Rose reluctantly said she would go too. But expected to see nothing.

Pat had the idea that even if she *did* see evidence on Jennifer's security camera's, she would even be more miserable than she was now, as she would have been proved wrong. Pat thought *I have worked you out, lady*.

They got their hats, coats and boots together and put them on. In fifteen minutes from hearing about Jennifer's camera's, they were out on the cold streets again. It was sunny and the sun shone off the snow brilliantly. They walked out of Our Doris's cul-de-sac and onto the main road. Not one person was out and about. Maybe it was too cold or maybe there was no one else left. Wee Renee kept looking at the other houses windows. She wanted to see another human, or at least a curtain twitching. She was disappointed.

Laura's Uncle did not live far from Our Doris. They knocked, but no one came to the door. She tried both of her cousin's houses. No answer again. This wasn't looking good for them. Laura was quiet and deep in thought for the rest of the journey.

Jennifer did not live too far away, just the other side of the Main Street. They walked into the centre of Melden. The local council had installed the Christmas Lights. Silhouettes of candles, holly and stockings were high on the lamppost's and strings of white lights joined all the shops together. Sue looked up at them. She wouldn't get to enjoy these at night. Who was seeing them now, only Anne and her wolves. How sad.

There were a couple of shops open, which had no customers. Gary and a few of the others had decided what they were all having for the evening meal and had given Wee Renee a list of items, which she would pick up on the way back.

Wee Renee was excited to see a haberdashery, but unfortunately it was closed. She had promised to try and darn Pat's tights and needed special thread.

The roads were still impassible even in the centre, where the gritters last were. The snow had built back up to an equal level across the road. There was no chance of anything coming through the village. They found plenty of footprints, which they could see going in and out of shops. Even though this was lunchtime, the Chinese takeaway and the kebab shop were open, which really was quite heartening to see. It was also very strange. They didn't usually open for morning or lunch trade. Wee Renee could see that there was still plenty of food in the shops, as they walked past the glass windows. A good indicator was whether they had milk and bread, which were usually the first things to sell out. They did, so even though this must be now a couple of days old and would not last much longer, she thought she would replenish Our Doris's freezer with a few loaves, and buy some cakes, biscuit and toilet rolls.

By the time they got to the other end of the street they had still not seen anyone else in the village. Following Jennifer's lead, they turned up a small side street and at the end, it stopped becoming a street and became a driveway. This was their destination.

With tall tree's either side, it took them about ten minutes to walk up it. It curved once to the left and once to the right. At the end, they were rewarded with the view of Jennifer's house. It was surrounded by a high wall, which made it seem very secure. At the centre of the front wall were electric gates and there was indeed a camera over the gate to show anyone that might ring the bell. Jennifer keyed in a pass code and they went through into large grounds.

Sue estimated that this house, which was quite new, had about seven or eight bedrooms. 'What a lovely house, Jennifer. You must be doing very well for yourself.' Sue said.

'It is down to my husband's efforts really. He always works away. There is a price for everything, isn't there?' She said sadly.

They walked up to the front of the house and Jennifer opened the door. Inside was very plush. Sue could tell that Jennifer employed at least one cleaner to look after this house. It would be a handful for anyone.

Jennifer took them through to the back of the house, through the kitchen and into the conservatory. She pointed upwards to the roof of the conservatory.

'I will look at that one first.' They could just about see a camera on the back wall, which was close to the conservatory pointing out to the fields behind. 'There is a footpath that cuts off a lot of the main road so you can triangulate through Melden and quickly get to the other side. It's very well frequented, and I would be surprised if they *hadn't* used it. Especially if she has local people with her. Everyone uses it. You can cut fifteen minutes off your journey.'

Jennifer said they were to all go into the sitting room and take a seat. Her laptop was in her office, but they should all sit on the sofa, as she wouldn't be a minute. Rose said she would put the kettle on for everyone whilst Jennifer did that and off she went. The others got the idea that she did not want to spend any time with them on her own without her sister, Jennifer as a backup. Brenda went to help her.

Jennifer had a similar large picture to Our Doris's, over her fireplace. Her husband looked like Cary Grant. Suave, tanned and with swept back hair.

'Two for one, do you think Rene?' Pat smirked gesturing at the picture.

'Aye, I bet neither Jennifer or Our Doris need BOGOF's, Pat,' Wee Renee chuckled.

'He looks like a ladies man, he does,' Pat commented. The others murmured in agreement. 'You can tell a mile off. Sexy pig!' Sue heard creaking footsteps on the wood flooring and nudged them in case they said anything else they might be embarrassed about later.

Jennifer appeared and put the laptop on the coffee table in front of them. Clicked a few icons on the screen and connected it to the CCTV feed. A list of dates came up and she clicked the top one. Brenda and Rose returned with the drinks and sat down beside them.

'We will check last nights, first,' Jennifer said. 'What do you think? Start at five pm?'

They all agreed, and she moved a bar across the screen to five pm. The footage appeared on the screen. It was in black and white and it was split screen.

'We will scan through pretty quick and if we notice anything we can have a look at that screen in particular and blow it up to full screen. Keep your eyes peeled.'

They started watching the speckled dark screen and at seven thirty two, on the clock below, they could see figures in the distance on the screen from the conservatory feed. Out of the black grainy picture they came like ghosts. Spectres with flashing coins at their eyes. At first, one person became clearer and more visible and then there came another and another. Four figures. Bright dots were shining low beside them and after a moment this was clear that they were the eyes of five wolves. They got closer and then the picture became very clear. There was Anne, large as life with her vampires beside her and surrounded by her wolves. Laura's uncle and cousins were not amongst them.

The general movement of the vampires seemed to be quite jerky, but maybe this was because the camera only took so many frames per minute. It was apparent though that they were sniffing the air. The three ladies from Friarmere had not seen the vampires do that at the Christmas concert. It was as if these infected creatures were on some kind of illegal drug. They seemed to not be able to stand still. They stopped in a circle for a moment and Anne seemed to address them and they all replied in unison. What a pity there was no sound.

'We are witnessing a wee gathering. How marvelous.' Wee Renee said in awe.

'Look!' Brenda said pointing to a particular person on the screen. 'I know her, she is in her sixty's. She doesn't look like a normal woman at all. Look at the way she moves. She could be eighteen years old. It doesn't sync with the look of her body, does it?'

'Well you've seen it now,' said Pat. 'What do you think Rose?' Pat really had to try hard to not finish it off with *I told you so*.

Rose did not seem very happy at all and said she didn't want to think about it and it still might not be what they thought. She had murmured her reply, with her head turned away. Rose was obviously embarrassed and too proud to admit she was wrong.

'Come on,' said Brenda, 'of course it is what it looks like.'

'We've all seen it now, it should be crystal clear to you,' Sue said.

'If you don't believe us, you must believe your own eyes,' said Wee Renee.

They waited for one, but Rose didn't reply. It started to feel like they were ganging up on her a bit, so they all shut up.

'Do you see them again throughout the night, Jennifer?' Sue asked.

'I will have a scan through.' Jennifer picked the laptop up again and placed it on her knee. Within a minute she was nodding.

'They are here again, coming the other way.' She turned the laptop towards them. Following their Mistress, Anne, one of the vampires was dragging a dog behind them and another one held what looked like two wild rabbits. Rose's complexion took on the pallor of a grey rainy day. Sue asked Jennifer to check again. Jennifer checked over and over again and showed them each time. The vampires were observed on the back camera, six times.

On checking the front gate feed, Jennifer jumped back as she found more footage. For one alarming minute, Anne stared at the camera, as if to challenge the occupants. She was shouting something into it, not knowing that there was no sound recording. After each unheard sentence, she gave a quick cruel smile, which did not reach her eyes. This terrified Jennifer, as she had been in the house alone at the time.

'The villagers know the only house behind that wall is mine. That was to me alone. Well, I am convinced.' Jennifer said with a sigh. 'No question about it. I believe you.'

They had seen various animals taken by the vampire's throughout the recordings. Another dog, three cats and what Wee Renee thought was a young fox.

'I think I might need another cup of tea, if you don't mind Jennifer, just to get me back home.' Pat said.

'I'll make it.' Rose muttered and got up, taking the empty, teapot and cups out with her. Jennifer looked at them all, before saying.

'I am sorry about Rose, she is a little closed-minded, and you have to admit this is quite hard to believe. She will come round. Don't worry I will have a chat with her later.'

After a few minutes, Rose came back with the tray. They all sat and drank their drinks quietly and thoughtfully.

After the tea and more cake, they felt more equipped to tackle the journey back in the snow. Rose had asked them to walk her back to her house and Jennifer stayed behind in her own home.

'You are welcome to stay with our crazy gang, you know.' Brenda offered.

'I will stay here tonight, thank you. Now I have got over the initial shock of it, I am okay. I will see what tonight brings but I am quite safe in here. Tomorrow, who knows, I might get a bag packed and bed down with you at some point though, Brenda.'

'Well I hope you have a good night Jennifer, God Bless,' said Wee Renee.

Putting a chain across the gate, as they made their farewells, she said she would watch the cameras all night for activity and report back tomorrow.

Rose only lived two streets away from Jennifer on that side of the village. She walked in front of them and as she got near to her house. She turned to them.

'I'm fine now, you can go.' She said flatly.

'Thank you, my lady,' Pat replied and saluted her. She ignored her, making her way through the snow. The others watched her go.

'She's a piece of work, that one.' Pat said.

'Sshh Pat. Blood's thicker than water,' Wee Renee said quietly. She nudged Pat and indicated Brenda standing beside them.

'I fully agree,' said Brenda. 'Why shouldn't I admit it. The whole family have been putting up with her nonsense for years. Freddie can't stand her. Didn't you notice I only invited Jennifer to stay with us? Freddie would end up doing time if Rose moved in!'

As they walked through the village this time, they saw the odd person walking around shopping. It was now a quarter to three in the afternoon, and in an hour it would be dark again.

The four ladies went into the grocery shop each of them picking up a basket. Between them putting in the ingredients for an *All Day Breakfast* that Gary was making. One of his famous fry-ups he said, as a treat. None of them had heard of his fry-up's, so they couldn't be that famous. But with so many people in the house, Brenda was happy not to be on kitchen duty for a night. Although she had agreed to be his wingman. They picked up bacon, eggs, sausage, black pudding, beans, hash browns and some loaves of bread. Wee Renee also found quite a lot of cloves of garlic, which she happily picked up. She put in two tins of corned beef.

'Has Gary asked for that?' Pat said.

'No, but I thought I could make corned beef hash, if his fry up is more infamous than famous, if you know what I mean. Our Doris has got a sack of lovely potatoes in the garage.'

'Well thought out, Rene. It's a good standby anyway for another day, if the snow starts again and we don't want to go out. Who knows, Gary might be a budding Gordon Ramsay!'

'Ooh Pat, wouldn't that be special. But alas, I have a feeling in my water, that he could be more Fanny Craddock.'

'Not to worry, I'll be in there as well,' Brenda added. Wee Renee went through the list to check she had everything. Her lips moved as she read from top to bottom.

'Tampons! Who has asked for them?'

'Well, it wasn't me. I'm guessing Gary doesn't use them in his fry up either. It must be Laura or Liz.'

'Oh Pat, imagine it. All this, and God's wee curse on top of that. Poor love, whoever she is.'

'They're for me actually,' Sue said wandering up. 'Mystery solved.'

'Bad luck!' Pat said and sniffed.

Wee Renee's carried on with the list. Her final two items were unplanned, but she felt, necessary. A Yorkie Bar and as a last minute thought, a punnet of grapes for Our Doris.

When they got back the others were very interested to see if they had observed anything at all on the cameras. After they told them about what they had seen - the wolves, the three vampires and Anne passing the house seven times, they were in shock. Sue told them with dread, about the dead animals they carried and was naturally upset about the dead cats, promising vengeance.

Brenda told them about Anne shouting at the camera and challenging any occupants inside. Which horrified them.

'Was her face dreadful and scary.' Liz asked.

Pat could see where this was going and wanted to nip it in the bud.

'I thought she just looked a silly bitch.' Pat said shrugging and Liz laughed. The tension eased a little.

'I thought it was amazing to behold. There was a wee gathering of evil brethren. A circle of unnatural souls, hunting their prey. Very rare to see. I felt privileged in a way. How many people have witnessed that,' Wee Renee said in a quivering voice.

'Great,' said Bob.

'Weird,' said Andy.

'Exciting!' Our Doris concluded.

11 – September

Excerpts from Anne's Diary.

3rd September
I have decided to hold a thank you party for The Councillors and their top employees this month. Our wine will be flowing that night. The trouble is that losing a lot of blood, to add to the wine, is a big drain on my own body's resources. I am lucky I have a full cellar at moment to help me replenish but I may have to *lose* more of my tenants soon to keep the stock up.

15th September
Well, the party was a roaring success. Everything was planned down to the last tiny detail, even to the extent that I paid for taxis! This meant that no one had an excuse not to drink. And how they did. I have noticed that free wine goes down very well here. Aren't I just the lucky one!

There will be a few sore heads after that night. Not least from me, poking about in their deepest thoughts. There was one worrying thing however, Norman seemed to have got wind of my party and turned up unannounced. It seemed that this visit was all about a Melden villager that he had spied and wanted. He is keeping her here for a while until she is ready for travelling. Norman is making her into one of his special ones. The ones that seduce men. I don't make them. Pointless.

28th Sept
A crate of wine is being delivered today as part of a raffle to help the needy being run by the Council drivers. I am such a generous soul. I couldn't resist and I need to step up the pace. I want EVERYONE to drink my blood. I need to hunt for humans tonight. They are still walking on the moors in the autumn rains and winds. The other day it was thundering and lightening. Still the fools are out. Supposedly feeling nature on their faces. Now they feel my teeth on their throats, my syringe in their arms. How things have changed for them. I am all for enhancing their experiences.
 What the Triangle does not provide, the tenants will make up. After all, I use it to feed, and for my beauty regime.

I have told my two brothers for years (centuries actually), that this fortifies me. And what is good for me, will be good for them. But do you know what, instead of thanking me, they look at me as if I am disgusting! Me! Norman has told me off. He says I am a threat to him and Len. He said I am dangerous. More than the authorities, a stake or a silver bullet! What? I know what I am doing. Him and Len are there, infecting one or two at a time! Where is that getting them? Not very far. Amateurs. I know. Anne knows. It is up to them if they don't want to take over this Island! We could do it. Especially if we worked together. But they won't. I want us to sit on three thrones with everyone bowing and scraping to us. Great farms of humans, for our delectation. But if they don't want in – so be it. I will be Queen alone. Me. Anne. The best. They don't need as much blood as me. They don't think of me. A lady needs to bathe in blood. That takes a couple of fresh humans. This bad attitude is all Len. I know. He can say he is the eldest as much as he likes but he is SHIT and I don't care!

12 – Metal Mickey

With a little help from Brenda, Gary did indeed cook a fine All Day Breakfast. There was absolutely mountains of food and they all enjoyed it greatly. Bob had copious amounts of tomato ketchup on his, which made his mother feel ill, especially after seeing the vampires with all those poor dead animals. Luckily for her, most of the people had brown sauce on their meal. After all the dishes were loaded in the dishwasher, and their pots and pans had been washed and put away they heard their first wolf call of the night. The reality hit home again. Anne was now a constant threat. A threat they knew they would probably have to deal with.

At the exact time they heard the howl, Norman was talking about the same thing in Friarmere. He had voiced his concerns as to the whereabouts of the missing bandsmen to Kate, Christine and Michael. He needed to pick their brains, bounce his ideas off them. Maybe these three, could work it all out.

'I am wondering if they had got over the hill, and are in Melden. What are the chances of that?'

'It's certainly a possibility because there is no sign of them here. I have walked it with Stephen in the summer. It's doable. Even in the winter I suppose.'

'Ah, then, if you say a human could do it, then that is where I think they are. Fine.'

'They could also be in Moorston, although that is a bit further. The hills are a little steeper. I would say it could take them nearly twice as long to get to Moorston,' Michael said.

'We'll try Melden first then.'

'They could be gathering an army there.' Michael said. 'Very dangerous.'

'They could be bringing a lot of burly policemen over here too. Chrissy could help you with them.' Christine said. They ignored her.

'What do you think Kate?' Kate smiled serenely.

'Bad luck them, if they have,' she replied.

'Why?' Michael asked. He didn't like Kate and Norman having little secrets away from him.

'They are in for a massive shock. Haha. My sister Anne, has a quirky sense of what she should be doing and has released her children into the wilds, for the most part. Encouraging them to eat animals before humans, which keeps their animalistic nature strong. They roam the village freely. Melden is theirs. It would be better for the missing humans, if they had made the trek to Moorston. For their sakes.'

After their evening meal, a few of them settled down to watch a film. Wee Renee asked Bob to sit next to her and when he did she put the quilt over their laps and gave him the Yorkie Bar, that she had bought earlier on. Wee Renee asked Bob what the film was called, and he told her. She had no idea what that was about and hadn't heard of it before.

'Well it's about robots that turn into something else. Good ones and bad ones.'

'Ooohh!' Wee Renee shrieked. 'Robots give me the willies,' she shivered. 'I didn't like that Metal Mickey from the eighties. Did you ever see him?'

'No.'

'He was dreadful. Really ghastly and they used to put him on at Saturday teatime as well. *A Saturday teatime*. It was still light. No warnings on at the beginning or anything it was really horrible. I couldn't have it on. I had to get out. Then once, I happened to be walking past Rediffusion, and he was on about ten screens in their window, as large as life. And the shop was shut! What do you think about that? He was following me.'

'Mint. Well, I don't know what he was like. He sounds good, I will have to Google him.'

'I ran, you know Bob. And at that time, shops didn't open late at night, so I had to go the Outdoor Hatch in a Working Man's Club. I bought two milk stouts and I ran over to Pat's house, which was close. Luckily though, I managed to evade him or else I wouldn't be here to tell you this tale.'

'Bloody Nora.' Pat said, coming back in from the toilet. 'Has some fool brought up Metal Mickey?'

'I didn't mind that dusty bin though, he was alright, Bob.'

Freddie looked over the cover of an Atlas he was reading. Intrigued by the two with the quilt over their laps, now sharing a Yorkie Bar. A strange conversation from a strange pair. *The mind boggles.* He looked back down at his atlas.

'Anyone for Horlicks?' Brenda asked.

The film finished and everyone started making preparations for bed. There were some upstairs and some half way up to the stairs when they heard the howl. It was very loud and very close. They could feel it vibrating through their body. Sue felt her bowels turn to jelly and went weak. She was halfway up the stairs, so grabbed on to the bannister. Liz felt her temples begin to throb and Our Doris's muscles where taut like steel wire. Haggis bared his teeth. Our Doris stroked him and he licked her hand. Freddie was near the front door and grabbed his special stick. They turned the light off in the living room and every one of them made their way upstairs.

Our Doris had a window that looked out over the front but she had yet to turn the lights on. The curtains were shut. Behind the curtains, she had vertical blinds.

'Don't turn the light on,' she whispered. Walking over to the curtains, they split themselves into three groups. One looked through the middle gap, where the curtains met and two at either side of the window. They had to slightly open the vertical blind, with their fingers, so they could see out. They were in pitch darkness so no one could see them. Right outside, halfway up the cul-de-sac stood the group, with their wolves.

They looked like they were out on patrol and were looking at each house as they moved up. Sue could see that apart from one extra person, it was the same group that they had witnessed last night. There were five wolves flanking the vampires. The wolves were loose. They did not stray further than ten feet away from Anne. Again the people seemed to walk in weird jerky movements, almost the same as their lupine friends with them. Wee Renee noticed that as Anne's head moved to the left, the wolves' head's would move to the left and then as it moved to the right or centre it would follow again. The wolves seemed to have a pack intelligence and Anne seemed to be able to control them as a collective force. Every eye of the monsters looked at wherever Anne looked. Checking out a house, for a new brother, or maybe a tasty snack. This pack of vampires and animals were very, very dangerous indeed.

They were all shocked to see this and Our Doris, still poorly, was being supported by Brenda and Freddie. She was terrified for them to see her, feeling that they would physically force her to join the group. Our Doris backed away from the curtain, not being able to see anymore made her feel better for the moment. She sat on her bed in the darkness, feeling lost and vulnerable. Pat walked over to her and so did Bob.

'It's not a just a chance that they were checking homes in this cul-de-sac,' Our Doris began to cry. They put their arms round her.

'We won't let them get you.' Said Bob gently.

'I think they were after me. They can smell me can't they.'

'They weren't,' said Pat, 'they are just patrolling, just the same as at the back of Jennifer's house the other day. And they were looking through *her* camera and she hasn't been infected, has she? They are just after people all the time, to join their gang.'

The rest of the group continued to watch the wolves and Anne walk around the cul-de-sac. As they got close to the bottom Anne turned round and looked straight at them in the window and smiled. She gave a brief cheerio wave and was gone. Andy gulped.

'Promise me that they weren't after me.' Said Our Doris from the bed. 'I couldn't bear it if I knew I was just a magnet for them and I was putting you all in danger being here. I can't cope with it.'

All the others remaining at the window realised that she was probably right, but it was going to do no good telling her that. So they came away from the window and told the three on the bed that they had gone now.

'They are just after more mates or food. Don't think about it one second more Our Doris.' Pat said standing up and putting her hand's on her hips. 'I don't know about you Our Doris, but I could really do with one of your brandy's after that.'

'Yes, you're right. That's just the thing for this. Well, have away with a little whisky everyone, or whatever is your fancy. Help yourself, I think we all need something to calm us down after that. Will someone bring me a whisky please? I won't make it down and up again. And please, don't leave me on my own, while you get it.'

'Right,' Gary said, 'me and the lads will bring up the glasses and the booze. Who wants what?' Everyone told them. Even Bob was allowed a small nip tonight and he chose dark rum.

Whilst they were drinking their nightcaps, Wee Renee was mulling everything over. She stared absent-mindedly at Our Doris, who was applying cold cream to her face. Bob was telling her a joke. She sipped her whisky and thought about the wolves. They were a lot bigger in real life than through camera, and a lot scarier. Larger teeth and heads, sulky looks and doleful eyes.

The fact that they were working as one system was quite terrifying. She could not tell what their fur was like on the black and white footage, but they were a brownie grey. Wee Renee took another sip. Wondering what kind of wolf they were.

Something at the back of her mind wanted to come forward but wasn't quite there yet. At the moment she did not seem to have all the facts. At the back of her mind, she somehow knew what this was all about, and what Anne was. It would come to her. Then when she knew the beast, she would be able to kill it.

Excerpt from Anne's Diary

Saturday, 10 December
This evening I walked and patrolled the village, whilst my wolves howled. I love to hear their voices calling out to me. We were patrolling a small street when I recognised a smell. I discovered by chance that there was one of my becoming there. One of my future children, a partial turn, was in that street. I suppose you could call them a foetus.

When I was patrolling the street, I could see people watching me from an upstairs window (night vision is so handy). I realised that this was the house where my unclaimed child was and I really needed to get to her, but I could smell that there were too many people in the house. Many mixed human smells. Also, the cheesy smell seems to be coming from there. I would be outnumbered. I gave them a quick wave as I walked away, just so they knew I had seen them. I hate my brother Len. I wish we were back in Switzerland. Bad news. The mix of the rabbit and cat did not work and this morning I found the fat man I had injected dead. He will not go to waste as my wolves and children will enjoy him. Nothing goes to waste here. So now there is an empty sad, stained mattress and a bucket, with no owner. I will rectify that tomorrow. I have a waiting list for my sheltered housing, so I will create a vacancy. Oh, what a good idea it was for me to put lonely and needy people in those houses that could easily disappear. I still am receiving rent for most of them. Ha! That is the funniest bit! Or is it when I come at them with my syringe. I do wish they would not cry so much downstairs. Sometimes they scream so loud down there that I fear that other people may hear in the village. That is why I love my wolves. Their sweet voices cover so much. I am 'running' a bath now. I have had to use two humans for this but it really is the Fountain of Youth and I am so worth it!

13 – Anne

Norman sat in the green room at The Grange. With him were Christine, Kate and Michael.

'I think I have to let you into a few facts about my sister, Anne. Kate knows some of this, but not all of it. My sister is older than me. We also have a brother who is the eldest. Anne has settled in Melden and likes it there.'

'She sounds like a nice woman.' Said Michael.

'She's not! You couldn't be farther from the truth. Why did you say that?'

'I like you, so I will like her, won't I? She's your kin.'

'Stop trying to please me all the time Michael. I can see right through you. It's embarrassing.'

Christine looked at Michael, a slow wry smile spread on her face. They were constantly competing for The Master's attention and favour. This was a win for her as much as anyone.

'Where is your brother?' Michael asked.

'My brother is in Moorston. He only arrived the day before the great snow came. So a few weeks after myself and Anne arrived in this area.'

'What's his name? Will we meet him?' Michael questioned.

'Too many questions Michael. I will answer these and then that is it. I am trying to tell you about Anne. My brother's name is Leonard, or Len as he insists we call him. You are a lot more likely to meet Len than Anne.' Michael briefly nodded, then laughed quietly.

'What is it now?'

'I can't imagine you being someone's little brother,' Michael replied, obviously amused.

'If I may continue, from a young age my parents realised that Anne wasn't quite right. In fact, if I had to name what she is I suppose it would be a lunatic.'

It was on Christine's mind that to say that *'he can't say that anymore. It's not politically correct'*. But at the last minute, she thought of being put down in front of Michael and she bit her lip.

'The turning point was when Anne was in her early twenties and the man she loved, married someone else. He, of course, had no idea of her obsession. Something I have experienced quite often. Anyway, I digress. Anne wanted to cross her DNA with other creatures and did, in fact, find a way to do this. However, it was a long process, hampered by unsuccessful attempts. Finally, she worked out that only just a few animal/human crosses thrived.'

Norman shook his head. It was obvious to the others that there had been problems with this experimentation. 'The process seldom worked out and even with her best efforts.....well, it made it clear to me that this was all wrong.'

'What has she been doing?' Asked Christine.

'Trying to mix her blood with another creature so that she produces hybrid offspring. As a young child, she always liked dogs and then wolves. Anne could always connect to wolves and ironically this was the best DNA fusion. She also had some success with crows.'

Michael looked very confused at Norman. 'Apart from what you said about crows, are we talking about a werewolf?' He asked.

'I suppose that that would be the closest thing. Or what you might be able to understand best. Although, they are still more vampiric than wolf. Anne believes that this makes her offspring stronger and we cannot convince her otherwise, but her hybrid strain is *weaker*.

For a start, only a few of her offspring actually turn into functional creatures. If the subject is too young, or too old…. or ill, the strain of turning into the hybrid makes it harder to thrive. The turning gives a high fever. She will actually yield less vampires this way. The subject's die during the last stage, mostly.' He shook his head.

'Also, the process of turning is longer and more complicated and there can be more interjection from outside parties. The subject can be saved down the line before completion. If signs are seen, as it is a longer time, their family can take them away and it is all over for Anne.'

'How does she do it, Sweetie?' Christine asked.

'It is a three stage process. The first thing is that they have to consume just a small amount of Anne's blood, just like the way I do it. In this way, it prepares the subject and makes them ready for change and as a marker for us to find them, if we lose them. Anne has been injecting herself with the blood of her wolves for many years. It does not harm her. As well you know, technically she is not alive. But it does make a difference when the humans ingest her blood. They smell different from my flock instantly and are being prepared for her particular strain, you see? The problem with Anne is that she marks everybody, so they all start having vampiric symptoms. She does not think about infecting a few and then turning them. Then starting off a new batch. I had to go over to Melden a couple of weeks ago, to deal with a matter arising from that. Nearly one hundred people were ill and having nightmares. Anne does not cover her back, so myself, and Len have to. Her irresponsible efforts at her party meant that not only hers, but my discovery was imminent too. It was quite taxing, wasn't it Kate?'

'Yes.' Kate said and crossed her legs. She didn't elaborate.

'And we couldn't ever tell Anne because she would have gone berserk and thought me a traitor. She still doesn't know. So, back to the process. Next, the subject has to be physically bitten by a wolf. This cannot be left out of the chain of events. Anne discovered whatever creature she uses she has to have the saliva, with all its cultures, entering the body of the human. She had tried their blood and other ways, but this killed the host. Just the saliva. Then she has to wait at least three days for this to work. What is happening, is that the slow virus of the real wolf and Anne's blood fuse and attack the human together. Part of that human's cells change. The final stage is when Anne returns, when they are only partly changed and turn's them, the normal way, into a vampire. The vampiric virus as you know is very quick acting, but it will not change the cells already changed by the wolf DNA in the saliva. So the subject becomes a hybrid.'

'No wonder there has been problems. You can see there would be many a slip between cup and lip there.' Michael stated, nodding. 'Very interesting though. Amazing.'

'What a faff, sweetie!' Christine commented, not to be left out.

'Quite. As you can imagine, this also means that Anne has to keep a party of wolves close by. She found a way around this by obtaining a Private Zoo Licence, which means she may keep these with her at all times. As I said before, she has had success with the crow. Transforming them, in the same way, using the crow for the middle interjection. But these hybrids are not as useful as the wolf hybrids.'

'What is the difference between us? What problems or advantages does she have?' Kate asked.

'There are many problems, beautiful one. Take their food, for instance. These wolves prefer to eat dead flesh rather than live blood. That is their first difference to us. Also a few physical differences. They may have a thickening of the nose and mouth but not too much as to be a dog's muzzle. They will always have a bruising of the hands and feet as their bones were trying to turn into paws or claws before the vampiric virus was introduced. So they are half and half and because, to be a vampire they have to become for all intents and purposes, dead, their hands and feet never heal or turn to either a normal hand or paw. They do feel a certain amount of pain for the rest of their existence. Being part wolf, they scream out, using their wolf voice in pain, not their human voice. It is a dreadful sound. A cry from the bottom of their soul, if they still had one. Anne see's it just as a way to find them, however.'

'What is the point of all this?' Michael asked. 'Why would she bother doing it?'

'For the advantages. The subject is more vicious. They can live on animal flesh forever and can just eat dead animals that they find. Their ideal diet is raw flesh, so they can eat our leftovers quite happily, animals, and people. Whatever they find. It is easier to keep her children fed. When they run wild they are uncontrollable, but if Anne keeps them with her, they have a pack mentality and she can control the whole army better. Another main advantage is that this cross strain seems to confuse the law of admittance. They do not have to wait to be invited in, which is, I admit, a massive plus for Anne. Disadvantages are that the hybrid is slightly weaker, as they are not pure strain. Noisy too, with the howling, I like peace, my friends.'

'So do they look like us, apart from bruised hands and the pain. How will we know them?'

Christine thought this was marvelous.

'Oh, you will know. It is clear for anyone to see, there are many differences. The first thing that happens with that change is that the eyes become reflective, like you will see in cats and dogs. This, more than anything is how humans will recognise them from a distance at night. Of course, they have to know what they are looking for. But once they do, Anne's children become vulnerable. That aspect is a give away, and dangerous. If a human can see them from a distance, by just the eyes, well, he could get them when they were no where near him.'

Christine gasped at the thought and Norman nodded and continued.

'Using a bow and arrow, or gun. The human would be totally safe. The eyes are the main thing that you will see. Every one of Anne's children has them. But the other symptoms depend on how long after the wolf bite Anne manages to turn them. They come to an evolutionary fork in the road. Some evolve into one physiology, some evolve into another. If more cells are vampire they will be more like us but have these reflective eyes and Anne will have the ability to control them well. That is the best-case scenario for her but often even within an hour or two, if she is trying to turn quite a few, there will be a difference. Someone will be quite normal and someone quite disfigured. So you will get a range of looks, abilities and obedience with Anne's pack.'

'How are they disfigured?' Christine whispered, her hands over her mouth.

'Pointed ears, coarse hair growth, elongated hand bones, leg bones, curved spines. They tend to stoop more. Not have the upright human stance, you know. You can never tell, what was transforming, by the time she got to them. Myself and Anne's brother have tried to stop her doing this, but it is the way she likes her offspring and as I said to you, she is not a reasonable lady.'

'Are they like that just on the full moon?' Christine asked.

'No. They are the same every day of the month, due to our bloodline.' He said proudly.

'Bottom line,' Michael said, 'are you able to protect us from her.' He didn't like the sound of this Anne at all.

'My vampires are safe. They are stronger and they are past the point where she could introduce the wolf saliva to them. I will be going over there, with Christine and Kate. You for the moment will have to stay here. You are still too human for her not to want to kill or transform you. She kills indiscriminately, not thinking of saving a kill for later. Anne does not think of maybe not turning someone, and leaving them for the future. Common sense. She knows she cannot turn children or the old, but she will still try. If they die, they die. Anne does what she wants, as her wolves do not mind eating rancid meat. Her and her pack kill a lot, and then just eat them one by one, leaving some for several weeks. She would kill you, Michael, so I suggest you stay here in this house where you are safe with my children.'

14 – Hogwash

Our Doris had not had a good night. The sight of what she could become and, what was actually out there on the hunt for her, was too much. She would be like that, if Brenda hadn't been there. There was still plenty of time for it to all happen. If Anne could get to her she would. The situation was a ticking time bomb. She wished her husband was alive, or that it was summer and she could just jet away on a plane to Benidorm or somewhere. But the thought of being undead, eating cats and dogs, walking the streets with Anne in the snow, had been playing on her mind all night. What if she had to live in a kennel or on some straw with the others? She had tried to sleep, but kept thinking about it. Looking up at the ceiling, imagining the horror. Once they got you, there was no cure.

In the end, she had knocked on her sister's bedroom door, who had always been a light sleeper. Brenda had told Freddie that Our Doris was having a bad turn and she left the box-room to get into bed with Our Doris. They had chatted until Our Doris was so tired that she was able to drop off.

In the girls' room, throughout the night, there had been much talk about the difference in the monsters from Friarmere as oppose to Melden. They were at a loss as to how to deal with these.

'I mean if they are part wolf, if that is the reason for their movements and stance, we might have to use silver to kill them.' Wee Renee said. They had very little of that. Laura and Sue had silver charm bracelets on, but they thought prodding a predator, with a little heart or a silver treble clef wouldn't do much good. They had no chance of melting it down and making a silver bullet either. Every single one of them felt that Anne was in the cul-de-sac last night hunting for Our Doris.

In the boys' room, even though they did not want to say too much in front of Bob, they said that no matter what these things were, they were still flesh and blood. Not ghosts, not an invisible poltergeist. So they would just hack them up as best they could. Cutting them down, chopping and dividing until they were dead would work, whether they were a dog, a werewolf or a vampire.

When the welcome dawn came, it was a lovely bright day, without falling snow. Brenda made up a big batch of porridge and also toast was on offer again, with tea and coffee. They could pretend everything was normal for a while.

Tony had to use the downstairs toilet quite urgently, which sometimes he had to do in the morning. It was situated next to the front door. Being winter though, he decided not to open the window.

As was his way, he made an awful smell in there. Everyone was complaining and unfortunately, just then, they had visitors calling. There was no escaping the smell that hit them as soon as they walked through the door.

The visitors, Rose and Jennifer arrived earlier than usual.

'Which filthy pig has just done that?' Rose asked. No one told her. They had with them Rose's daughter Natalie and Jennifer's daughter Beverly. Jennifer's daughter was beautiful and enigmatic. She looked like she went to the gym or was very athletic. Rose's daughter was very much like Rose. She was a simple, large girl who took too much notice of her mother. Once they had gone into the living room, sat down and told Brenda what they wanted to drink, Natalie wanted to have her say.

'I want to know who you all think you are? What rubbish have you been spouting to my Auntie Brenda and Auntie Doris? There are just maniacs running around the village with wild dogs and that is all. At some point it will come to an end.' Rose nodded at her, agreeing.

'Well coached but not seamless! Speak on Rose!' Freddie said sarcastically.

'I haven't coached her to say that. Take it back, Frederick,' she snapped.

'Kiss my arse, Rose,' Freddie said. He got up and walked into the kitchen to help Brenda.

'You haven't just discovered all this, you know,' Natalie continued. 'I made a call just five minutes before the lines went down to complain about this to the police, but it said that I was in a queue, as they were experiencing an unusually high volume of calls.'

'I bet,' Pat snorted.

Rose took up the dialogue now.

'There is a tall tale from the man in the kebab shop. I would never have a kebab, but I heard it from someone who was in the Post Office. Apparently, he is saying he defended himself against some wolves and mad men with his kebab shaver, whatever that is, and a metal rod that he cooks the lamb tikka on.' Rose had a look of disgust on her face.

'All this is simply mass hysteria. This man in the Post Office said it is highly unlikely for a pack of wild wolves to be walking round. I said that I knew that was only a partial lie from the kebab man. They are not wild, they are zoo wolves, but they still could be dangerous. I will agree with that. The kebab shop man said it is affecting his custom. He is sending a letter to The Council with very harsh words and said that the dog warden needs to come up from Huddersfield. The man in the post office says even though the kebab man calls them wolves, he thought that they were probably someone's husky dogs that had got loose and are evading capture. He might be right after all. They still could bite, I suppose.'

'Oh aye. Even husky dogs have teeth, Rose,' Wee Renee said.

'What do you think about all this, Jennifer?' Sue asked.

'Rose is talking a load of old hogwash. I have looked again at my CCTV. All night the wolves and Anne were going past. I asked Beverly, to see what she thought. I didn't mention anything about it previously. She watched it fresh, with an open mind and instantly came to the same conclusion.'

'My husband works away too and my daughter is in boarding school.' Beverly was obviously quite wealthy too, she cast her eyes down. She was quite upset about what she had to say.

'So they are safe. At least Philip and Tara are safe. But I have some stables and I am so worried about my horses. They have nothing to defend themselves with. And my Auntie Doris. What hell has she been through? It's a violation!' She put her head in her hands and started to weep.

'A violation. Those were my words exactly, weren't they Brenda?' Wee Renee said. Brenda nodded.

Jennifer asked the others to tell Beverly all about what had happened in Friarmere as she knew she had inadvertently left parts out. She wanted to hear everything.

Wee Renee told the lot. Even remembering more facts than the time she had told Brenda. When she had finished, which took nearly an hour, Beverly had finished crying and was calmly taking all facts in, and processing them. Pat then told them what had happened the previous night outside Our Doris's house.

Beverly looked at her cousin, before shouting.

'Natalie! How can you sit here, know all this, and say these people are liars? Look at the state of them. They are all genuine people and you are just small-minded to think that this could never happen in our village. Wake up and smell the coffee.'

'She's more likely to wake up for cake,' Freddie said.

'Or pies,' Pat said, thinking out loud.

15 – Kebab

That afternoon everyone was quite disheartened, after the visit from Rose and her daughter. Also, the previous night had left them worried and tired from lack of sleep. No one wanted to cook that night. They decided to venture out whilst it was still light, to see if they could find a takeaway and put it in the oven for later.

It did not help their mood as the weather had changed. The sun drifted away to be replaced with dark clouds, which threatened more snow or storms. It was so dark that the streetlights, which were light activated, came on in Our Doris's cul-de-sac.

Two or three of them wanted to try the Chinese takeaway first, but Wee Renee said that she had a phobia of chopsticks. Everyone burst into laughter but she assured them it was a real thing, with a real name, and she would discuss it later.

'You don't have to eat your Chinese with chopsticks,' Freddie chuckled. 'We have forks in this house.'

She shook her head in horror and said she couldn't eat a Chinese without thinking about ticks, so they decided that if the chip shop wasn't open they would have a kebab. This would be an ideal opportunity for them to have a good poke around in there. Maybe, they could get the story out of the member of staff that it had happened to. Perhaps it was a load of rubbish. Rose was inclined to twist or ignore truths, they thought.

As mobile phones weren't working, and they wanted to make one trip, they wrote everything down to cover all eventualities. Brenda laid out two pieces of paper on the coffee table and wrote kebab shop at the top of one and chip shop on the other. Freddie took control and wrote the orders from everybody in his copper plate writing.

Wee Renee, Bob, Gary, Andy, Liz, Danny, Pat and Haggis were ready to go out, the lists safely folded in Wee Renee's coat pocket. Our Doris was quite insistent that Haggis went for a walk whilst it was daytime, as he was champing at the bit. She had not taken him out herself since the day of Anne's party. When her sisters came, Jennifer helped Brenda with the housework and Rose took Haggis out. He probably hadn't had a good time for a few days. Haggis definitely wouldn't be going out at night for the foreseeable future.

One of them would have to stand outside of the kebab or chip shop whilst they ordered the food, that was all. Bob wanted to take him out on his lead, anyway. Freddie thought it was a good idea as, if there were any problems, Haggis would bark, and give them an early alert.

 A couple of the group took their weapons and hid them inside their coats. They were fully prepared.

It was only afternoon, but with the heavy black sky and oppressive atmosphere, Our Doris's cul-de-sac was quite dark, even with the streetlights lit. As they set off through the snow, Haggis seemed to run from one lamppost to the next. He did not particularly want to use it in the typical dog's way, but he seemed to be sheltering in the light. He was afraid of the shadows in the bushes. Pulling Bob along, running fast through the dark patches, he waited in the light until the other's caught up. Our Doris watched him do this from her window. He had never acted this way at night, even when it was darker than this. It was very worrying.

At the end of the cul-de-sac on the main road, there was a big modern pub. As they walked past, Wee Renee looked through the windows and turned to Pat, wrinkling her nose. Pat looked closely through the glass, turning her head left and right, to see the length of the pub.

'It is not as cosy as ours, is it?' Pat said.

'No,' said Wee Renee, 'all bright lights and disinfectant in there.'

'Hmmm…..what's the betting, everything's served with sweet potato fries,' Pat said.

'And a *balsamic reduction*, naturally.'

They tried the chip shop first, which didn't have anything in the glass cabinets at the front. Wee Renee went in, with her list out and slapped it on the metal counter.

'Have you got any of that, pet?' She asked.

The man picked up the list with his left hand, still frying his chips with the right one. He mouthed the list as he read through, constantly shaking his head.

'Unless you want chips only, you are going to be out of luck. I have run out of fish, puddings, pies, peas and gravy. I can rustle you up a spam fritter, if you like?'

Wee Renee thought that there probably would only be her and Pat that would have one of those. Everyone else needed more sustenance than just fried potatoes. If the kebab shop wasn't open, she might get items from the shop to put with the chips.

'I might be back.' Wee Renee said thoughtfully. She did however, spy a large jar of pickled eggs on her way out of the door and Pat and herself decided to have one each. The man put the two eggs together in a paper bag and off they went to the see if the kebab shop was open.

Bob walked ahead of the others with Haggis. It seemed to be getting increasingly dark and Haggis seemed to be following his nose as he was pulling Bob towards the kebab shop. Bob was the first to see that it was open and shouted back to the group to say that it was. Gary said it was typical.

Bob, Andy and Liz stood outside on watch with Haggis. Pat and Wee Renee by this time had finished their eggs and they went inside with the rest of the group to pump the member of staff for information.

After ordering the kebabs, there was a brief moment where no one knew what to do. When the man asked if they wanted hot or mild sauce on their kebabs, Wee Renee, Bob, Tony and Danny had opted for the hot sauce but got mild sauce for everyone else.

There was only one man in the kebab shop, and they stood waiting at the shop window, whispering about what to do next. They did not know if there was some kind of shift system and there was a chance this man might laugh at them if they asked about the wolves. Wee Renee did not care about this and went straight for the jugular.

'Can you tell me anything about a tale I heard about wolves. Was it you that it happened to, or someone else that works here?'

The man, who was quite large but had a kind face, put down his knife and the lettuce he was slicing. He walked over to the counter and put both his hands on the counter, straightening his arms and locking his elbows. He looked Wee Renee straight in the eyes.

'The wolves, yes it was me. I am the only person that works here and i could never forget what happened. What did you hear?'

'Didn't you have to go outside and wave your kebab shaver at a wolf?' Pat asked. 'That is what we heard. Summing it up for you.'

'It seems that a few things have been lost and gained in the constant telling of what happened.' He laughed but not joyfully. 'About all this......well, it was far more serious than that. What is your name by the way?' Gary took the lead.

'I'm Gary, this is Wee Renee, Danny and Pat. Outside is Andy, Liz and Bob.'

'My name is Nigel.'

'Hello, pleased to meet you Nigel.' Gary said. 'I can assure you that anything you tell us in confidence and we will have heard and experienced worse, I can assure you.'

'I don't think you have. I think you have no idea what went on. If you think that I just shook our shaver at a dog....' He shook his head.

'Alright,' said Gary, 'I'll go halfway with you. What we are talking about, isn't mentioned in your story, or from what we have heard. Vampires and maybe werewolves?'

Nigel gasped. Danny smiled at him and moved forward from the window.

'Mate, we can probably help you a lot.'
Nigel checked the kebabs, then started to tell them. 'It was about nine o'clock last night. There had been no one in for a while and I was just thinking of shutting up. I was starting to put all the meat away in the fridge's and clean the surfaces down. When I turned around there was someone standing right where you are, from the village, who I knew was named Sarah. She had one of those wolf dogs with her in the shop. With her friends outside there was more of the dogs, or wolves or whatever they are. Lethal buggers, from the looks of it. Three of the people stood flat against my window staring in, pressing their faces against the window, so their noses squashed, moving their head from side to side. It was really weird. I have seen young teenagers do that kind of thing, when they are acting up. What I haven't seen are people in their twenties, thirties and forties do it. Standing pressed against my window with that gang mentality, trying to upset me! Straight away I was on my guard. I said to Sarah, you will have to take him out. I can't have dogs in here, it is against food hygiene regulations, you know, unless he is a Guide dog, which I can tell he isn't. You and your friends, stop doing that on my clean windows and vacate this area. I was pointing like this over the counter at the dog.'

He gestured with his finger downwards. 'When she grabbed my hand, and tried to bite it. Honestly she did. Luckily I was a lot bigger than her and I yanked my arm back, even though she raked her fingernails through it. I grabbed up this meat skewer here.' He picked it a massive thick skewer, putting it on the counter. 'I cook my Lamb Tikka on it and I picked it up and took a swipe at her. Now I am not a man that takes to violence, but with those looking through the window and the wolf dogs and her grabbing at me, I wasn't having it, I can tell you. I am on my own in here, you know. I don't have a panic button or anything. So, I got the skewer, I swiped at her and I poked her in the shoulder with it really hard. It didn't go through her coat, but I told her where to get herself off. I said I would shove it through her bloody throat if she didn't take herself, her mutts and her cronies away from my shop. She said that she'd be back and I tell you this, as soon as they went I rushed over and locked the door. Tonight I will be shut at four, whether I don't get much business or not. And I'll keep doing it until someone gets rid of that lot. You struck a chord with me when you said the word *vampires*. That is what they made me think of at the window. Crazy teenagers will usually keep on blinking, but these didn't. They were hungry and not human. White as a sheet, with a ghastly mouth. Gaping, open and red.'

'You don't know how lucky you were last night.' Gary said. 'We aren't sure whether they are vampires or some kind of wolf vampire,' he shrugged, 'but they aren't gonna be good for you. They would have killed you or turned you.'

'Who knows what they are planning,' Nigel said. 'I think that the wolves were after the meat. They had smelled the raw meat and had drawn the vampires here with them. I have had dogs wander in before when the door has been open in the summer, and you can tell they are sniffing the raw meat, so I think it was that. I aren't taking any chances tonight. Luckily I don't have to go off home. I live in the flat above. Once I have locked the door I am upstairs and safe. I have strong doors and shutters that I lock down here and the safe is upstairs, so I am okay. What do you know about all this? Have you seen them?'

'Yes we have seen them around this village. The wolves, and their leader who is an older woman. Perhaps in her seventies.' Pat told him.

'I haven't seen her. She wasn't with them last night.' Nigel admitted.

'Yes, she is an elderly woman. You will know when you see her, that she is the one. We are originally from Friarmere and *that* has been laid waste to by a vampire. I know it seems far-fetched and I hear myself saying these words and can't believe I am saying them, but we have all seen it.' They all nodded and looked at him.

'I believe you. Maybe one time I would have thought that they were some druggies or something like that. But the look of them, and the ages of them. What they were like. The electric atmosphere that came into the shop with her. The hairs stood up on my scalp. It's tingling now, just thinking about it.' He scratched his head to relieve the sensation. 'I just know you are telling the truth. I have noticed on occasion that there are people walking up and down at night, but I wasn't really looking at them closely. Obviously, I am going to be more vigilant from tonight. I haven't had much business yet and I might not have anymore because I am going to shut up early. But I probably won't even open tomorrow. Not until all this gets cleared up. It's not worth losing my life over.'

'Let's be clear, that *is* what we are talking about,' Danny said. 'Our friends, a lot of them from our band, have lost their lives, through not believing or not even finding out in the first place.'

Nigel finished their order and said he was so glad that they had come into his shop and he did not feel so isolated about the situation. They had made him feel fine about the craziness running through his mind too.

When the group got outside, they spoke to the other three about what had been said. Andy had heard bits and pieces through the door. On the way home, Haggis ran from lamppost to lamppost pulling Bob in jerky stretches, as fast as he could to his mistress. Wee Renee was quiet most of the way and as they turned into Our Doris's cul-de-sac, she stopped in her tracks. She knew what to do.

'I have an idea!'

'What is it?' Bob asked.

'I think it's time to feed the wolves.'

16 – Wrong 'Un

That evening just after dark, Wee Renee discussed with Pat and Gary the possibility of a trip to the pub. She wasn't interested in mingling with the locals, as she was getting enough socialising in the house, but just to see what the lowdown was on the village. To see if anyone was talking about missing people, sightings of wolves, or if there were new tales to hear. This could be crucial towards the fight with the new foe and to protect themselves. She also wanted to see if there were any others like Our Doris.

Gary spoke to the others and after much deliberation, most of them decided to go. Andy and Liz decided to stay behind as Liz was having a bit of a weak day, especially after the jaunt around the village for kebabs. Sue thought Bob might not be welcome in the pub.

Our Doris and Brenda also stayed behind. Our Doris thought that if Anne came after her whilst they were out, they were close enough that Bob or Andy could shout from the upstairs window and they would hear them.

Haggis stayed behind with Bob as they were already having a fun time. Haggis kept deliberately rolling his little ball under the sofa. Then he would yap and look at Bob and Bob had to scrawl over, stretch his hand under the sofa, get the ball and throw it. Haggis would fetch it and roll it under the sofa again. Our Doris never stopped getting amused about this.

Andy looked out of the upstairs window when the others were ready to go. There was no sight of the wolves or Anne. The group of friends stood on the front doorstep, looking up at him.

'Right, go!' He shouted. Andy watched them from his sentry post, walk quickly down the cul-de-sac looking from left to right. Seeing that they had got to the door of the pub safely, he relaxed a little. They had all agreed earlier that they would go for exactly two hours. Then the other people could go to the upstairs window again, watch their return and signal if there was danger coming behind them. Andy decided he would stay there, after they had gone. The two hours spanned the peak time for Anne's patrols. He didn't want to take any chances.

The pub had been recently refurbished. It was part of a chain, which did meals and posh cocktails too. The lighting was very bright inside, with new wooden tables and chalkboard menus. It had a salad bar and a carvery, which didn't look as stocked as it should be. There were about fifteen customers and five staff.

Inside the pub there happened to be Beverly, who was in deep conversation with a man. Another man lurked round the table listening. When he saw them look at him, he sloped off and started playing on a fruit machine.

On another table, Laura was very pleased to see that her Uncle Terry was in the pub, sitting with her two cousins Sally and Kathy. She was immensely relieved, as she knew that all three of these people were members of Melden Band. Laura could tell immediately that they were not vampires or werewolves, not at the moment anyway.

The friends went to the bar and Wee Renee felt quite giddy, with all the choice available and ended up splashing out on half a lager and lime. Pat thought this sounded nice but had a pint of lager and blackcurrant instead. Everyone else opted for cokes and beers. They did not want to be under the effects of strong alcohol if they had to run home very quickly.

Wee Renee bought two bags of nuts. One for herself, and one to take home for Bob. They decided to go and split themselves between the two tables. Laura and Freddie went to sit with Sally, Kathy and her Uncle Terry. Gary, Danny, Tony, Sue, Pat and Wee Renee went to sit with Beverly and the other man that was sitting there.

Laura's Uncle Terry, and her cousins, were very glad to see her too. There were lots of embraces and Laura introduced them to Freddie, who said he was from Friarmere Band.

'I called at all your houses yesterday. Where were you? I was having kittens,' Laura said.

'Sorting out music in the bandroom. It's been long overdue, so we thought we would do it over the Christmas break.' Terry said. 'Do you know what is going on here, Freddie? We have had so many strange happenings.'

'What do you know first. I'll fill in the missing pieces after,' Freddie advised him. Terry went on to tell them that apart from the woman walking around with the wolves, there was other weirdness afoot. Like the sudden departure of lots of members of the band, some who now seemed to be spending most of their time with this woman.

'Forty years playing in Melden Silver Band, man and boy. And they leave at the drop of a hat. I have never heard of the likes!' Terry said.

The three of them had heard of tales of missing or dead cats, dogs and sheep. If the owners found them dead, the corpses then went missing when the owner returned with a spade, to bury them.

They thought anyone could be responsible. Maybe the crimes were committed by totally different people. Maybe these people, who they had seen from afar, acting very strange were somehow responsible, the group of jerky people who used to be bandsmen and now were friends of Anne. Or was Anne taking these animals and feeding them to her wolves or allowing her wolves to just wander about and help themselves.

Sally said that people had had enough, and we're thinking of going over to Friarmere, until the snow has gone away. Once they were over there they could contact someone about taking Anne away as well. Probably in a straitjacket.

'Don't go that way, it is worse than here I think, but for different reasons.' Laura said. She was just about to tell them why but there was an interruption when the man by the fruit machine shouted loudly to the bar steward.

'Another pint of Guinness please. mein host!' Freddie looked at Laura and rolled his eyes.

'Oh,' said Freddie, 'that's embarrassing.'

'That is my brother, Malcolm.' Terry stated, blushing.

'I have put my foot right in it now, haven't I?' Freddie said, 'Sorry.' Kathy put her hand on Freddie's arm to comfort him.

'Not really, we all think the same in this family, and we are related to him.'

'You can imagine what Christmas's we have.' Sally said. 'The worst thing is, we can't ever get rid of him, because he conducts the Band,' she laughed.

The other party of friends had sat with Beverly. She was obviously consoling this poor man who was looking down into his glass. As they sat down, she smiled and gestured towards the man.

'This is Carl. He is in the band too, but he didn't go that night to the concert in crazy woman's house because his wife is missing. Although she was missing well before the concert, so he thinks this has nothing to do her disappearance. He can find no signs of her anywhere. Not one clue. It's fair to say she liked to go out quite a bit, so he left it a couple of days before he decided to report her missing. By the time he did the lines were down.'

At this point, Carl looked up from his drink and observed the faces studying him around the table. He had an uneaten lasagna with salad in front on him. Beverly took this opportunity to tuck into her steak, with sweet potato fries.

'She is beautiful,' Carl said. 'She is always getting attention off blokes and the like. Because I love her so much, I let her do what she likes.' Gary gave him a strange look, before saying.

'Oh lad, can you hear yourself?'

'Bloody stupid. That isn't how you keep a woman.' Tony said, taking a gulp of his beer.

'Tony!' Sue snapped whilst kicking him under the table.

'I know I am wrong. But I just think that I am punching above my weight and she is gorgeous. I am obsessed with her, and as long as she comes back to me at some point, I am kind of happy.'

Wee Renee drew her chair up right next to him and put her arm round him. Comforting him and speaking gently, she said that this sounded a very destructive relationship and he should have got out of it a long time ago.

'I am so worried about her.'

'The relationship is one thing, but her going missing is another, and serious. When did you last see her?' Gary asked.

'About three weeks ago. Maybe getting on for four now. I don't know. No it's more than that.'

'Didn't you get worried before this?' Pat asked.

'No she has been gone at least a week and a half before now. If someone asks her if she wanted to go on holiday, she will just go.' He started to cry a little. 'Always been a free spirit.'

'Well, I am sorry,' said Wee Renee, 'she just sounds more like free and easy to me.'

'I don't know why she would want a husband, if she still wants that kind of a single life.' Beverly said. 'I have known Carl for years and so many times she has hurt him badly. He has always loved her. Even when we were at school, she was under his skin. Now he has this new worry. She has been trouble to him since he met her, and he won't mind me telling you, he has cried on my shoulder many times. I have said to him that he is coming back to my house and stopping in the spare room but he doesn't want to in case she comes back to the house. I have said after that long she can bloody well wait for him.'

'Yes, listen to Beverly. You don't need to be on your own, if you don't have to. It is a good idea.' Sue said. 'She sounds like a *wrong 'un* to me.'

'What's the alternative to Beverly's, mate? Sitting on your own, looking at the same four walls?' Danny agreed.

'Eat your lasagna love. It will make you feel better,' Wee Renee said.

'I can't face it. I couldn't' get it past my lips. I didn't want it. Bev made me get it,' he said sadly.

'Are you doggie bagging it?' Pat asked.

'No. They can chuck it.'

'You've paid good brass for that. You don't mind if I have it instead of the bin, do you? I'll have a smaller supper then.'

'Go ahead,' he said.

'Watch it Pat. I think Our Doris has run out of antacids. You know how you are.'

'Don't worry Rene. I'll leave the salad. That's the bugger that will play merry hell with me.'

Laura wandered over to them at one point, to see what was going on at their table. She then returned and relayed the information about Carl back to her relatives and Freddie. All this required immediate action.

Gary tried to enjoy the pub for a moment, to shut out all thoughts of fresh horror and insecurity. He gazed outside, he could just about see the centre of Melden from here. A few red and green Christmas lights were lit. They reflected prettily off the snow. This could be a perfect night if he just tried hard enough to shut everything out. He needed the escape. When he opened one eye, Pat was smiling back at him, a large blob of lasagna was on her scarf, just below her chin.

'Dreaming of Father Christmas?' she asked.

Two hours easily passed and Freddie was checking his watch constantly. He got them to form one group, five minutes before the time was up.

It was agreed that the next day, that some of the people who had seen Anne and her monsters, would go to the bandroom. Terry said there were plenty of pictures on the wall of the band from years past. Hopefully, they would identify the bandsmen who were missing.

Everyone checked through all the pub windows before they set off. In every direction, there was absolutely no one outside.

They left the warmth and light of the pub. Out into the cold and darkness. Terry, Kathy and Sally went one way and Beverly and Carl went another. The Friarmere group quickly made their way down the cul-de-sac and could see Andy looking anxiously for them, out of Our Doris's upstairs window. From the looks of it Ovaltine had already been made, as Andy was talking sips out of a steaming mug.

Once their coats and boots were away, Brenda started to warm some more milk for the drinks and Our Doris wanted to know what they had discovered. Laura told them about what they had found out from the pub. About the cats, dogs and sheep. Andy thought it tied in nicely with what they knew about Lazy Farm and Friarmere. Pat brought up that they had obviously witnessed the missing corpses of some of the cats and dogs being carried about over the moors, from the footage on Jennifer's camera.

They told Our Doris about the girl that was missing and she said she knew her from Beverly's group, when they were at school. She could remember that this woman was always a beauty and a flighty madam.

'I'm not surprised that she has come to a sticky end. Although it is just a likely that she will just turn up after a long holiday in Barbados knowing her.'

'She sound's a bit of a go-er,' Wee Renee said and she looked around at the others, thinking she had been very risqué in saying that.

'Jezebel! That's what she is,' Our Doris said. 'I wouldn't trust her with Haggis, never mind a real live man!'

'Kinky.' Gary laughed.

'I feel a bit sick, Mum.' Bob muttered. They all agreed that they didn't feel too good. From nausea to bubbling stomachs, something had affected everyone.

'I feel a bit bilious, and I have a strong constitution,' Wee Renee said.

Sue pulled Tony aside and warned him about the state he had left the toilet in earlier on and to be mindful when he goes in there. His eyes shot open and as if that was an indicator for him to go, he got up and went into the hall. He was back two seconds later.

'Someone's on the throne, already. Bloody hell.' He said.

Freddie was moaning about it, clutching his stomach, saying it had to be the kebab.

'The poor fella probably doesn't have his mind on cooking, after his attack the previous night, bless him. We were all probably due for a colon cleanse. Think of it as a freebie.' Wee Renee chirped happily.

Brenda was so happy they had got from A to B and back again with no harm, especially as Freddie was with them. She did not care if they all had the trots, her husband and friends were safe. They had survived another evening. Andy had said that he had watched the whole time and had not seen Anne patrol their cul-de-sac once.

The reason that Anne had not been in the cul-de-sac or on the streets at all, was that she had had a visit from her brother Norman. As soon as it was dark Norman had set off to Melden. Although a creature of the night, and endowed with supernatural powers, he still had trouble perambulating through the snow. So a couple of weeks ago, he had ordered snowmobiles, which were put safely away, until required. Norman could get over to Melden in a matter of half an hour, only a little longer than using a car in the summer months.

He had taken Kate with him on the back of his snowmobile. He had another, which he had told Keith to drive and Christine sat on the back. Although Anne was vicious, aggressive and unpredictable in nature, Keith and Christine immediately felt superior to her as she was sullied. They were proud to be Norman's children. Kate had had dealings with her before and was not fond of her.

When they arrived they found Anne preparing to make her nightly walk. Christine desperately wanted a look at the deformed vampires. The ones that Anne had defiled with wolf DNA. Norman said, if she saw them by accident, then fine, but she must not poke about in Anne's domain. Anne would cause problems if this happened, which he would have to solve and they weren't there for that. That was not the priority tonight.

Anne and her brother spoke to each other in greeting, and matter-of-factly Norman asked if she had come across a party of people from Friarmere. She did not know if the people staying with one of her infected were the same group, but she thought there was a good chance of it. Anne told him that at the moment, she would be outnumbered and would not want to force her way in and become overpowered. Norman felt that he was impeded by having no invitation inside, so also could not find out. So for the moment, they would have to wait. Either Anne had to make a larger set of children or perhaps they could pick them off, a couple at a time, if they saw them.

Norman said he would really like to find out if this was the group, so that he could put an end to the search of Friarmere, and possibly all the villages. He asked what she suggested. Christine, Keith and Kate watched all this happen, they were told to never intervene. Christine hadn't seen Anne acting unreasonably yet. Then Anne threw her head back and laughed madly. All of a sudden her tone became accusing and sarcastic.

'You will have to you stick around then and hang out with your sister, won't you? As much as you don't like it. There are plenty of rooms in the house for them.' She jabbed her thumb angrily at the three other vampires.

' You will all stay a few days to see if we can pick some off or at least catch sight of these people. If I see them, I won't know it's them will I? So you need to stay. We can all patrol together or split into two groups. I'm telling you that is the way I will work with you. It's you who have come to me.' She banged her fist on the table in punctuation.

Even though Keith, Kate and Christine did not fancy this at all, especially after meeting Anne, they would have no choice in the matter. She seemed to be crazy, hot tempered and unpredictable. Norman decided what they were to do, and it seemed he had to play Anne's game to get what he wanted. To him, finding these people was his primary objective. All they wanted to do was to help his cause.

Excerpt from Anne's Diary.

Sunday, 11 December
I still have a spy in the village. He is managing to live amongst them. Just about. He hasn't got rumbled yet, as he is one of my own. Drinking my bloodwine to fortify himself. He is hiding in his chambers in the day but still mixing with them at night. He does not come out on the hunt with us, as he will be seen. He must appear above suspicion.

I wished I had more of him, willing to work for me this way. Not having the comfort of the pack. He is through the first two stages of turning, but not the final one. He is still alive, but so willing to be one of us. Already succumbing to carrion, he waits to be turned. He does not like the day even now, his eyes burn he says and his skin itches. He does not die however, and this will be useful. This is the problem with having my blood in them, they transform so quickly. Alas I should really ensure he has his food brought to him. It must be hard for him to hunt incognito. I will reward him for this. I have said that he should keep well away from all of us until the time is right. I believe that he is having some of the local pets for his meals. The way it is going, they are becoming more and more scarce to find!! Tonight I got a visit from Norman just when I was about to go out on patrol, which was wonderful, as I love him so much. I don't like one of his Lieutenants named Christine. She is loudmouthed and fat. I don't like fat people. Even to drink, really. I know we will clash. I keep myself slim. I have always had a body to die for!! (I made a joke, haha!) Norman is after a group from his village, Friarmere. I know that there is another group that are not from Melden staying with that one off my infected. The one in the little street. The reason I am outnumbered is because of them. I told Norman, blackmailing him into staying with me overnight. That also meant housing his children (Boo). I said that this is the only way that I would help him. I knew he was desperate. Of course he had to stay. He needs me. So, Norman stayed in the hope that he could find out if they are here. He is impeded by the fact he has no invitation into houses and cannot wander in to find out if the group is here. He needs me again. Who is clever now, eh? I am a little bit obsessed with Norman I agree. Norman wants to take over his village, while I want to take over the world. Why can't he see that he is thinking too small. He says this will be my downfall but I know that it is just Len talking not him. I will make him proud of me. I am doing it all for Norman so we can rule the world! (without Len)

17 – Succulent

Somehow, the next morning they were filled with new hope. Wee Renee, Pat, Bob and Haggis went out for a walk in the crisp morning.

When they got back, Brenda, Sue and Laura had cooked a lovely bacon breakfast for everyone and they were very glad to have it, after being out in the cold. There were about two-dozen fried eggs, on the hotplate, for everyone to take. Pat had four bacon and egg *barm's*, with brown sauce and maple syrup as she said she was famished. Sue banned Tony from taking any eggs, after having embarrassing conversations with the others, about Tony's toilet habits.

They had agreed at one o'clock to meet Terry, Sally and Kathy at the band room. Carl who had agreed to stay the night at Beverly's house, said that he would also be there. Some of the Friarmere party had seen the group of people with Anne, *and* the vampires in Friarmere. He wanted to rule out the fact that his wife, Kate might have been amongst them.

Terry said there were about fifty group pictures of the band on the wall of the bandroom. Right from the early 1900's to the present day. If the Friarmere group could look at all the recent pictures, they could identify people they had seen. Carl knew of a couple of other people in the band who were missing. Some had seen various members of their family in Anne's gang who no longer contacted them, just wandering about through Melden. Horrified, but unwilling to make an intervention, they went home to lock the doors and hope the relative had forgotten where they lived. But some other people were still totally bereft as to what was happening in their family. *Were their relatives, dead, undead, alive, or requiring medical assistance?* If they were in this gang, Carl could let the relatives know and there would be some kind of closure for them.

Laura, Wee Renee and Pat decided to go as they had seen the people twice on the camera and once in real life. They called at the grocery shop on the way there. Wee Renee bought a lot of raw meat with her pin money and a tin of chocolates for Our Doris to say thank you for having them.

They met up outside the bandroom. Pat and Wee Renee looked up at the golden sign. *'Melden Silver Band'*, very grand. Carl was stamping his feet against the cold and rubbing his hands together. He looked nervous.

Terry, Kathy, and Sally were with Carl, all looking anxiously for the Friarmere group to join them. They said that a couple of other relatives of the missing band members, were joining them but had not arrived. So everyone had to wait a bit longer. They looked out at the silent morning. The semi-detached house's with their closed curtain's upstairs and downstairs. Each one the same, at one o'clock in the afternoon. Wee Renee had seen this before. Laura watched her head go from window to window. She knew what she was thinking, but also Laura had the feeling that the walls were closing in on her. She wanted to get out before she had to have another battle with a supernatural creature. They had gone from one massive trap to another. *Time is running out for us*, she thought.

Soon a couple of other people joined them. Terry took out his keys and started to walk up the path. The other's trailed behind him in silence.

Once they passed through the main entrance to Melden Silver Band, there were three separate doors, opened with three separate keys, and a corridor between each of them.

'Have you got the crown jewel's in here?' Wee Renee asked.

'You'd think so wouldn't you.' Kathy replied.

Terry had keys to all doors. He also owned the house next door, which housed his business, *Melden Smiles*, the dentist.

Melden was an old band and had an old bandroom. It was nearly one hundred years old and contained a lot of old memorabilia. The main room was quite dark and to add to the atmosphere, every wall had oak wood paneling, which was covered in pictures. It smelled musty and felt damp. There was a door to one side, and this led to the upstairs of the house that the bandroom used to be. Up there now was the bathroom and the place where the band kept all spare instruments. The music library was also up there. Laura had been in here a couple of times when she had deputised for players on behalf of Melden band if they were ill. As a percussionist Laura valued the quality of the percussion in this band room, it was extremely good. If she played here she would be worried about the xylophone or marimba getting mouldy. It really was too damp. Laura's cousin Kathy played the cornet, Sally played the horn and Uncle Terry played the big Bflat Tuba.

Kathy snapped the light on, and they were suddenly confronted with the sight of Malcolm sat in the Conductor's chair waiting for them. They all jumped back, he had scared them. Pat clutched her heart.

'What are you doing here?' Terry asked.

'I thought I could help and I got too cold outside waiting, so came in.'

'Fair enough. Why didn't you put the light on?'

'Thrift. And I wanted to be alone with my thoughts. There is a lot going on, isn't there.'

'You're not wrong there,' said Pat.

Laura had a feeling in her water about him. She thought Malcolm had been acting strangely last night, snooping on conversations and today, he didn't look too well at all. Laura wanted to pull her Uncle Terry aside and ask him if Malcolm had been at Anne's party and was infected like Our Doris, but didn't get the chance.

Although very pale, Malcolm was quite talkative. He was talking to Pat and Wee Renee about their story and what had happened to them in Friarmere. They told him their story until their arrival in Melden.

'It sounds terrible. What an ordeal. You had to kill your own fellow bandsmen too! I can't imagine doing it. It must have scarred you for life. How many of you got out?'

'Eleven are here. But there might be others left in Friarmere, we don't know. We hope so anyway,' Pat replied.

'Of course yes. And all that musical talent gone to waste, along with the waste of life. Are you safe now, here in Melden, do you think?'

'No. There are new threats here, which I obviously think you are aware of. But we think we are safe from the Friarmere threat. I mean it was a long way for us, and it will be the same for him in the snow. He won't have any idea we are here, he will be looking high and low in Friarmere, I imagine.'

'Of course. Where are you staying by the way?'

'We are with Freddie's sister-in-law, you know........' Wee Renee quickly put her hand over Pat's mouth.

'Sshh! Loose lips sink ships. You don't know who is listening to your conversation.'

'I'll tell you another time, love,' Pat said to him smiling.

Malcolm seemed very concerned about it all and Pat thought he was quite a likeable chap. He reminded her of Michael Thompson, before he became evil, but an improved version. A people pleaser and a bit too nosy, but generally good hearted.

Wee Renee started looking at the old pictures laughing, it was funny how things have changed.

'These are marvellous, I could look at them all day,' she said.

'Can we just get on to a few identification's please,' Carl said, clearly agitated. He didn't know if he wanted to know or didn't want to know now.

The recent batch of pictures from Melden Band had been in their sections. There was not a whole band picture, so they went from one to the next looking at the various groupings. Wee Renee recognised one straight away.

'That lady there. She is one. She has had her hair cut since this photo, though. A wee bob, she has now.'

'That is my Sarah.' One of the men said touching the picture gently with his hand as if he could bring his old Sarah back.

'Ah,' said Wee Renee. 'I think she made a visit to the kebab shop the other day as well then, if that is Sarah. You'll probably come across her sooner or later I imagine.'

Another lady was looking for her sister and Pat was able to identify her too. There was a teenage youth who was looking for his father and they had to tell him that he was amongst one of these people roaming around Melden, also.

'I thought he would be. I just wanted confirmation.'

'Are you ok. Do you have people to be with?' Laura asked.

'I'm at my mate's house.' He wandered out alone, which they felt very sad about.

Laura and Sally quickly followed him, and managed to catch him in the last corridor and tried to talk to him. It was hard work. They asked him if he was okay, but he shrugged off all their good wishes and said he just wanted to get home quickly so he didn't meet his Dad.

As they arrived back into the bandroom, Wee Renee reached the last picture on the wall, which was of the horns.

'This is a nice one of you, Sally.' She said as she moved along the picture. Then she squinted at it and gasped. 'Who is this person here?' She pointed to the attractive woman who was holding the flugelhorn in her hands. Carl and Sally walked over to look and followed Wee Renee's finger to the lovely brunette woman.

'That is my wife. That is Kate.' Carl said. Wee Renee took down the picture off the wall. She passed it to Pat, who looked down, then back up at Wee Renee. She passed it to Laura, who didn't know it was coming and the frame dropped on the floor, smashing the glass. Laura bent over, picked up the frame and walked over to the small metal bin, tipping all the broken glass into it. She could now see who Carl's wife was.

Wee Renee put her hand on Carl's arm.

'I am sorry to tell you that she has become one of his succulents,' she said gently. He put his hand over his mouth. Then realised he didn't understand what she was saying.

'Who is *he*? And what is she again?' Carl asked.

'The *he* is Norman. She is in Friarmere with him and was at the Christmas concert. Liz told us she was at the bonfire party and she is a wee succulent.'

'Okay so I know who he is now. But I still don't know what you mean. I don't understand what she is. Are you saying she is a cactus? Are you saying she is something he sucks on? Or that she is prickly?'

'No, no. A succulent you know what I mean.' Sally was watching all this and was winking one eye and thinking.

'Wee Renee do you mean a succubus?' She asked.

'Yes, that's what I mean. A sexual vampire. That's what she is, a succubus. I always get those words mixed up. I've been in the garden centre asking for succubus's before now!' Laura and Pat laughed and clapped her on the back.

'You are a one,' Pat said still hysterical. Kathy and Sally looked at them with extremely wide eyes and then glanced at Carl. Pat got her handkerchief out quickly and pretended to sneeze. 'Oohh, the dust in this bandroom.' She said, trying to stifle the laughter with the handkerchief.

Wee Renee looked at Carl who was devastated. He had crumpled onto one of the chairs and his head was in his hands. Wee Renee put her hand on his shoulder.

'Take no notice of Pat, love. She suffers from nervous laughter. I can assure you she is as upset as me.' She looked over at Pat and mouthed the words *you silly bugger* over the top of Carl's head and this started Pat off again. She rushed out into the corridor where she obviously thought she couldn't be heard. Pat took her handkerchief off her face and fully let rip with the guffaws.

Wee Renee decided to pretend she couldn't hear it and stroked Carl's head, saying *there there*. Carl looked up at Wee Renee.

'What is she doing there? What is happening to my Kate?'

'Well she is a vampire and she is a sexy one, that's all I know,' Wee Renee said. 'Plus you can safely say you wouldn't want her back, I think. I think a succubus does her Masters bidding, seducing men into becoming vampires at his will. And other dark deeds. At least you can grieve now. I just hope she doesn't want you back, or else you have a problem.'

At this point, as their conversation had become a little uncomfortable, the other people who had come to identify the last missing bandsmen wandered off with their heads down. Maybe their loved ones were in Anne's gang. Better that than a succubus.

One of the men entered the corridor. He tapped Pat on the shoulder.

'What does she mean exactly by a succubus? How far would they go?' He asked her quietly.

'Oh hello, saucy!' Pat said.

'No….I want to know because my sister is missing. I want to know the full facts.'

'Oh, sorry. They follow the Head Vampire's orders by doing it, this way and that with men, you know. Or creatures, who knows,' she said loudly.

'Ah!' Replied the man simply, put his head down and walked away from Pat. The whole conversation had been overheard in the bandroom and there was a tense silence. Pat had calmed down now and wandered back in, with a smile on her face.

'I will kill him.' Carl said.

'Now listen. You might feel like that,' said Pat sternly, 'but you won't on your own. You would never do it on your own in a million years. You haven't seen them. At some point we will go back, with our little army and you can come with us, if that is what you want. Then you can get revenge for your Kate. But let's be clear about this, she can never be the same again, and at some point one of us, or you, will have to kill her again. Don't forget she is already dead.'

18 – Shopping Bag

Wee Renee had put her shopping on two chairs. The meat on one chair, and her bag of chocolate's, on another one. Malcolm had shopping with him too and he had put this on the floor lying next to the Conductor's Stand. It was a brown paper bag inside a clear plastic bag and Pat noticed that it had been leaking.

'What's happened to your shopping, Malcolm?' She asked.

'Smashed it on the way. I slipped on the snow and knocked it against a wall.' He picked up the bag, and wiggled it a bit. They could hear the broken glass. It's a jar of beetroot, so I have put another bag around it. Luckily I had a spare in my pocket, from taking the dog out. He's missing now. I will have to sort it and wash the beetroot off all the shopping when I get back.'

'That's a swine,' Pat said, 'you haven't got 'owt in there that's absorbent have you. Like icing sugar?'

'No. Just a few tins of potato's and mushy peas.' He replied. Pat seemed content about these delicacies remaining unspoiled.

'I need to go upstairs in the archives and have a look at some paperwork up there. I have received a letter and it needs some personal details filling in. There are more pictures upstairs if you are interested? Really old ones. You ought to see some of the hairstyles,' Terry laughed.

They all trooped upstairs after Terry. The upstairs was very orderly with filing cabinets and a photocopier. At one end there were piles of instruments in brown and black cases with stickers on. Across the length of one wall sat a large dining table, which they used to sort out music. Above this table on the wall were all the old pictures. About half were black and white and half were colour. Wee Renee enjoyed looking at these thoroughly. Some of them were pictures of Terry's grandfather with a large moustache and sideburns. Sally brought up the fact that there were only ladies in the pictures from the 1980's and how it was wonderful how *banding* had moved with the times.

They had not noticed that Malcolm was still downstairs. Malcolm wanted to get a message to Anne. He knew everything now. How many there were and where they were staying. He would be able to inform Anne and Norman that some of the Friarmere party were here and there was a chance if they got here soon after dark, that they could be taken out tonight, leaving less to kill tomorrow. He would be in favour for this. Malcolm might even get a special reward. Perhaps they would finally turn him. He rushed off whilst he had his chance. There would be no questions from that lot upstairs. He just had to get his timing right, darkness wise. They would never know it was him.

'Is this the bathroom Uncle Terry? I probably should go.' Laura asked.

'Yes, that's it. It's fine to use, but don't judge us on the sanitary ware.' Terry said.

Laura went in and shut the door. There was an outer room with a mirror and sink, which she didn't look at, as she was desperate to get to the toilet. It was indeed a very old style toilet. A strange shape, small with quite a lot of pink flowers on its cracked surface and a small hole for the waste to go down. The flush was above, with a black chain and handle. She was glad to see that there were at least six sheets of toilet paper left on the roll. She looked for another to replace it, but there was none.

When she had used the toilet she went back into the outer bathroom area to wash her hands. She turned on the tap and washed her hands shaking them dry, thinking about what a pickle they were in. Laura glanced up at the mirror over the sink to check herself. What a mess. Her hair needed dying, her skin was dry and her eyes were dark underneath. At least she was alive. And thankful. It was then that she remembered about the empty toilet roll. There was a cupboard under the sink, which she checked. There they were, two unopened toilet rolls, she pulled the packet out and it was then she noticed there was a post-it note stuck to the top. It was an anonymous note. It said….. *I am so scared. Our conductor is now one of them. I have seen him with her. He eats animals. I am scared. Help.*

Laura took the note off the toilet paper. She reread the note and realised who they were talking about. Laura came out of the bathroom, and observed the group of people in the music library. She could see that Malcolm wasn't there and then remembered that she had not seen him since they had been upstairs. Gesturing for the others to come over, she put her finger to her lips, to prevent Malcolm from hearing them downstairs. She passed the note to Terry. He read it and then she motioned for him to pass it round. They all read the note and were shocked. Wee Renee clutched hold of Pat's arm. They stood there for a very long time listening.

'Malcolm!' Terry shouted suddenly. There was no reply.

'Dad! He could be fully transforming down there, all his fur growing and stuff. Now he will remember we are here again.' Sally said

'He'd have to grow a spine first wouldn't he?' Pat said. 'Yellow, two-faced bastard.'

'Yes Sally. They don't turn into a proper wee werewolf. He won't be doing that.' Wee Renee informed her.

'What are we going to do?' Kathy whispered.

'We will have to go down at some point. He hasn't done anything up to yet. We should be fine. We'll act like we don't know.' Wee Renee said. Laura took the note, folded it in half and put it in the back pocket of her jeans. They walked to the top of the stairs but were frozen to the spot. Pat walked to the head of the stairs, turning to the others.

'Let me go down first. He'll regret starting with me.' She whispered and off she clumped downwards. Pat was not bothered whatsoever.

She poked her head out of the stairwell carefully and then went a bit further. They all stood behind on the staircase, she was totally blocking their view, so they were depending on her. Their muscles were tense, ready to storm Malcolm at a moments notice. It seemed to be taking an eternity. Wee Renee sighed.

'What's going on Pat, I can't stand it any longer.' Pat didn't answer and Wee Renee feared the worst for her friend. She jumped down the last few steps and took a crouched position ready to spring. She quickly picked up a music stand to defend herself with, only to see Pat coming back in from the outside corridor.

'He's not here,' Pat said, 'It's safe to come down.' They all descended the last few steps and saw that she was right. Malcolm had mysteriously disappeared.

'This isn't giving me a good feeling,' said Wee Renee.

'I just checked all the corridors and popped my head outside. He's definitely gone.' Pat stated. 'I think he's gone to fetch some vampires to pick us off.' Terry muttered shaking his head.

'So do I.' said Sally miserably.

'How dark was it outside, Pat?' Terry asked.

'I wasn't thinking about the dark when I looked.'

'Let's look outside and see how bad it is.' Terry said. The whole group made the trip through the corridors and looked outside. It was already quite dark.

'We might have five to ten minutes to get home, but the fact that people could be on their way here, well……I'm worried we might not get out.' Terry said.

'How have we been in there so long?' Laura asked.

'I think we stood upstairs for ages, making our minds up about what to do.' Pat replied.

'It can't be helped now. The options are, we try and make a run for it, or we can stay in the dentist next door and, if they can come back here they won't find us.' Terry offered.

'What about our tracks. They'll know we are there.' Carl said.

'We will run around and make loads of footprints. There's enough of us to do that quickly. We should be able to confuse them on that part at least.' Sally said. They all agreed that going to the dentist was the best option. 'Right then let's lock up for the night, then they will have to waste time getting in. We have that much time at least.' Terry got his keys out of his pocket.

'Yes, he must have been gone fifteen minutes at the most and my shopping is inside.' said Wee Renee. They all rushed back in, Wee Renee picking up her two bags. It was then that she noticed that Malcolm had left his shopping by the conductor's stand. She opened the bag and noticed that there was not a smashed beetroot jar in there. Or several tins of potato's and mushy peas. What *was* in there, in fact, was a dead tabby cat and a smashed bottle of Swiss red wine.

'Oh my God!' gasped Wee Renee. 'Poor wee fella. If only we had checked.' The group looked at her in shock, their eyes going to the bag.

'What is in there?' Terry asked.

'You don't want to know. Only that it is a dead giveaway. I have seen bags like this in Friarmere. Let's just say, I'm glad Sue wasn't here. Pat and Terry chose to go and look. Terry closed his eyes as he saw what was inside.

'Nasty little rat,' Pat said and Terry nodded.

'Come on, let's go.' He said.

'I'm taking this poor wee soul out of here. This is one they won't eat!' Wee Renee said.

'You take your shopping, Rene. I'll take this little lad with me. Let them try and take him now. Barbarians!' Pat said, picking up the bag containing the dead tabby cat. They filed out and Terry locked the doors behind them.

'Now run around like mad.' Terry said. Whilst they did this, running around the street making higgledy-piggledy footprints in the snow, he walked to the next house. He took out a separate set of keys. Once the door was open he shouted, *'Right! In!* ' One by one they stopped running about and entered the dentist. Terry locked the door. They breathed a huge group sigh of relief. It was now fully dark. They would be here soon.

19 – Dentist

Terry got into the dentist and locked the door behind them. Immediately they were in complete darkness.

'Wait,' whispered Terry and he walked a couple of steps. They could hear his arm dragging on the wall. Suddenly about ten feet ahead of them it became slightly illuminated. Terry was framed in dim lights in front of them. He had switched on some fan shaped wall lights that had very low wattage bulbs. 'Follow me,' he said quietly. They walked behind him into the dentist waiting room, at the end of the corridor.

This room was furnished with quite a few soft chairs and sofas. It had the smell of clean antiseptic about it. The walls looked a mocha colour, the carpet chocolate. There was a large fish tank on one wall, which was lit by a bright aquarium light.

It illuminated the glittering fish, the water reflecting all over the walls in relaxing patterns. There were several pictures on the walls. These were of lovely serene landscapes, pools of water, forests and snowy mountains.

'This is nicer than our dentist, Rene,' Pat whispered.

'Yes, by a long shot,' Wee Renee replied.

Terry walked behind the reception desk and opened a cupboard. He fiddled under there for a few seconds and turned on the switches. Terry also got a bottle out of the bottom of the cupboard and placed it on the counter.

'Right shouldn't be too long now and we will be a bit warmer. I have put the heating on, but I'd wait a bit until you take your coats off. I am just going to splash this disinfectant across the entrance, so that they can't smell us. I don't know if that is what they can do, but better be safe than sorry.'

'Good idea Dad,' Kathy said.

'I am also thinking, we need to splash it over ourselves, just in case they can smell us through the door,' he said.

'Aye, good idea Terry. I think we need it on our shoes. I'll do them all. Lets leave them on though, shall we Pat,' Wee Renee said as Pat began to pull off her boots.

Terry walked out of the waiting room and Kathy went with him. The entrance hall had several doors leading to rooms for different purposes. One said *Hygienist* and two of them said *Dentist*. The one they were in said *Reception*. There was also a door opposite the reception that said *Toilet*.

Terry went to the front door, Kathy opened it quickly and he tipped the bottle of disinfectant upside down whilst wiggling it. Several loud glugs of liquid splashed across the steps. She shut the door quickly, as soon as he had finished. When he came back, he was just about to enter the waiting room, when he suddenly cocked his head towards the door. He said he could hear something outside that sounded like a motorbike. Which was unusual in the snow.

Wee Renee quickly went to his side.

'I will look take a look. I'm good at beaking.' She said winking at him. Walking past him, she opened the door that said *Hygienist*, which would have a view of the front of the property.

'Don't put the light on!' Terry said, just as her hand was reaching for the switch.

'Oh yes, silly me.' Wee Renee giggled. She struggled through the room, and round the dentist chair and all the paraphernalia, to get to the window. In the half-light, which was weakly coming through the blinds, she just managed to navigate her way around without knocking anything over. It was slightly brighter outside than inside, due to the streetlights. She positioned herself to one side of the window, looking through the gap between the blinds and the window frame. She observed what was going on for a long time. The other's watched her from the door of the hygienist, trying to be as quiet as they could. She stood and blinked and watched. They could see her eyes moving from left to right, recording every detail. The rest of the group desperately wanted to ask what was going on but they did not dare. They could hear small noised outside too, muted by the snow. One of them stepped forward as the tension was unbearable. Wee Renee heard the floorboards creak and put up her palm to stop them in their tracks. She put her finger to her lips before carrying on. They saw her swallow and then they heard more noise and voices.

Wee Renee continued her surveillance for another five minutes, mentally making notes. Then she backed away from the window looking behind her, so that she did not bump into anything and make a noise. By rolling the balls of her feet on the floor, she managed to walk really quietly to the door.

She pulled the door shut, but not fully closed, behind her. Poking her finger towards the waiting room, they all quietly walked back in and sat down. She shut the door behind them, so slowly that no one heard it click, to try and block out their voices. In a loud whisper, she began to tell them what she had seen.

'I have just seen the vampire, Keith who used to be in our band. *He is a policeman*!' She advised the others who did not know. 'And a plump woman who lives near The Grange where Norman lives, that is *also* a vampire named Christine. She was sitting behind Keith, on a kind of snow bike, with wee runners instead of wheels.'

'Do you mean a snowmobile?' Terry asked, raising his eyebrows.

'Yes, I think that's perhaps what they are. Keith and Christine came and waited, sitting on their snowmobile. They seemed excited, but seemed to be waiting outside the bandroom for something. There were a couple of wolves running behind them, who also stopped. Then they started roaming around the area, sniffing. They seemed confused with the scents from the bandroom. Maybe as there are a few of us and by running around we jumbled up the smells. Finally they came here and sniffed right up at the door, but I think your disinfectant made their noses tingle because they sniffed, squinted and buggered off. They didn't like it at all.'

'Are we talking about real wolves or Anne's gang?' Pat asked.

'Real. Keith and Christine sat there and waited but did not speak. She was wearing an evening dress. *An evening dress!* A strappy one in this weather. With no coat! Her hair is looking very dry as well, more like a blonde fright wig.'

'That'll be going on a bike. That's happened to me.' Pat sniffed.

'So another man turned up finally, I don't know who he was, and Malcolm. He held out his key and all four went in. The wolves stayed outside, to keep watch, it looked like.'

'So he *did* tell them where we were,' said Pat, 'that's it for him. And to think I liked him. I feel like a right old fool. I'll teach him.' And she drew her finger across her throat.

'I'll help you,' Laura muttered, 'dirty cat murderer!'

'Well, it looks like we are here for the night then.' Terry said resignedly.

'They will just find that we aren't there and then go, won't they?' Sally asked.

'This is how I see it,' said Terry, 'tell me if I am wrong. To get home we would have to walk through the streets knowing they are trying to find us. They were already out patrolling, trying to find Laura's group, before this.'

Laura nodded and Terry continued.

'If two vampires are here from Friarmere the others might be here too. The whole bloomin' gang, as far as we know. Plus we haven't seen Anne and her group. They'll be somewhere terrorizing some poor beast, no doubt. Then there are the wolves, sniffing round trying to catch our scent to follow. Don't forget too, there could be those kind of traitors, like the man you told me about, that stood in the centre of Friarmere on the last day. Still human, and more than happy to tell Anne and Norman about us, or to pick us off themselves. Apart from that, even if they aren't looking for us, they are after fresh victims every night. More and more people are becoming like them. Maybe watching, spying from their windows. No. It will not be safe until morning, so let's think of the best way we can settle in here. As soon as it is fully dark, any light that is in this dentist will shine out. I know that, as I have driven past at night and realised that a light has been left on. The only thing I can think is that we stay in here, as this room has no windows but we have the light of the Fish Tank. I think is it dull enough for them not to see, but bright enough for all us to see our way around. Let one of us look and see that they have gone, and then maybe we could have a drink. There is a fridge in the back, it will have milk in it, so that we can have a tea or coffee. There might be some food in there too, that someone has left. We have the toilets down here too but I suggest unfortunately that we flush it sparingly, because of the noise.'

'So it might mean if it's yellow, let it mellow,' said Pat and laughed, 'thank heaven's Tony isn't with us.'

'Oh, it doesn't bear thinking about does it,' Wee Renee said. Laura laughed.

'What do you all think? Do you think that is a good plan?' Terry asked.

'Yes, but all the others will be worried back at the house.' Laura said concerned. Wee Renee put her hand on Laura's arm and spoke to her frankly.

'Yes, they will. But what can we do about it? It is better that they have some worry tonight and we get back safe tomorrow than taking the chance of never getting back to them at all. I will have that bag from you, Pat if you like. I have a facility that I could use to sort out the dead fellow.' Pat passed over the bag.

'Thank you, Terry, I was wondering what to do with him. Eee, I hope the other lot aren't too worried about us. The silly buggers might put themselves in danger to find us!'

The others where in fact worried about Wee Renee, Pat and Laura. They knew that once it started to go dark, this probably meant they would not see their friends tonight.

'I hope that they had found somewhere to safe to hole up in overnight.' Our Doris said anxiously. Brenda, Our Doris and the rest of Friarmere Band, were really worried. They kept talking about it, going over various awful scenario's and generally were making each other feel a lot worse. Gary, of course, felt extremely guilty as all along he thought he should have gone with the three ladies. Once they weren't back by dark, he promised himself that he would listen to his instincts next time. If they had been killed, he would never forgive himself. He paced up and down Our Doris's living room, looking through the window each time he passed it. Gary was anxious and to add to it, he had started to get a headache. They were only supposed to be helping a few villagers with identifications. Maybe something had happened and they were still there. Perhaps for some reason, they had to take Carl back to Beverly's and thought they would *err on the side of caution*. Our Doris thought that they had gone into Terry's Dentist's Surgery, as it was very comfortable. Gary didn't see why they would be, but he supposed it was possible. That was a least three possibilities. He realised how much they all depended on mobile phones. How he would have loved to use one now.

'What are we going to do? Should we try and send out a search party?' He said.

'No! You're not thinking straight, Gary,' said Freddie. 'They will be safe, I know it. They have Pat and Wee Renee with them. I would pity the vampires or wolves that tried to attack them. All three of the girls have weapon's, I checked. They will be absolutely fine and I am sure we will see them tomorrow. It's just going to be a bit of a long night. I am hoping that they found somewhere to stay too. Obviously, something has happened so that they could not get back here before dark. But they are sensible and experienced. Those three know what they are playing at. They are big tough girls and clever ones at that.'

Wee Renee decided that she would like to go and watch the street again from the blinds, in the Hygienists room. She said she had seen exactly who had come in, and she would know who had or hadn't gone out. If they had left someone in the bandroom, she would know. She felt, as she had not been observed before, that she obviously had found the ideal place to watch. She positioned herself again and Pat stood by the door, just in case she had to very quickly indicate to them that they were coming this way, or for another emergency matter.

In the waiting room, Terry quietly walked around, having a look in the fridge and strangely, the filing cabinets. Trying to find out what sustenance they had to last them overnight. Kathy and Sally had known their father far too long to know that he would not be finding any biscuits or chocolates in this dentist. He was very strict about those kind of foodstuffs and it did not set a good example for his receptionist to be eating them, when he was telling patients not to eat them at all. Sally had the idea that they might have to live on toothpaste samples at this rate, but at least she wouldn't be worried about getting on the scales at slimming club next week.

Laura, Carl, Sally and Kathy sat on the sofas. Laura looked at the fish tank. It certainly was relaxing. She watched one fat black fish go to the bottom, pick up some gravel, swim to the top and spit out he gravel. It cascaded down and he happily wiggled his tail. Then he dived down again. She wished life was as simple for them. Just happy with a bit of flake food and throwing gravel up and down. There was something to be said for the life of a mere fish as opposed to a human. This life was now harsh and dangerous and sharp. Carl was facing the fish tank too, but not really watching the big black fish. He was still every so often releasing a tear down his face, which he wiped on the sleeve of his coat. Carl was not thinking about anything only Kate. Laura got up from the sofa and took a big box of tissues off the reception desk. Wordlessly, she placed them on the arm of the sofa next to Carl.

Sally and Kathy were watching their father walk around checking cupboards, pulling various bits out of them and putting them on the receptionist desk. All of a sudden, a thought occurred to Kathy.

'Wait a minute, we should have worked this out about Malcolm. He went to that party at the big house and then last week when we were at rehearsal he slashed his finger open on one of the old music stands that he was trying to force open for someone. When he did, I saw that it was a really big cut, but do you know, I haven't thought about until now, but no blood came out of it.'

'Yes!' Sally said. 'He quickly got his handkerchief out of his pocket and wrapped it round his finger but it never bled and he wasn't bothered about it the rest of the night.'

'It doesn't add up,' Kathy said shaking her head. 'If he is one of them, how come he was out in the day?' The others looked crestfallen. This would have tied up everything nicely. Everything was explained apart from that fact. He had been at the party, had been cut but had not bled. There was the bag with the dead cat and the smashed wine. Apart from the fact that he was a traitor. Terry thought hard. There was something they were missing. Then he knew.

'Well he wasn't out in the day really was he? Malcolm was already in the band room. He was already here when we got here. He could have been in there since it was dark this morning, waiting.'

'Extremely creepy,' said Laura shivering.

'And last night when we saw him in the Pub it was already nighttime. I can't remember when I last saw him in the day.' Kathy said.

'What about just?' Sally asked.

'He probably slipped out the second it was dark and then went and told them where we were. It all fits. He hasn't been out in the day.'

'Or he could have been hiding in the wheelie bin until it was dark!' Kathy said. 'Who knows, with them kinds of folk.'

'Oh no.' Laura put her head in her hands. 'Not only does he know where we were tonight, he tricked us into telling him exactly where we were staying and how many of us there are. Now Anne and Norman know everything.' Terry cleared his throat.

'Yes, we are all in even more danger now. And the other group stopping in Melden don't even know it!' Terry said as he run his fingers over his bald head.

20 – Fang

Even though they were talking quietly, Terry could hear everything they were saying. He stopped putting stuff on the counter and took a deep breath.

'Listen, everyone, Malcolm visited me a few days ago. He was pale and anxious. I noticed he was slightly hyperventilating and I was very worried. It took him a long time to tell me. At one point I thought he wasn't going to at all.' Terry stopped at this point and stared at the wallpaper, recalling the day of their meeting. 'He was heavily sweating, his face looked …..waxy. He said he couldn't go more into it but he had developed a strange addiction. One that he was a little worried about. He wouldn't give me any more details, no matter how hard I pressed him.' He shook his head. 'I thought it was marijuana. I really did. I called him the next day, left messages, heard nothing.'

'That was really strange Uncle Terry, didn't you wonder about it?' Laura asked.

'No. Malcolm liked attention and had a tendency to make things up. He was a bit of a Walter Mitty.'

'As well as that, he has always been secretive Laura, that's the way he is. He is always saying things that are enigmatic and not telling you the full story but tempting you to constantly ask him about it. Then he won't tell you and you keep asking. He has always been the same.' Sally added.

'Yes that is his way. I thought if he wants me to know he can just bloody well tell me, but I'm not going to play one of Malcolm's games. But I got too worried. I didn't hear anything from him for nearly two days. Then I went to visit him. He didn't allow me to enter the house. I stayed at the door. He said the place was untidy. Why he thought I would mind, I don't know. It was always untidy and I had never mentioned it. It was obviously not the right reason. I asked him about his addiction, and what it was again. Malcolm said that the addiction was still there, but perfectly fine and that he could probably see that at some point, I would have it. He didn't hint as to what it was and naturally, I thought it was the drugs messing with his brain.' Terry put his hands over his face. 'Why didn't I see this? I could have stopped it. *I could have saved him*.'

'No. You could not have worked this out' Laura said to Terry. He looked a bit devastated, as if he should have been able to pre-empt this situation.

'You didn't know about the cut that didn't bleed. Sally and Kathy didn't know about him saying he had a strange addiction. Also the reality of what has really been happening in Melden has only hit you within the last couple of days, since you have seen us. There was no way you could work out what was going on with Malcolm. Everyone had one piece of the jigsaw.'

'There is something else I need to tell you. I just want to check what is going on at the front.' Terry tip-toed out of the waiting room to join Pat in the corridor. He touched her shoulder gently.

'Anything going on?' He whispered.

'She hasn't said anything to me. She is still watching.' Pat replied bluntly. Wee Renee stepped back and turned her head towards them. She could hear them from the window even though they were talking in the quietest tones. Wee Renee shook her head as if to say there had been no movement.

Terry walked back into the waiting room, slightly closing the door behind him. The other's waited to hear for any news.

'Nothing yet, they are still in the bandroom.'

'So what else has been going on then, Uncle Terry?' Laura asked.

He sat on one of the chairs opposite the group and took a deep breath. Rubbing his hands across his face, he took a deep breath, before speaking.

'Two days ago a strange case presented itself to me in the surgery. I attend to all of this particular family's teeth, and it was the son, that had the problem. His mother told me that only the previous day she had seen an unusual tooth starting to form in her son's mouth. He had come to her complaining that his mouth was hurting and when she looked she had seen the point of a new tooth, cutting through the gum. He seemed to have a fever and was very tired. She had given him children's paracetamol for the pain and he had gone to bed. The next morning, the tooth was fully formed on the corner of his mouth here,' Terry pointed at his own gum, 'at the side above the canine teeth. There was the start of one the other side too, in exactly the same place. So she called the surgery to get an emergency appointment, as she was extremely worried about how quickly these teeth had appeared. Her son was in quite a lot of pain. When she presented the boy I witnessed an unusual tooth indeed. All I can say is that it was more like a fang, rather than a tooth. I did not remove it, but gave him some antibiotics. as there certainly was swelling on the roots of both new teeth. Until I could reduce his infection, I wouldn't see how far the root system went. Also, regretfully, my x-ray machine had broken down and the technicians obviously couldn't get to me, to repair it. I booked him in for an exploratory today, with a view to having the teeth removed. Or to check the growth of both of them, if I couldn't. I also was going to refer the boy to the hospital. The child looked generally unwell, and I saw on his neck a superficial wound, but I thought there was nothing unusual about this at the time. However, I told them to book an urgent appointment with their Doctor as the fangs, weren't the only symptoms he was presenting. But these were the only ones I could deal with.'

'How old was he?' Laura asked.

'He was eight years old.'

'Did you notice anything else, besides his neck and the fangs?'

'Yes, I was concentrating on his mouth, obviously, but for a moment, I noticed a strange reflection in his eyes. In addition to that, when he was under the lamp he was also closing his eyes to the light. That is why I told them to get an urgent appointment at their Doctor's Surgery. Meningitis was at the back of my mind. I was certainly worried though, as we are cut off from all the hospitals at the moment. I don't know if she listened to me. I think she probably did. Whether they have seen their Doctor or not, I don't know. How could I? Communication wise we are living in the dark ages.'

Pat then entered the room with Wee Renee close behind her. They shut the door behind them and Wee Renee told them that everyone had come out of the bandroom, disgruntled and had now gone. They could now maybe talk a little louder. Perhaps use the toilet or kettle.

21 – Antibiotic

Pat and Wee Renee sat down and said they were tired from standing up. They needed to rest for a while. Terry suggested that they all have a cup of tea, and relax for a minute. Sally and Kathy asked what everyone wanted and set to work as quiet as they could, putting the kettle on and making teas and coffees for everyone.

Whilst they did this, Terry told the two women that had been in the hygienist room, about the tale of the child that had visited him.

'The plot thickens,' Pat said.

Sally and Kathy brought over the drinks. Terry had found a box of cereal bars that his receptionist had had in the drawer. There was just enough for all of them to have one each.

Again Terry looked as if there was something he was going to have trouble imparting to them.

'We need to discuss something else too.' The group put down their cups and waited for him to start. Terry gazed at the fish tank from where he sat. At one point Wee Renee thought he had forgotten he was supposed to be telling them something. Then he bought it all out, in one mouthful.

'You have forgotten that I went to that party too. I ate and drank the same as everyone else.' Carl felt a knot tighten in his stomach. For the first time that evening, he looked up from his hands and slowly regarded Terry. He pushed himself back against the chair.

'What are you saying? Are you going to turn on us as well? Have you and Malcolm been planning this? Are you some kind of vampire? Have you been eating cats? Have you eaten my cat, Terry? Is this what you are telling us? Was that child one of your new bloodthirsty mates?'

'No. Hold your horses, Carl. I've never been asked so many questions in all my life! No not at all. It grieves me to have to tell you that I did eat and drink what they were eating. Since then I have felt a bit ill, but I have been very busy in the dentist and until now, I did not realise the severity of it, or recognise the symptoms, or even imagine what it could mean!' Terry was clearly upset and they could see he was worried. He picked up his cup and took another drink, his hand shook and he had to hold the cup in both hands to steady it.

'Right Terry, lets sort you out. Have you succumbed to eating flesh?' Wee Renee asked.

'No, not at all! God no, I haven't! I have felt strange certainly and had weird dreams. I have definitely been tired in the day, but just drank more coffee. I thought I was coming down with something. I missed my flu jab this year, I thought it was that.'

'The lady we are living with, Our Doris,' said Wee Renee, 'is having those dreams too. But she is so bad that she cannot get out of bed. She has hardly eaten too. This doesn't add up. How else have you been suffering?'

'I've just had the tiredness really. Been a little achy, I suppose, but I have been able to carry on working. Since I knew about how this situation was developing, I have been thinking it through. It is great that I haven't had as severe reaction to it as others, but there must be a reason. I wondered if it is because I was already on a course of antibiotics before I went there. If this is some kind of infection or virus that she introduced to our village, then maybe this is what has saved me. If I consumed exactly the same amounts of virus, it can be the only explanation.'

'What were the antibiotics for Dad? You never told us you were ill.' Kathy asked.

'It is a bit embarrassing really.' They all jumped to the same conclusion. Pat smiled at Wee Renee and she pursed her lips.

'Go on Rene,' Pat said encouragingly.

'Aye, Terry. It's clear you have had a problem with a private area. You are going to have to tell us, we are all friends here. We won't judge you.' Wee Renee said kindly. Sally and Kathy looked at each other shocked. Carl's mouth dropped open. Terry was a dark horse, indeed. Pat moved her head forward, a hand on each knee. She didn't want to miss the details.

'Go on, love. Spill the beans,' Pat said.

Terry didn't know what they were trying to say, and then came in at the last minute.

'Oh right, no nothing like that. I am on about my toe that had gone really septic. My big toe. I have a funny toenail. It keeps happening. I had to have strong antibiotics for it.' Pat sat back again in her chair, clearly disappointed with Terry's ailment.

'Oh Terry, you got me in a proper to-do there. I thought you were going to turn out a right *rum 'un*!' Pat said.

'Dad,' said Sally, 'why didn't you tell us about the toe or about feeling ill. You have been going through all this on your own.'

'It's not a big deal. It was a bad toe and a bit of tiredness or that's what I thought. Now I am worried, but I didn't have all the pieces of the puzzle back then.'

'What is this infection anyway? Or virus?' Carl asked, frowning at the others. 'I am confused as to whether it is vampires or is it werewolves? Surely we can't be so unlucky as to have both. It must be one or the other.'

'I don't really know, to be honest. This is what I can gather.' said Wee Renee. 'In Friarmere there is a man named Norman he seems to have been here in Melden before, and it looks like that is when he took Kate. I think Kate *is* a vampire, a succubus. He then infected our band with wine and food, which contained his blood. Which marked them for his approach. Norman then turned them one by one, apart from one person who fought the compulsion to become one of his. Being a vegetarian helped Liz resist the urge for meat or blood. As far as I know, the people from Friarmere are pure vampire. Now, as well as all that, a farmer had some sheep stolen. They were eaten or mutilated. Both of those things I think. He thought he heard wolves howling. Which obviously now ties in with this. At one point there was a battle, which seems ages ago, but was in fact, only last Wednesday. We lost some good people. At this battle, a Christmas Concert, all the people that had been made into vampires, came out of the woodwork. Between us, we managed to get some of them but we also witnessed them make others. They blocked the village off. We were all trapped. The vampires were now picking people off one by one. We saw two people from the band, The Cooper's attacking a lady we knew named Mary. We got away by the skin of our teeth. When we arrived here, we spoke to Our Doris. She went to a similar party but there was a lady named Anne, who was the host. Our Doris has never clapped eyes on Norman. Anne also invited the band from Melden. What a coincidence?

And it looks like this Anne, infected them with her blood too. Her blood is different though it seems. Our Doris had different symptoms and dreams than Liz. I have witnessed the vampires in Friarmere and the infected people over here in Melden. There is definitely a big difference between them. Physically they look different, stand and walk differently. Plus there is the aspect of the wolves that are roaming with the group of predators and this lady named Anne. They work as one intelligence. I have seen her command them with her mind working them one way and another, shifting like a flock of birds. These people still look to be mostly regular. They are not covered in hair, so are not werewolves. But what the people are, I don't know. From a distance I would say their heads and hands are slightly different, and they walk more crouched or bent over. The vampires in Friarmere are just pale imitations of us. If you saw one from a distance, you would never know. They can act the same as us at will, but are a deceiving bunch of monsters.'

'So, there is a difference. Would you say the Friarmere lot are clearly vampires, but it is unclear what they are here?' Terry asked.

'Yes I would. I am no expert, but I have read a little. Whether what I read is a myth or a truth passed down, I don't know.' Sally couldn't imagine what Wee Renee was going to say next.

'Some of the books I have read might explain the Melden lot, one way or another. I am not saying what I know is gospel. You must understand. But I admit a lot of things fit with something I have read. I can't remember it all either. The books are sitting in my wee house right now, with all the answers we need. Just waiting for me to find them!' Wee Renee said.

'Tell us please,' asked Sally. 'Tell us what you know.' The room was quiet, the fish tank bubbled every so often. As Wee Renee spoke, there was a feeling that they had been sent back to ancient times, when Old Wives told tales around the fire. Where the world was still flat and anything was possible. Their wide, shining eyes watched Wee Renee. They absorbed every word.

'There is no doubt that there are many legends about vampires and werewolves and some of them go hand in hand. There is a Russian legend about a monster called the Strigoi, who is part werewolf and part vampire. Bram Stoker's Dracula is like him. A Strigoi. Where do the bats come into it? Maybe people saw something else flying in and feeding on people. Something black, and they naturally put it together with the vampire bats that mostly feed on cattle. The engravings of The Strigoi are truly terrible.' Terry swallowed loudly, before Wee Renee continued.

'Also there is the Irish goddess of death called The Morrigan, that I have heard of. She can transform herself into a wolf or a crow and signifies death and fate. A crow – they are black aren't they, like a bat. Is that too much of a coincidence? Imagine this. What if this Anne is a lot older than we think? What if she was in Ireland hundreds of years ago and *The Morrigan is her*! Tales passed down from generation to generation, changing with each telling. Maybe, she was just a vampire who owned wolves. I don't know, there are so many legends, I only managed to read a few in the first days between us realising what we were facing, and leaving Friarmere. Like Terry, I didn't know what I know now. I wasn't looking for a vampire werewolf connection. Just vampires.'

'Wait a minute. Isn't Anne's surname....Morgan?' Laura asked.

'Yes,' Pat answered.

'Talk about tales being changed with each telling. How much is Morgan like *The Morrigan*?'

They all held their breath.

22 – Snowmobile

Wee Renee was just about to say something else when they saw her stiffen.

'Shhh!' she said. They all listened intently and they started to hear it too. There it was, the sound of a motorbike again. In fact, it sounded like two of them. Wee Renee quickly and quietly got up and walked out of the waiting room. Pat followed her and the others filed in behind Pat. Wee Renee quickly resumed her position of viewing and watched what was going on. She was there for a long half an hour again, watching as quiet and attentive as a cat. Then suddenly they began hearing more voices, and shouting. Wee Renee stepped back a little from the window. Even if they had been speaking at normal volume they probably could not have been heard for the amount of noise outside.

They were all very worried, breathing shallowly, thinking that at any moment they would be discovered. After a short while, the noise seemed to transfer inside. Shouting, bangs and thumping could be heard against the wall that joined the bandroom onto the dentist.

In the next house, they certainly were having a thorough search for the group. Wee Renee came away from the window, shooing the others in front of her. They quickly paraded back into the other room and shut the door slightly behind them.

'Listen carefully,' she said before telling them what they most craved to hear. Her eyes were large and her breathing quick. They stood in a circle. The atmosphere was electric. 'There were five wolves, and six of what I would consider three people infected by Anne, rather than Norman. They were waiting. I don't know how long they had been there. I take it they hadn't heard us speaking or else they would be in here now. We will have to be careful. If we hadn't heard the snowmobiles as a warning, we could have been doing anything in here and given ourselves away. Just as I got there the first snowmobile arrived with Keith and Christine again. Then, I could hear the other snowmobile and they all turned facing in one direction and waited, in reverence. There he was on the second snowmobile, The Beast himself, Norman.' Wee Renee stopped and touched Carl's arm. She looked him directly in the eyes for a long time. 'And sitting behind him, on the snowmobile was your Kate.'

Carl's knees buckled and Terry managed to grab him quickly at the side. Between Terry and Pat, they got Carl into a seat, where he sat pale, glassy eyed and still staring at Wee Renee.

'They would have killed us. All that amount of people.' Laura said.

I have no doubt,' Wee Renee said. 'Norman looked excited and so did Kate. Keith held back all the others until Norman got there. The Beast went in first, whether that was so he would have first dibs, I don't know. They never even glanced in this direction. I'm going to do more beaking now, but it's no use looking out there now, they have gone inside.'

Wee Renee took a glass that was on the receptionist desk. She walked over to the area in the corridor where the noise was loudest and placed the glass against the wall and then her ear against that. She started to hear the conversation a lot more clearly.

No human was in the bandroom. They had been though. Keith had even knocked over all the filing cabinets to check that people had not got behind them, or even inside. They had been into the bathroom and had looked everywhere in the lower level of the premises.

It was quite clear that there was no one here. Norman could sense there had been a group here not too long ago. Malcolm had not lied to them. He had just not been quick, or covert enough. Malcolm had been clumsy and their prey had worked it out. He had told them a few of the names that he thought were there. While this meant nothing to Norman, he could recognise the scent from Friarmere, and knew they were some of the group he was hunting.

'Malcolm, please repeat all the names to Keith.' Norman said through gritted teeth.

'Pat, Laura and Wee someone.' Malcolm said, looking at Keith hopefully. He really needed these names to be on Norman's list, as this triumph could very easily go south, he could tell.

'Those are three of the names from Friarmere Band. They were part of the group that resisted us at the Civic Hall concert.' Keith replied, a sly smile at one side of his mouth. Then the atmosphere changed from Malcolm being in danger to him being the hero again. Norman was ecstatic about this. Now he knew where they had gone for definite.

'Yesssss.......!' But his triumph turned to ashes in his mouth once again. Realisation hit home. Knowing where they had been, wasn't much good to him. He was still in the same position as he was yesterday.

The eleven missing people were not in his hands, were they? What was it with this group that they could keep getting out of his clutches? Did they have some kind of guardian angel? The mood changed again as this made him angry and for the briefest moment he thought that he would never get them. No matter how hard he tried, how many vampires he had, plus Anne's children, he was always one step behind them. He started to throw chairs and music stands around the room.

'This place stinks of humanity and life and happiness. You will all be witness. I swear I will put an end to all that for these people.'

Malcolm watched from the corner of the room. This situation was very volatile again. What was it with this guy? He didn't think he would bother spying again. It just wasn't worth the hassle. All his dreams of being in The Dark Mistress's favour had come crashing down. Malcolm closed his eyes and imagined of going back to Anne's house, and chowing down on a nice fat badger.

Wee Renee took the glass away from the wall and went back to the group to tell them what she had heard.

'Malcolm repeated our names and Keith confirmed we play for Friarmere Band. Little weasel.' She hissed. They had all heard the last part where he was really angry and throwing stuff around for themselves, as it was so loud.

'I think I will pop more disinfectant across the steps whilst they are in there.' Terry said, who walked back to the waiting room to get the disinfectant. The group trouped back into the waiting room. Terry pushing past them now with the disinfectant to get the job done before the vampires came back out.

Carl had remained seated. He looked very tired. His eyelids were heavy and the whites of his eyes were red. He rubbed at an imaginary spot on his jeans. The others sat with him.

'Well what now?' Pat asked.

'For sure we are stopping here tonight, no question about that. You haven't seen them Pat. We don't stand a cat in hell's chance with them roaming the streets tonight. I know for a fact he can smell us in the band room. It wouldn't take long for the wolves and him to catch our scent. Those snowmobiles are fast. We couldn't outrun them.' Wee Renee said. She then turned to Sally and Kathy. A very serious look was on her face and they instantly felt anxious about what she was going to say.

'I think I am going to upset your Dad.' They wondered what she was going to do or say that was that serious.

'Although I am very grateful for the cereal bar and although Terry might not agree, I am going to open a tin of chocolates that I had bought for Our Doris as a thank you. I need the chocolate girls. I'm starving. It's the nervous energy. And I think for Carl, it is a medical necessity!' Terry stood at the door of the waiting room, the empty bottle of disinfectant in his hands. His daughters looked up at him, expecting fireworks.

'I don't have any problem with that at all. In fact I will be eating as many as you. Cavities seem less important today than they used to be.'

Wee Renee opened the tin and they all took one out, opening it in silence. They sucked on the chocolatey goodness, looking at the fish tank's reflected water on the walls. If they tried hard enough maybe they could block out the bangs and crashes they could still hear from next door.

Excerpt from Anne's Diary.

Monday 12th December
Well, what a night!! The spy that I had in the village came good. He ran all the way to me at the time I was in my bath, or spa as I call it. I cut the treatment short to see him. He told me that there is a group in the bandroom that he thinks are the ones I am interested in.

He told me that they are a mixture of Melden and Friarmere people, so it must be them. I have to meet people from The Council tonight about secret matters. I cannot go with Malcolm. It is very important that I attend this meeting and get them to do something for me. After they have done that, I can make them my own. Again if they resist then they will just have to expire. I need to bend their will tonight, hence the early bath. I have got to look my best (if you have got it, flaunt it!).

Norman and Kate were out, enjoying the moors on the snowmobile, so Keith and Christine went out to investigate on theirs. I let them have some of my wolves, Malcolm of course, and another one of my children. Off they went to the bandroom, and I continued to make myself beautiful. It wasn't long before they were back.

They had come to ME, to ask what to do. When they got the place Malcolm had last seen them, the mixed group were no longer there. They could smell that they had been there, but they were either hiding or had just left. We all had a chinwag about it over a spiced blood drink which is my new invention! We felt that as it was dark they could not have chanced getting home. Keith and his group would have seen them in fact. So they are near to where he last saw them. If they are hiding in the bushes, waiting for us to check there before doubling back to the bandroom, then they have a false sense of security. As we won't be giving up!! Norman returned to hear the news. Excited he went straight back out with Kate, Keith and Christine. Again I let them take some of my wolves. I am not using all of them tonight, am I? What a lovely sister, I am! Maybe Norman will see how useful they are! I could sort him out with a pack very quickly. Again the bandroom was empty and there was no fresh scent. Malcolm got into a lot of trouble for letting them slip away. I was told Norman was very angry, but he had a line that he didn't cross. That is why I love him so much. I will turn Malcolm now. The pretence is over. His cover is blown. He will get his prize now. They left two wolves there, to wait outside the bandroom. They also stationed two wolves at the end of the little street where my infected child lives. Sophia stayed with me whilst I was on my way to see the people for dinner. Anyway, what should happen when I was out and about with my new friends from the council? I came across two

*of Norman's children roaming around Melden,
unsupervised. (I think they did not have permission to
be there, as he has never mentioned them!) One was
a fully formed child vicious and powerful, I was happy
to see. The other was semi-infected but I knew he
was a full daywalker minion of my brother Norman.
They were natural brothers when they had both been
alive. I could smell it. Ordinarily I would maybe have
tried to turn or kill the one that was still alive. I would
have fancied my chances against Norman's child, if
he had defended his brother, but as I am trying to be
a good sister. (aren't I, just?) I left them. Of course, I
was with unsuspecting humans anyway. So it was
meant to be. I sent Sophia to retrieve the two wolves
from the bandroom and the two from the street at
five o'clock. Norman now says he has to return, sadly.
I did not inform him of his two wayward sheep, that I
had come across. They may well bleat my tune in
time! There are matters for him to attend to in
Friarmere. We both made a plan. He has left me with
a message for them, which will I will faithfully deliver
tomorrow evening. I will make him proud of me I will
show him I can take over the world. I can be trusted.
Finally he will be proud and I will be his favourite, not
damned Len!!*

23 – Poison

After a short while they could not hear any more noise from next door. The two snowmobiles started up and their noise gradually disappeared into the night. As they had not been checking the window, they did not know if there was anyone still inside. Wee Renee quietly walked to the Hygienists window again to have a quick check. In the street, she could see two wolves hungrily pacing and one of Anne's people standing outside. It looked like they were waiting to see if the bandsmen came back. Wee Renee watched them for about ten minutes but nothing changed. When she came back into the waiting room she shut the door and addressed the group quietly.

'I have been thinking about what Terry said earlier. About the fact that he was on antibiotics and that this seemed to have staved the infection off. Do you have any drugs here?'

'Yes, this is a dispensing dentist. I only have drugs here related to dentistry. I do have antibiotics here, but they are meant for oral infections and not broad-spectrum antibiotics. I see where you are going with this. I just don't know how well this would work.'

'It's worth a shot though, isn't it?' Pat said.

'Oh yes. I am wondering also, about when I finish this course of antibiotics. Will the symptoms come back?'

'I don't know about that,' said Wee Renee, 'but Our Doris certainly has improved and she has had no antibiotic or intervention. So I think time is also a healer in this. Slowly your body either adapts or gets rid of the infection.'

'What about your other friend, infected with the Friarmere strain?' Terry asked.

'The same. She is certainly improved from how she first was. Liz couldn't eat at all. She is still affected and very weak, but she is a different person than she was a while back.'

'Don't get me wrong, I still know there is something wrong with me.' Terry said. 'I don't think antibiotics totally obliterate it. I think it just keeps it at bay. It's no miracle cure.'

'Alright,' said Wee Renee, ' looking at the facts. We have got you. You have had antibiotics, but had started the course before you were infected. You are infected with the Melden strain. I suggest that we try some of your antibiotics on Liz who has the Friarmere, or pure vampire strain and Our Doris, that has the strain from Melden which is the same as you. The difference being, she is having the treatment after infection and not before.'

'Wait a minute, I don't know about this.' Kathy said. 'We are just using these two people as guinea pigs. This is a weird situation. A strange blood virus, that is changing them. We aren't qualified to do this, even Dad. We can't mess about with people's lives.'

Pat stood up and stretched, then turned to Kathy.

'Love, lets get this straight. We are giving them something that is tried and already tested on humans. It cannot hurt them. Only, maybe make them better. What is wrong with that? It certainly looks like it has made a difference to your Dad and for all we know these dental antibiotics might not work the same as the one's for the septic toe, but I think if there is a chance we should try it. But, lass, we won't force it on them, they will have a choice to take it or not. I know I would if, I was in the same boat.'

'Don't forget Kathy, I am nearly out of my tablets too. I will have to take oral antibiotics just the same as everyone else. Or else I might revert back, who knows. When I take these, I still might revert back. But I have no other options in the interim period. I have no Doctor's and I don't need a sore toe on top of fighting monsters. I am happy to take them.' Her father said.

Carl seemed to become attentive as a thought struck him. For the first time since he had found out that Kate was in the next building, he spoke.

'Yes! We might have discovered the cure. I could have my Kate back!'

'Hold your horses there, Carl. You've not been listening. I have said that it isn't even curing *me*. It is keeping me in a holding pattern.' Terry said, laying his hand on Carl's knee.

'As much as I would like you to be able to have Kate back, we are talking about three people that are *not dead* taking it. Who are all consciously fighting this hostile takeover! Not someone who has embraced it. That have not eaten human flesh, they are still made of it. We are working with the living and an infection. Surely this cannot work on someone dead. No drugs work on the dead. I know that much. Also we have the fact that the three people, one of which is me, I would say would be mostly willing to take it and want to be cured. Whereas your Kate will not want to be cured and be resistant to the idea. How do we force it on her? I don't know about the future and how this will work on the other two ladies infected, but I don't think for a minute this treatment would work for a corpse effectively. It will be hard enough to not only get rid of the infection, First, I would have to breathe life into her. Like some kind of Frankenstein's Monster.'

Pat was shaking her head at Carl gravely, she added to the conversation.

'I have seen these suckers in real life. They aren't the same as us any more Carl. I am so sorry to say but all their normal stuff has gone. All the bits we have inside. They're gone. All the kidneys and livers, the sausage bits that were hanging out of Ian....'

'The intestines, Pat,' Wee Renee informed her. 'Them. Yes. What's left is sort of greeny-black and putrifying. Powdery with no blood. I can't say any more but the texture of them is different even from the outside. They change so much and there is no humanity left.'

Carl was looking at his lap. For a long time, he had been flattening everyone's chocolate wrappers and then folding them neatly into little squares.

'I'm sorry, love.' Pat said gently. She took another chocolate out of the tin, unwrapped it, popped it in her mouth and gave him the pink foil wrapper. 'Here, have that.'

'Do you think Terry, that antibiotics will work the same on the vampire strain as well as the strain that you and Our Doris have suffered?' Wee Renee asked.

'I don't see why not, if the person is still alive.'

'How much antibiotics do you have?'

'I have an awful lot, I had a recent delivery luckily. Enough for at least four months here of a normal dispensing dentist. So definitely, we could treat a few people for quite a while. Lets hope it works. By the time we have run out, we might be right as rain. Or if we aren't, we have sufficient to last us until the snow thaws and we escape to normality and a free range of proper medication at a hospital or specialist centre.'

'What other drugs have you got?' Asked Wee Renee.'

'Erm…. what do you mean?' He replied intrigued.

'I have had this idea. One which might help us a little.' She lifted her carrier bag up. It was heavy with the contents, and she had to use both hands. 'This is full of raw meat. I was going to try and poison the wolves with something from Our Doris's house. To try and kill those wolves off. But I am wondering if you have something that is more undetectable and would either poison them or knock them out for a while. If we wanted to make an escape or have a confrontation it would put them out of the equation.'

'That's very clever, Rene,' Pat said.

'Yeah, I wish I'd have thought of that,' Laura said. 'It's got to help.'

Terry thought for a while. The others watched him in anticipation. This could be a game changer.

'I have several drugs in the dentist that would do both. It is up to you. I could combine certain items and the dosage would be too great for them to take or we could just knock them out for short while, make them discombobulated.' Terry stopped and was obviously still weighing everything up. 'There might be a slight taste though.'

'From what I know about wolves they will eat quite old, warm gamy meat. This is why I haven't been concerned about putting this meat in the fridge. Hopefully the smell will be stronger now, which would attract them to it and also cover the smell of any drugs that we put in. My only worry is getting it to as many as possible. I will have to put it in a few places to ensure that each wolf gets a bit, instead of one greedy wolf scoffing the lot.'

'That's a good point, Wee Renee. I have got enough drugs to do a lot of wolves over a few nights. But you would need more meat than that.'

'That not a problem. This can be just the first day's smelly offerings. I will just buy some more.'

That night, Freddie slept downstairs. Slept wasn't the exact word he would have used really. He had decided to be on the ground level, so that he could open the door quickly if he needed to. When he closed his eyes, he had visions of Pat, Wee Renee and Laura running up the cul-de-sac, the wolves and Anne in hot pursuit. In his visions, Anne had a whip. She cracked it down and the noise echoed through the snowy landscape, driving the wolves to run faster and faster. In this scenario, he would fling open the door, the three ladies would tumble in, and the pursuers would crash against the front door, thwarted.

He lay on the sofa, listening to the radio, which was on a very low volume. Every so often he walked to the window. Freddie kept his eye on the wolves. He could just about see them at the end of the cul-de-sac, in the bushes. They were lying in wait, knowing not everyone was in the house. Ready to pounce.

White Christmas started to play on the radio. Freddie took another sip of his whisky to rid him of the outside and inside chills he suffered. Chills of the soul. He got back onto the sofa, pulled the blanket over himself and picked up his stick. It lay down the length of him, like a crusader, the point glistened in the dim light. The bung that covered it, long discarded. It would be a long night.

24 – Swede

The group in the dentist whispered well into the night. Laura wanted to know more about *The Morrigan*. She was sure they were on the right track with her. Wee Renee couldn't help her anymore than earlier. More information was available, she knew. They would get to that in Friarmere. Wee Renee was full of questions for Terry. About the fanged boy, the drugs and Terry's infection. Pat, who lay next to Carl listened to him tell her about all his wonderful experiences with Kate and how much he loved her, whilst she gently snored. Kathy and Sally played I-Spy. Occasionally Pat would come round for a second and shout out the answer. Then proceed to unwrap another chocolate, pop it in her mouth, give the wrapper to Carl and say to him. 'Go on love, I'm listening,' before closing her eyes again.

As the conversations dropped they sat watching the patterns of water from the fish tank on the walls, the slight noise of them flipping their tails every so often or nuzzling round in the gravel was comforting. There couldn't be a more relaxing atmosphere and in time, all managed to fall asleep, apart from Carl. Their eyelids heavy, bodies and minds exhausted, they could not listen out for Norman any longer. Carl was listening for Kate's return.

The following morning they woke up quite late. It was just after nine, and well and truly light. Wee Renee had a stiff neck, with no cushion, her head had flopped to one side resting on her shoulder. Pat had used the tin of chocolates as a pillow and felt great. Carl's eyes were red and swollen from a full night's crying. Whilst not having the worst nights sleep ever, they had certainly had better ones. At least they were alive and would fight another day. The group quickly gathered their belongings together. They had made quite a mess in the dentist's waiting room, but Terry did not mind one bit, and said he would sort it, if life ever got back to normal. He gave Wee Renee several lots of antibiotic and said that it would be enough to last an infected person seven days. They could revisit the situation after that. The medication was the strongest one he had, but he said that they might make the patient slightly sleepy, which wouldn't be good if the patient had to fight.

They went out into the bright cold morning. There were many pawprints and footprints outside the dentist, scattered everywhere along with the tracks of the two snowmobiles in the street.

'I was thinking,' Carl said. 'Why don't we just burn her house down now, this Anne? Then tomorrow daytime, go to Friarmere and burn his house down.'

'It seems a good idea doesn't it?' Wee Renee said. 'But she might have living people in there. Victims like us. Waiting to be rescued. Poor souls that they are feeding on, or God knows what they are using them for. Plus I am sure both of them have thought that we might attack in the day. They will have some measure against it. They are wily folk. Remember they have people they control, who are alive and could watch the house for them. There is no reason these people can't be saved in time too.'

'Yes, Carl. It seems a no-brainer. Very tempting. But could make you a mass murderer!' Terry said.

No one was out, as they could see anyway.

Wee Renee definitely thought that Anne had herself an individual, like Michael Thompson. One that could go out in the daytime. Maybe they weren't guarding the house. Perhaps they were nearby, waiting to grab them. If she did have someone, it didn't look like he was outside the dentist. Would they see them in the main street? Positioned just like Michael had been, watching in any direction to trap them.

None of them ever considered going back into the dark of the bandroom. Surely there would be at least one monster in the darkness, waiting for them at the end of the many doors and corridors. Lying amongst all the debris of Norman's tantrum last night. Laura could picture them there. In a half state of wakefulness, ready to be activated. Grinning when they heard their voices. In the darkness, they would have the upper hand.

Terry, Carl, Sally and Kathy said they would come round to Our Doris's house the following day. Terry knew where she lived as she was one of his patients. Carl said he would ask Beverly. The group of survivors split up and made their separate ways home. It was about fifteen minutes walk to Our Doris's house. During this time, the three ladies voiced their hope that the predators were too preoccupied with them last night to be bothered about the inhabitants of the cul-de-sac. The village was empty. No sign of Anne's spies.

Freddie had been watching the bottom of the street constantly for any signs of them. He had not moved for about an hour. He would not be shifted and was on his second cup of coffee, supplied by Brenda. He actually felt pretty wretched. Freddie figured he had dropped off about twice all night, for a full total of twenty minutes and he felt guilty about that!

Sue, Bob and Tony were going to take Haggis out to see if they could find them, if they weren't back soon. Although Our Doris said that he wasn't the best at bloodhound duties, being a westie.

Suddenly Freddie became animated shouting out. 'They are here! Put a brew on. They're back!'

'All of them?' shouted Brenda from the kitchen. 'Yes all three.' he said. Liz flung the front door open. They could tell by her face that she had been anxious all night. This whole few weeks had put years on her and she looked older than her mid twenties. She ran out of the house and down the drive towards them as they trudged up cul-de-sac smiling. Liz took Wee Renee's bags off her and they looked up at the house. All the rest of their group was looking through the windows at them, safe. Everything was alright again.

The four ladies were soon inside. The three returnees were hugged and kissed within an inch of their lives. Bob who had been particularly worried about losing his two new best friends Wee Renee and Pat, was visibly relieved. His little face was anxious and his eyes will large.

'Where did you stay last night?' Gary asked.

'The Dentist,' Wee Renee replied.

'Didn't I tell you it would be The Dentist!' Our Doris exclaimed.

'You did,' Freddie said.

'I felt it in my water,' she said knowingly.

'It's certainly an accurate barometer of any situation, is your water, Our Doris,' Freddie replied. He was just about to turn away from the window, when he saw Jennifer and Beverly walking up the cul-de-sac. Beverly had her laptop bag over her shoulder. Freddie laughed as he saw that Jennifer looked like she was openly carrying a kitchen knife in front of her.

The door was still open and the two visitors walked straight in, Andy shutting the door behind them. Freddie gestured towards the knife.

'What's this all about then?' He asked.

'I have gone past the point of caring now Freddie. They are going down, if they come near me.' Jennifer said angrily.

'Fair enough.'

'We have got something to show you. More excitement!' Beverly said, tapping her laptop bag.

'Two ticks then, whilst I finish the drinks. What do you two want?' Brenda asked. They both wanted coffee. They took their coats off. Jennifer laid her knife on the living room windowsill, ready for the return journey. Beverly got a cable out of her laptop bag and walked over to Our Doris's large television. She started to fiddle around at the back of it and plugged one end of the cable in. She then knelt on the carpet attached the other end of the cable to her laptop and fired it up. Freddie watched her work, intrigued and Bob asked if she needed any help, which she didn't.

Sue, Our Doris and Liz were helping Brenda make the drinks in the kitchen. There was a lot of clattering and in came the ladies with teas and coffees, plus two packets of biscuits. Chocolate digestives and ginger nuts. At one point Bob looked strangely at Pat's head as she sat beside him.

'What's that in your hair, Pat?

'Where?'

'Here,' he said plucking out a blue square of foil out of her hair.

'Busted! Haha!' she said laughing. 'It's a toffee wrapper!'

'Have you seen Carl? He was on his way back to you. He hasn't had a good night at all,' Laura said.

'Yes, I gave him my key. He said he wanted a long sleep in safety. I'll look after him when I get back. Give him time to have a kip,' she said.

When everyone was sitting down Beverly started to go through what she needed to tell them.

'Ok, some of you don't know where I live, but I live at the north end of the village. Up the hill on the road to Friarmere. I checked on my CCTV camera from last night to see what was going on.' She turned to her laptop and clicked it a couple of times. There was a still grainy black and white picture on the screen.

'I didn't know you could do that with my telly,' Our Doris said. 'Whatever will they think of next?'

'First look at this.' Beverly said. There was a shot of the main road going up to Friarmere, which the bandsmen had walked down, just four nights ago. The group was silent as she played two clips. 'The first one is not from last night, but the night before.' They saw Norman, Kate, Keith and Christine travelling over on the two snowmobiles.

'So they were here the night before. Hell's teeth!' Andy said.

'The night we went to the pub, hmmm!' Freddie said.

'I've checked and they don't go back that night.'

'That's one spooky sleepover at Anne's house!' Bob said.

'I wonder if they were all in onesies?' Wee Renee said. They all looked at her. 'You've got to laugh about it, or you'd bloody cry wouldn't you?'

'They probably all had sex together,' Pat sniffed.

'Well, winter nights are very long aren't they,' Tony said.' This is my argument with Sue!'

'Dad, no!' Bob said.

'Yes. No Tony,' Sue agreed.

She stopped the recording and moved the pointer to another place she had highlighted.

'Ok, this is last night,' The footage showed Norman and Kate riding past several times in a short space of time.

'Joyriding!' Freddie said.

'Whilst we were *shitting it*!' Pat grunted.

'This is the other group, I particularly wanted you to see. I don't know about these though. Are they some of your lot, because they are in danger here if they are!'

The camera again showed the white moors as a backdrop. From a distance they started to see two people walking down chatting. Freddie moved forward on his chair, pointing at the screen.

'That is Michael and Stephen Thompson, not aided by a snowmobile apparently!' he said.

'Looks like they have come over uninvited, if their past lives are anything to go by.' Andy snorted. Gary got up and walked to the television. He pointed at Michael. He addressed Our Doris, Jennifer and Beverly. The three people who didn't know anything about Friarmere Band.

'He is the one who isn't a vampire, who met us in the middle of Friarmere. The one who threatened us. He can go out in the day. Very dangerous. That is his younger brother Stephen. He is a fully turned vampire.'

'Okay,' Beverly said, 'so they are both our enemies?'

'Yes,' said Danny, 'definitely enemies.'

'So then I have this.' The time stamp was 2.32 am. First they saw the two black snowmobiles go up the main road, back towards Friarmere. Beverly forwarded the recording on forty minutes to show Michael and Stephen Thompson walk up the road behind them.

'Christ! they've gone.' said Freddie, 'They are not in Melden. That's at least six people we don't have to kill.'

'Last night I thought I heard motorbikes which was very strange when it was snowing. At a distance though, not close.' Our Doris said. 'About ten o'clock though, Haggis was getting nervous and pacing up and down, so I peeked out of the curtains. I saw her wolves sniffing the length and breadth of the cul-de-sac. I thought they had gone afterwards, but two of them sat at the end on the main road. You couldn't see them from this window, but I could from my bedroom, I got the others to take a look. They were still there at five in the morning, when I got up to use the little room.' The rest of the group digested this fact and Our Doris had a drink before speaking again. 'So what happened to you lot? You've not told us yet.'

Wee Renee, Laura and Pat told their tale about the band room and discovering who Carl's wife was. Liz was amazed.

'It's a small world, isn't it,' said Gary. Bit by bit the ladies went through the evening and night events. The betrayal by Malcolm, hiding out in the dentist and the discovery of the antibiotic remedy. The rest of the group were shocked at the tale of the fanged boy.

Wee Renee also told of her plan to poison the wolves or drug them, so they were no longer a threat. She then showed them a whole bag full of tablets for Liz and Our Doris. Pat passed her a large brown box, that she had carried home. In that were lots of liquids that she had instructions to mix together for the wolves and some syringes.

'A lot has gone on then,' said Freddie. 'I would love to help get rid of those dirty beasts. I think it will be very interesting, to see the results.'

'I would like some help please, Freddie, just to check I am getting the mixture right. I don't want to bugger it up.' Wee Renee said. 'Liz and Our Doris are you happy to take these tablets? It is just a regular type of antibiotics that you would be prescribed if you got a bad gum boil or something.' Both of them agreed at once. 'Before I give them to you Liz, Terry said I have you ask you, if you are allergic to penicillin? He knew that Our Doris wasn't, as she is his patient.'

'No, I'm fine with it,' Liz said.

'You can take them then.' They both took a packet each and read the instructions.

'You take them three times a day. They are quite strong.' Wee Renee got out another two packets and gave them one each. 'You have to take these alongside it. Don't ask me why, he didn't tell me. Let's see how we go shall we? Don't expect miracles. Terry thinks that it has saved him. At least from the worst symptoms. Let's face it, he has been able to carry on as normal mostly. He had exactly the same infection that Our Doris had, and was infected at the same time. He is nowhere near as ill. Hopefully it kills off all the bad and evil things that are coursing through your blood. You will know if its working won't you?' Wee Renee said to Our Doris, whilst pointing down below. She was trying to keep it secret, but by her actions, everyone knew now and it was in the public domain. Bob raised his eyebrows. He knew all too well.

Wee Renee said that she wanted to go to the shop again and get more meat. She also admitted to Our Doris that she had bought her some chocolates that sadly they all had to consume to survive, the previous night.

'I am so sorry, I had bought them as a thank you for your hospitality.'

'You are all welcome and I don't need to have anything, as a thank you. I know you are grateful.'

Wee Renee said she was insisting, so that was that. Everyone thought that with the night they had all had, Wee Renee and the others should really be resting, so Bob, Sue, Tony, Danny and Gary said that they would get all the groceries required from the shop, and off they went.

Jennifer and Beverly, enjoying the company said they would stop for lunch. It was a simple soup and bread affair, which was served as soon as the others returned from the shop. Beverly had done some sport's therapy when she was younger, so massaged Wee Renee's neck as it was very painful after her crooked sleep on the dentist's sofa.

For a couple of hours they didn't think about vampires, wolves or infections at all. They just sat together, talking, laughing, and eating cake. By mid afternoon, Jennifer and Beverly said that they had better make their way home, as in an hour or so it would be dark. It would take them half an hour to get there and they wanted to be well and truly home with the house locked up, before there was a hint of darkness. Plus, Beverly had Carl to attend to. Jennifer had decided to stop with her daughter Beverly, as the sightings in her cameras, at the back and front were very frequent. Anne kept staring up at the front camera. Jennifer thought they were unaware that they were being filmed at the back of her house too.

Worrying, she thought it was only a matter of time before Anne's group made a serious attack on her home. She was on her own, with no weapons and knew she could not defend herself, so Beverly had offered to have her over there.

After they had gone, Brenda said she was going into the kitchen to start preparing the evening meal, which was going to be sausage and mash. Liz, Sue and Wee Renee and went in to start peeling potatoes. Pat and Our Doris were having a long conversation about Our Doris's Haggis, because Pat used to have one a few years ago and it was remarkable how similar they were in behaviour and idiosyncrasies. After a while, a lot of noise could be heard from the kitchen. Brenda was shouting and there was a lot of banging. Pat was nearest to the kitchen, so quickly got up to see what was going on, obviously knowing that nothing too bad was happening or else Wee Renee or the others would have shouted them to come in. The men turned their heads towards the kitchen, dropping their conversation too, waiting to see what the cause of the fuss was. Pat popped her head back in, a grim look on her face.

'I am just going to help Brenda attack a particularly hard swede. I will be back Our Doris.' Our Doris laughed.

'Ooh, I love swede in my mash. I am hoping for onion gravy.' Our Doris raised her voice so that it would be heard in the kitchen.

'You know that's what you'll be getting, Our Doris.' Brenda shouted back. Her sister smiled appreciatively and put her head back on the armchair

'Your Easter Egg is still nice and big,' said Bob.

'Thank you, Bob. That's what I like to hear,' she replied.

They whiled away the rest of the afternoon, chatting, cooking and calming down a little. When the meal arrived, which was, sausage, mash, onion gravy, peas and Yorkshire Pudding, they ate it with gusto and didn't leave a scrap.

25 – Message

It was their way now, especially once it got dark, that whenever one of them got up to walk around, they took a glance through the window. Several of them were in the kitchen filling the dishwasher and washing the pots and pans. Andy took a glance through the curtain and saw that Anne, her wolves and five of her children were calmly walking up the cul-de-sac, looking as if they were coming to visit Our Doris's house. Andy closed the gap in the curtains quickly and turned around to the others.

'I don't know for sure, but we might be in for a bit of trouble.' Freddie's stomach lurched. He thought that's typical. After an enormous amount of mashed potato and sausage at dinner, he was probably going to fight for his life. What were the chances?

Freddie had been hoping to not move off the sofa all night, in the hopes he could digest it. Gary took a glance out and said they were standing at the bottom of Our Doris's drive in a *congregation*, definitely looking towards their house.

'What are we going to do?' asked Brenda. 'I am certainly not inviting them in, for a cream tea.'

'We are safe in here, as long as no one asks them in.' Sue said with a tone of certainty.

'Don't count on that.' said Wee Renee. 'I don't know what kind of creatures these are. The wolves definitely could wander in. They are just animals.' Pat walked to the front window and flung open the curtains as hard as she could.

'Bloody sod it,' she said, 'let the dog see the rabbit, so to speak and the rabbit can see the wolves.' Most of the group stood looking outwards through Our Doris's bay window.

Anne and her monsters were sniffing out the air. The wolves pawed the ground and some of them licked their lips and glowered as they now saw the humans safely indoors.

'I wonder how long this is going to go on?' Bob asked.

'I don't know,' said Freddie, 'it is getting very interesting. We seem to be in some kind of a stand-off position.'

The wolves and Anne continued to look through the window at the people and the people looked back. It seemed to go on for a long time and neither group was budging. Anne looked at Our Doris and beckoned with her finger.

'Don't do anything!' Gary said. Both groups still stared at one another. Our Doris got the idea that Anne could do this all night. She couldn't. She thought this had only lasted a few minutes and the stress was already taking its toll on her.

'I am not going to stand for this!' Our Doris said abruptly. 'I am going to open the front door and see what the hell is going on.' Everyone secretly wanted to stop her but no one said a word. They realised they couldn't take the stress of it all night either. Playing Anne's mind games? No thank you. Wee Renee, Pat, Gary, Danny and Bob, holding Haggis's collar, walked behind Our Doris automatically. They went as a party into the hall.

'Don't open it fully, Our Doris.' said Freddie from the window, 'so that you can ram it shut, if they start.'

'I know what I am doing Freddie, don't worry,' Our Doris said. She braced herself, straightened her shoulders, then fluffed up her *Easter Egg*. She opened the door halfway. The people who were at the window, saw the predator's gaze move from the window to the door.

'What do you want?' Our Doris shouted.

'I have important things to tell you.' Anne said loudly. Anne wore a plain black long gown with a high neck and no jewellery. On her feet she had black lace up shoes. She could have worn it in any century. Anne was one of the ugliest women they had ever seen, beady eyes and a hooked large nose. She had a small wet mouth with protruding teeth. Her crowning glory was a thin bit of short grey hair. Haggis growled at the wolves, as he just managed to catch a glimpse of them between the humans standing in front of him.

'Why should we be interested in anything you have to tell us, you old witch.' said Wee Renee 'What have you got to say to us? You are evil incarnate, I can tell that. Be gone.' Wee Renee made the sign of the cross on her chest.

'I am sorry to hear that you feel that way; I hoped you would see me as a new friend. Especially you,' she said, focusing her gaze on Our Doris. 'I have been told to pass on a message. I don't really want to shout it from the bottom of this drive,' said Anne.

'You can come up to the end of the garden, but no further than my holly bush,' said Our Doris. 'And just you alone. I don't want your dirty wolves or your monsters coming up my drive, right?' Anne put her hand up in the air to say that she understood this. She slowly walked up the drive, her gaze constantly on Our Doris. She got close to the bottom of the holly bush.

'Here. I have stopped. Is this fine for you?' She said in a slow condescending voice to Our Doris.

'Not really, but it will have to do.'

'You know, tiny one,' she spoke directly to Our Doris now, her eyes opened, attempting to hypnotise her, 'you are nearly one of my children too. Come with us tonight, we can have such fun.' Wee Renee put her forearm across Our Doris and in case she felt that the compulsion to move forward and would be trapped outside. Spirited away by Anne. Even if she did not know anything about her, she would have taken an instant dislike to Anne. When she talked, she looked down her nose at them, as if she thought she was better than them. She was also, putting on a fake *posh* accent, as she would start in the Queen's English and then all of sudden forget and she would fall back into her plain accent again. She twisted her shoulders this way and that, throwing them back as she spoke. Wee Renee had only seen that before on teenagers with attitude! Who did she think she was?

'Say what you have to say, daughter of Beelzebub!' shrieked Wee Renee. 'Love and light protects us all here, and you cannot get us. Say what you want filth, then be gone with your many beasts, to eat your carrion. I can smell the blood on your breath, you dirty devil. Now speak, or bugger off.' Wee Renee reached into her turtle-neck sweater and fished out her large gold cross necklace. She held it at the base and waggled it at Anne. Whilst Anne didn't back off, or run for the hills, it was clear that she didn't like looking at it and averted her eyes.

'Yes, sling your hook, we've got better things to do, like watching paint dry,' Pat shouted, echoing Wee Renee's sentiment.

'Well if that is how you feel, I will have to come back for you won't I, when you are more amenable,' she said directly to Our Doris. 'But what I have to say tonight, is that I have a message for the people of Friarmere, from your good friend Norman.'

The group at the door were in silence. Everyone who was standing in the bay window could hear everything too.

'What does that swine want? And what's he to you?' Pat asked.

'He is my little brother.'

'I take it he got all the good looks of the family.' Pat scoffed. Anne scowled at her. Maybe it was the wrong thing for Pat to say.

'Shut up cattle, and listen. He says he has all the children of Friarmere. But best of all he has a special prize, in your friend Adam,' Anne said and looked directly at Bob. Bob felt his shoulders drop and his grip lessened on Haggis's collar. He felt Danny's hand take the collar and put his other hand on Bob's shoulder. 'Norman says time is running out for them, as well as food. You have a couple of days to come back and exchange yourself for the children of Friarmere. When your time runs out he will gobble them up, one by one. Him and his children. They are all very hungry you know.'

'Tell him and his henchmen that we won't fall so easily, into that kind of trap.' Wee Renee shouted. 'So you can all sod off now. You've given your message, get off the drive.'

'You have two days,' Anne said. She turned and walked away.

'Shut the door, Our Doris.' Freddie said. She immediately shut the door. All the occupants of Our Doris's house stood looking desperately at each other. Our Doris's shoulders dropped and Gary closed his eyes. What were they to do now?

26 – Trap

The group from the hall, walked into the living room. Freddie still stood watching out of the window, Brenda stood beside him.

'They are going,' she said, 'they've done what they came to do it seems, for tonight anyway. Who knows what will happen another night. I didn't hear all of it? What did she say about Norman?'

'He has got some kids and Bobs friend, Adam. He is going to kill them if we don't come back,' Danny said.

'It sounds like a massive trap to me,' said Sue, 'I don't like it at all. In fact all my knees have gone to jelly just thinking about it.' She promptly sat down.

'Of course it's a trap!' Gary exclaimed. 'A blind man on a galloping horse can see that.'

'What is he getting out of it? I don't understand. Apparently he has got plenty of kids to eat. Why does he need us then?' Our Doris asked.

'He doesn't want us to tell anyone, Our Doris,' said Freddie. 'It is obvious, dead man don't tell tales. If he can kill us all off, we won't be able to go and warn anyone.'

'Then he obviously see's us as a threat!' Pat said.

'Yes, that's an interesting thought.' Andy mused. 'You would imagine that he thinks we are just slugs he can squash under his feet. But he doesn't.'

'Well actually I have been worried about Ian, anyway.' Liz added.'

'Ian? What's Ian got to do with it? I can assure you he wasn't being resurrected. There was half of him missing for a start,' Freddie said.

'No, I know he won't become one of them. But for all of us who haven't been turned, even if they are dead, I want to treat with respect. After all, Ian killed one of them for us and we have all managed to benefit from his butcher's knives. He was a hero. Ian deserves not to hang in his own shop and be someone's dinner. Just rotting forever and ever. I would like to take him down and put him somewhere.'

'Well, the ground is too cold and frozen to dig up,' Gary said thoughtfully.

'I know, but if we put him somewhere safe where they couldn't get to him, then maybe when all this is sorted out, we could give Ian a decent send off. Make contact with his family, so at least they could bury a body.'

'That image isn't out of my mind either, Liz.' Laura muttered. 'I do see your point in that. After all this, what if his family go into the shop, looking for him and find him like that. That would be even worse than us finding him.' The group mulled over what Laura and Liz had said. They did want to save Ian's gruesome, mutilated body from more dismemberment. It was a sobering thought, to think of finding one of their own family in that state. Yes. It needed sorting.

'Ugly, isn't she?' Freddie said.

'Anne? Ugly as sin,' Our Doris agreed. 'The clothes don't help either.'

'Aye, it's an extreme look, there's no denying it.' Wee Renee commented.

'What's her brother like? We could only really see him from the side and for a moment on the CCTV.' Jennifer asked.

'He's a right dishy bloke,' Pat said. 'Ooohh, if only he wasn't a bloodsucker,' she sighed. 'I'd show him what a real woman could do.' Gary thought instantly about Pat's feet and thought Norman would probably pass on that delight, if offered.

'I wonder why she's so ugly then,' said Freddie.

'Forget her, what are we going to do about Adam? Norman will be waiting to eat us.' Bob interjected.

'We will just have to be more cunning than him then, won't we? If it's a trap we will seek it out and go to Friarmere *our way*. Attack him *our way*. Get those kids back *our way*.' Sue said.

'Yeah,' said Bob, 'I can't leave Adam. Just think of him, sitting there, waiting to be rescued. His mother will never do it, whether she has been turned or not. She didn't give two monkeys about him. I can't go forward knowing that Adam is still alive in Friarmere.'

'No,' said Tony, 'As much as I don't want us to go back, Adam has been a good friend to you. If the roles were reversed, I am sure that he would come looking for you.'

'It's not just about him. It's about all the other kids and how terrified they must be, without their parents.' Beverly said.

'Remember this is a massive trap won't you, while you are distracted, thinking about all these kids and running head long into danger, we are basically sprinting down the barrel of a gun here, you know,' said Gary. 'What I want to know is, if we are such a problem and he knows where we are, and we know he can get here, why doesn't he kill us? Why doesn't she kill us? They know we can't get a message out of Melden at the moment.'

'That's right. They could just wait, get loads of vampires over here from Friarmere. Anne could get her gang of furries, and they could storm all of us. Smoke us out or something. I don't know why Norman doesn't do it here either,' said Danny.

'That is one thing to think about. When we're thinking about this trap. Is it really about the kids? Are the kids just a way to get us away from *here*, and not to get us over *there*? Is it about being in Friarmere and *not* being in Melden.

'Yes, maybe he doesn't trust his sister,' Pat said.

'I have an idea that he wants us over there, because he wants to turn some or all of us. Why, I don't know, but I can't shake the idea. Maybe we are of value, in some way. If we are held over here, the chances are that she will turn us into a wolf person and we will be working for her, so to speak. If we are over there, then we are turned through his blood line and we are his to command.'

'That is a very plausible opinion,' Freddie said, 'we need to have a good think about this.'

Anne walked through Melden. She was annoyed at how her brother had just used her as a messenger and she had just done it. Now he had gone, and helping him couldn't be farther from her mind. She felt like a lacky, a servant. Why did she agree to all his request's when he asked her? She hoped that he would repay her, if she had a group that one time escapes from Melden to Friarmere. The fact was that currently, she did not have enough vampire werewolf children to storm the house. When she did, she would do it.

Currently, she was able to smell exactly what was in there. There were thirteen people in the house and one dog. One was infected with her strain and one was infected with her brother, Norman's strain. For the moment, she was still outnumbered, but she would change that. If they had not gone tomorrow, she would solve Norman's problem for him and say that they were never going and determined to stay put. So at least the problem was going to be over one way or another. One of her female children was at the rear of the group and kept glancing back to the cul-de-sac, as they walked away.

She halted the procession through the village and pointed to the one at the back and beckoned her over.

'Tell me child, what is the problem?'

'There are remnants of my life in the house. That is all Mistress.'

'Ah, very interesting,' Anne said, 'remnants that you would like to keep, or remnants that you would like to discard. It is entirely up to you. I know what it is to want someone as a constant companion.' The female growled at her.

'Keep.'

'Then it shall be so.'

27 – Flugelhorn

'So are we decided then? Are we going back?'
Gary asked.

'Yes we are going to go back and rescuing those
kids. He can't be lying about all of it. We are also
thinking about Ian. No doubt there will be other stuff
to deal with too,' Liz replied.

'I am thinking about my cats as well. Naturally,'
Sue stated.

'I am worried about Friarmere, and the state
that it is in at the moment. That is my village, I was
born there and I want it sorted.' Laura said. 'We
might be able to get my Uncle Terry and cousins to
come and help. Maybe some others.'

'A great big gang with torches, that would be
great wouldn't it? We certainly need to tool up,' Gary
said. Bob sat on the floor quietly. He was stroking
Haggis and was obviously going through a lot. His
face looked pinched and he looked extremely
worried. Pat listened to all the discussion from the
other people but her eyes were on him.

'He shouldn't have to have all this on his shoulders,' Pat said, 'it is bloody tragic. If I didn't have reasons to hate them already, I would now.' They all took her words in. No matter how bad they felt, they knew he was feeling it the most. His best friend captured, Bob was destined to return to a terrifying situation.

'Well we know *he* has gone back to Friarmere, from Beverly's camera,' Freddie said, 'waiting for us.'

Tony watched his son for a moment before replying.

'Yes, you are right. Tonight I think it is safe to say, we won't be under attack. I can't see him sending a message for us to go there, if he is going to come back here. And she gave us the message, so wants us to go too. Or else why tell us? I think we can relax tonight.'

Wee Rene was not saying very much, which was not her usual way. There were a lot of things she wanted to say about the journey back and the arrival into Friarmere, but she only had one thing on your mind. She had recognised someone that was amongst the followers of Anne. She had not noticed her on the cameras before and would easily have recognised her if she had. Wee Renee had worked with this lady for thirty years and she was still a good friend.

They met up every couple of months and sent each other Birthday and Christmas presents. She knew she would be able to count on this lady, if she was ever ill, and Pat couldn't help. Now she was one of Anne's undead wolf people. This was the first time that someone, who was quite close to her, had been affected by this situation. This had hit her like a ton of bricks. Yes she had known Ian, Keith and the others, but they were not personal friends, who she socialised with outside of the Band. Only finding Pat as an undead monster, could have made her feel worse.

There was one thing Wee Renee had decided though. That she was drugging that meat. There was no question about it.

'What are we going to do then? What's the plan?' Danny asked.

'We will have a bit of time to formulate a plan, I suppose. It will take us a while to travel over. That journey we know is long and hard going. We will have to do most of that in the daylight. We can do lots of planning on the journey,' Tony said.

'We don't know where they are, and so we will have to find them. Try and be as discreet as possible. So, it may be a glorious idea to have two hundred villagers with torches, but it might not be the best idea. He may kill the children if he feels threatened and sees our numbers are strong enough,' Gary said. They all agreed this was a possibility; not knowing how an undead predator would react was hard to judge. 'Okay, so what we have to do then, is to walk around, find out where he is keeping the kids. Maybe whilst we are looking, try to find pockets of people to join us. We can't be the only ones left from the whole of Friarmere Village. There must have been a couple of thousand villagers I would imagine. He can't be hungry, if he has eaten *all* of them. So I don't think he has. If we do find more folk, we will descend from different directions, to not give him a warning. What about that?' They all agreed that it was a good idea. Especially as they could build on this skeleton plan as they walked back over to Friarmere. Bob seemed to be coming out of himself a little, as the plan was coming together to save his friend.

'What about weapons? We know we have to use a certain amount of force to kill them, as I tried to stake one and it didn't work,' Bob asked.

'Did you?' asked Laura, 'I didn't know that.'

'Neither did I,' said Gary, 'that's worrying.'

'Yes, we sharpened our drumsticks at the other ends. I picked one up and shoved it in Colin. It doesn't work. He didn't like it. He kept hitting it, but not touching it. Kind of trying to waft it away. Like it burnt him. Then he ran off, like a swarm of bees was after him.'

'It wasn't a plastic one was it?' Laura asked. 'We have to make sure about this.'

'No, it definitely wasn't. Plastic ones don't sharpen do they? I will show you the other one,' Bob said. He went over to his bag, rummaged around and took out the stick. 'I mean, don't get me wrong, it sent him running, so he couldn't attack anyone else and it really freaked him out. It didn't kill him though. I suppose it is really good for poking eyes out. The thing is though, it definitely doesn't work because I am sure I hit the heart. There!' Bob put the stick into Laura's hands. 'It's not plastic.'

She looked down at the stick in her hands.

'It's not wood either!' she smiled and looked at him. He raised his eyebrows. 'This is bamboo, Bob. Are you sure this was the other one to the pair?'

'Yes, definitely it was this one. I was thinking it was nice and light to hold.'

'Then it is bamboo mate. That is why it doesn't kill them.'

'We aren't necessarily saying that wood does either, are we?' Pat asked.

'No, but at least it means that we haven't had a proper test. We could do really well with all these drumsticks, as long as we don't pick the bamboo or plastic ones.' Laura said. ' What this means is, at least drumsticks aren't out of the mix.'

'Gary, you bought your flugel, didn't you?' Wee Renee asked.

'Yes,' he said.

'Would you play for me? It relaxes me – the sound of your flugel.'

Gary was only too happy to play. He went upstairs to the boys' room and fetched it. The lights were low and Our Doris gazed into the fire. Gary began to play, not from music but just a rich, slow tune. Melancholy and haunting, that came deep from his heart. They all listened and thought about what they needed to do. Gary's playing was sweet and after the first tune, Brenda put her hand on his arm.

'Please play some more. Some more like that,' She said. Gary played the saddest song they had heard. His flugelhorn sounded like the aching heart of a woman for her lost lover. Our Doris closed her eyes and Bob slowly stroked Haggis, who lay against him on the floor. Wee Renee had her hand on her heart and tears began to stream down her face.

Anne did not know whether they would decide to go Friarmere or not, as it was so obviously a trap. She had told them two days – that included one day of travelling. So whoever hadn't gone tomorrow night, wasn't going. Anne had to have a good plan. She would make sure that she could deal with the situation easily the following night. She gathered her children around her.

'Tonight animals are off the menu. People are *on*. We have a few houses to visit. Potential children that I have infected. Tonight, this is the priority. The *only* objective.' Anne kept her wolves close as she needed them to do her bidding tonight. She just hoped that all of the changelings were strong enough to take the final stage. 'The infected will be the first. Then we force others to ingest the wonders of our nature.' She would enter the homes of her future children. Her clan could then take the members of their family currently uninfected and probably objectionable. There would then be new people to force her blood onto. A gift they would so happily relish in time.

The group in Our Doris's house decided to have their Ovaltine at about ten that night. They had noticed that Wee Renee had been quiet all night, but knew that she was the type that would only tell them in her own time what was wrong. They made plans and were happy with the weapons that they had.

They reconciled the fact that they would have to walk the long reverse journey tomorrow. The same hazardous trek that they had made a couple of nights ago. They were a lot wiser and healthier than they were then, so it should not be as arduous.

Anne visited sixteen people that night. Some were quite resistant to the group's advances and unfortunately she lost ten of the sixteen people that she wished to make. But she did not consider this wasteful. She was quite used to these people and knew that in the long run they would be detrimental to her cause, so it was best that they were eliminated early in the game. Anne had six healthy new members to add to her group. She would now be in a better position tomorrow night. Anne would be fighting too.

Excerpt from Anne's Diary.

Tuesday 13 December
I went to deliver the message this evening after my bath. I took five wolves and five of my children with me. I saw the bitch that had ingested my blood. She needs to continue the journey. She has to understand that. The rest of her existence means nothing. She will feel wonderful of course! I will make sure Sophia bites her, to take her through the next stage

. One of my children has a friend in there from Friarmere. They still mean something to this creature and they would like them as a companion. She has opted to keep the human rather than kill her; it really makes no difference to me. Let's just hope she survives the change. I do not know if she is old or young, but is she worthy? Tonight I visited sixteen people that I have previously marked with my wonderful juices. Ten of these did not make it either by resisting (futile and stupid) or by them not taking to the next stage correctly (Why? Note: More experimentation required). Six of them became new children of mine tonight. I have never been a mother in the traditional sense of the word (passing a baby out of THAT!) but I cannot be prouder or love them anymore than I do!

Again I tried to get in the big house with the walls around it. I love it. I shouted in the camera that this was their last chance to have any money from me and that I would take it from them anyway. But they did not come out to see me. The truth is that I don't think I will be able to get past their security to take it, so if they won't give it to me, I won't be having it! Hmmm….. vexing! All this is quite tiring me out. That led me to drink wine, which I mixed with blood, instead of pure blood, which I usually drink. I should not drink alcohol. It does not keep me fit. It dehydrates me, but I cannot relax tonight. There is so much to do. I am excited about tomorrow!

28 – Parkin

By the time it was light, there was already a hive of activity inside Our Doris's house. Some of them were packing and Our Doris was going through her cupboards finding provisions for the journey. They still had the tarpaulin, sledge, tools, nails and all the backpacks so they would be camping over in Bob's den that night. Pat had been downstairs for a while and had laid out her own and Wee Renee items out, not knowing how Wee Renee wanted to pack them. When she was still not down at nine o'clock Pat made the trek upstairs to see what was holding her up.

Wee Renee lay in bed. She had the quilt pulled up over her shoulders, and from the door, she was just a lump with a small head on the pillow. Wee Renee was turned towards the wall and Pat could not see if she was awake or asleep. She clumped around the side of the bed and looked at Wee Renee. She was indeed awake but her eyes were sad.

'Come on Rene, it's time to get up. We will be setting off soon.'

'Well good luck to you and all. I hope you save them all.'

'What?' Pat said. 'Aren't you coming?'

'No,' she replied, 'I am not coming.'

Pat dropped herself down on the bed.

'Why ever not?'

'I can't do it anymore. I can't be strong for anyone or myself. I'm worn out and tired and sick of doing it. The situation just gets worse the more I fight, not better. We can't win. I'm sick of fighting. Swimming against the tide. This is not me. I don't want to do it anymore. I just want to hide here, in this bed.'

'What's going on? You were fine yesterday.'

'Nothing!' she snapped.

'You are a bloody liar,' Pat said, starting to work everything out. 'I know you are.' Wee Rene had cast her eyes down but said nothing. 'I saw that you were quiet last night and hoped it was nothing more than that. I didn't know it was going to turn into something like this or else I would've nipped it in the bud. Has that Anne put the willies up you?'

'No it wasn't Anne,' Wee Renee took a deep breath, then said after a moment, 'it was one of the other people that was there.'

'Who was that?' Pat asked.

'One of the women I worked with for years. You will have heard me talk about her, named Carol.'

'Carol was one of those?' she asked, shocked.

'Yes, Pat.'

'Which one was she?' asked Pat.

'The one with the wee dowager's hump,' she said.

'Oh, right. I noticed one was young. I don't suppose that is who you are talking about.'

'No, she is just slightly younger than us. Carol was a lovely lady.'

'Was she in Melden Silver Band?' Pat asked.

'Yes, she played the baritone.'

'Well this shouldn't surprise you then.'

'Anyway, I saw her and she clocked me as well. I have been thinking about it all night. I haven't even managed to save one of my friends after everything I've done. I don't want to bother anymore, what's the use? What's the use at all?'

'I can't believe this is my Rene saying this. You will get your Mojo back, don't worry.'

'It's just been a bit of a kick in the guts to see Carol. I am right at the bottom of the chip pan this morning, Pat,' she said. 'I can't go with you all. I would be a detriment to the group. I think there are a couple who going to remain here. I am going to stay with them. I might get my sparkle back, and then I would be useful here. Especially if Anne comes back. I would also like to see Carol. I know it is probably out of the question, but I think I would like to see if she is fully beyond hope. If there is one small chance that I could save her, and she could be human again, then maybe that would be worth it.'

'Have you heard yourself? This is exactly what Carl was saying and you helped talk sense into him!'

'Aye, it's hard to take your own advice, Pat. I do understand his need for some kind of closure now though. So for the moment I have to stay here. I won't be going over to Friarmere.' Pat put her hand of top of the lump of quilt that was Wee Renee. 'There is too much unfinished business. I feel so low, Pat. I just don't know where I am going to find the last bits of energy. There is no fight in me.'

Pat thought for a moment. She looked towards the curtains that were still closed. She looked way beyond their fabric, towards Friarmere. She thought about Melden, Anne, wolves and Rene's friend. She couldn't think of going on that journey and leaving Rene here.

'I will stay here with you,' She said quietly.

'Pat, I don't want you to. You wanted to go back to Friarmere.'

'Yes, because I thought you wanted to go as well. I'm alright here, Rene. I bet whatever happens, I will still be fighting and doing good somewhere. The fact is *I would be a detriment* if I was there constantly worried about you, you silly bugger. So let's get you up and help the others get off. Make sure they will be as comfortable as possible. Get your nightie off, get some clothes on and have a wash. I will sort you out some breakfast. It'll be alright now, don't worry, you've got your old mucker Pat with you.'

Wee Renee felt a little better confiding in Pat. She did not want it broadcast that she was low, as she did not want to bring the rest of the group down. They had to face an awful task in Friarmere, and the journey alone was dreadful. She lay back down, then thought *what are you doing Wee Renee? You are just sinking back into your dark place. Get up and get on with the bloody mangling.* She sat up, threw her quilt back, dropped her feet to the floor and stood up.

When she went downstairs, there was the smell of bacon wafting around the sitting room. Everyone was in an awful rush. People darting one way or another, putting stuff down then picking it up again. No one knew what they were doing, all running around like chickens with their heads cut off.

'Let's get all this sorted,' Wee Renee said. They were all glad she was here to take control. She started to help people to get their bags together.

'What about you?' Gary asked.

'Oh, I am not coming,' said Wee Renee matter-of-factly. 'I think we need some people here. I don't trust Anne. Pat has agreed to stay too. We will see what help we can be. At some point we will come back, don't worry you haven't got rid of us forever.' Quietness descended on the group, as the fact sunk in. *They would not have Wee Renee and Pat with them.*

'Are you sure about this? Can't we persuade you?' asked Gary.

'No, love. For various reasons, I know my place is here for the moment. That will change. I need to get my ducks in order.' She smiled at him. 'You won't persuade me. You will be just wasting time, if you try to. So let's get you all sorted and off, daylight is burning away, friends.'

'I'm not going back either,' Freddie said. 'Our Doris isn't fit enough. Brenda needs to stay with her and I need to stay with Brenda. I'm sure you understand everyone.' They did. No one imagined the three of them would be coming. At least Anne couldn't get them inside the house.

Pat was in the kitchen. She had made Wee Renee a bacon sandwich and cut off all the fat for her.

'Here you are Rene, nice and light for you.' She smiled at her, as she passed over the plate. Pat put her hand on Wee Renee's shoulder. 'I have put a bit of brown sauce on and here's a nice cup of coffee. Are you feeling a bit more like yourself, Rene?' Wee Renee nodded and smiled back.

'I've told them we aren't going. I've squared it with them,' Wee Renee said quietly.

'Alright love,' Pat replied. Wee Renee felt her eyes starting to fill up, but quickly blinked away the tears. No one saw but Pat.

Our Doris was in the middle of making a mountain of sandwiches, in a world of her own. She seemed to be in some kind of regular, vigorous rhythm, with slicing, buttering, filling and bagging.

Pat walked into the living room, trying to locate Bob.

'Where is your bag?' She asked. He pointed to his backpack on the sofa. She stomped over to it. Her feet were pushed so far forward into her open toe slippers, that most of her toes, were off the slipper and onto the carpet. Leaving two inches of spare slipper at the back. She had several sandwich bags in her hand, which she shoved into his backpack. 'I have put plenty of our favourite sandwiches in, braun. Also, some of my best-loved biscuits, fig. You'll like them. You have the same taste buds as me.' She slapped him firmly on the back and trudged back to the kitchen. Laura smirked at Sue, who did a silent giggle. They both quickly looked away before Bob noticed.

'What have we all got?' Danny asked.

'Tinned salmon or cheese.' Our Doris replied, who was carrying a tray piled high with sandwich bags. She stopped suddenly with her tray, looking crestfallen.

'You do like tinned salmon, don't you? I've put salt, pepper and vinegar in it.' They mostly nodded and she continued.

'I have sliced up a couple of parkin cakes as well. They are in two foil parcels. Divide it up. I have got some drinks here for you too.' There were some pouches of orange drink, with straws taped to them.

They all stuffed their bags full of the goodies from Our Doris. Not knowing when they would get food again, this was precious. The one good thing about this weather was that as it was so cold, it would keep it fresh for the maximum time. Pat could not see Wee Renee in the living room, but she found her in the kitchen eating a bacon sandwich with one hand and getting the raw meat out of the fridge with the other. On the kitchen counter she had a bag full of the drugs that she had been given by Terry.

'When they set off, I am putting this meat out,' she said.

'Let's do it together. We will sort it quicker,' Pat offered. They got some of the chemicals and syringes out that Terry had given them. He had written the directions on a piece of paper from the surgery. They quickly injected each chunk of meat with the cocktail that he had devised.

'I am going to put some outside here. Some outside Jennifer's house, we know they are there a lot, and some outside Beverly's. Jennifer and Beverly are in that house, on their own. We will pick up some more from the shop after we see what effect this has tonight.'

Maurice knew that there was going to be a trap. He had seen a couple of the vampires out on the hunt, when he had been on the wander the other night. Maurice only saw vampires now at night. He hadn't seen any normal people in the dark for nearly a week. If there were any left alive, they were very sensible. It was so desolate and uninteresting now. All that they wanted to talk about was how much they loved being a vampire, blood, killing and how marvellous Norman was. Those were the only topics of conversation and he was bored with it. He still made conversation however, just to snoop. What he had picked up, was that there was a plan hatched up by Norman. He had somehow got a message to the group that apparently had gone over to Melden. Maurice had found out and had been tipped off, that any day now they would be back. Norman was planning to eliminate everyone.

Maurice had to think of what he could do without The Master finding out. He wracked his brains, but they didn't seem to want to work for him. Maurice could think about this day and night, until they got here. He wanted to save them from death and even worse, the monotony of vampire's conversations. Yes, better off dead than an eternity of that. That was an idea for him really. Once he had done all he could do – when he was no use whatsoever to his friends, he might as well lay outside in the daylight on a bed of stakes. That would do it. Good and proper!

29 – Virgins

The group was still making their final preparations when they got two sets of visitors. The first to arrive were Sally, Kathy and Laura's Uncle Terry. The other visitors were Beverly and Jennifer. They came within five minutes of each other up the cul-de-sac. When the two ladies were had taken their coats off and were walking out of the hall into the living room, Freddie happened to look through the window.

'I have a feeling he is after us!' Freddie exclaimed. They all walked to the window and looked out. A man stood alone, looking from one house to the next. He had a backpack on his back. Carl squinted up at the cul-de-sac and immediately knew which house to go to as it was jam-packed with people, milling around inside with backpacks themselves.

'Oh, that's Carl, the succubus's husband, I was telling you about.' Said Wee Renee.

'Probably better to call her Kate, if we have to. Or just to avoid the subject completely,' Terry said.

'Aye,' said Wee Renee

'Ah right, yes,' Beverly said. 'He's been home to call for some stuff. He said he was coming here.'

Wee Renee went to the front of the others at the bay window waved and beckoned Carl up. He smiled and quickly walked towards the house and entered with a relieved sigh. Wee Renee shut the door and then gave him a massive hug.

With lots of loud chatter they all congregated in Our Doris's living room. There was quite a crowd of people now, who stood in a rough circle. The excitement was palpable.

Freddie told the new arrivals about their visit the previous night from Anne and her pack. He said that even though it was quite obviously a trap some of them had decided to go back. There were other reasons to go too. Even if they managed to save one child, it would be worth it.

'I want to go too,' Beverly said suddenly. 'I have a child, even though she is in boarding school. I am all for *walking a mile in somebody else's shoes*. What if I was in the position of one of their parents? How dreadful that would feel, and how frightened the children would be? I am definitely going. I couldn't sit at home, knowing it might be me that could have made the difference, and I was too chicken to go. If we could quickly call at my house, so that I can pull some brief things together, I will join you. It's on the way out of Melden, as you know.'

'You're a good girl. I was going to go past your house anyway to drop some poisoned meat off,' Wee Renee said.

Carl said he had planned to go anyway without this visit from Anne. He had called to tell them, and had planned to go alone because he wanted to save his wife Kate.

'I am so happy that you lot are going. This gives me a much better chance at getting her back,' Carl said. They could see he had so many plans in his head about his future. Some of them looked down at the carpet, unable to burst his bubble.

'Kate is beyond saving. You must understand that. Get it out of your head that your life with her will ever be the same. I have seen her. I feel cruel, but it is what you need to hear. I am sorry,' Laura said.

Carl sat down on the sofa, his eyes looked from one to the other.

'Alright, yeah. I know what you are saying but my brain won't seem to accept it. I need to see Friarmere for myself. I need to see *her* for myself. If the unthinkable is true, I cannot stand the thought of her wandering around in her shell. I will have to sort it one way or another. It is no one else's responsibility. If I let her murder innocents, and I know about it....well....it is like I am consenting to it. If she was a shell of Kate, that didn't kill people, I would still let her walk around. I would want her just to be in the world somewhere, as beautiful as ever. I suppose that makes me a very sad man. I don't know what to think anymore. But if she is a killer, she has to go.'

His words resonated with what Wee Renee felt about her friend Carol. She came to sit beside him and put her hand on his knee.

'That is fair enough. At least you have company now.' She was holding back her tears. The whole group felt terrible for Carl.

'I am going too,' Sally said. 'I need to help the children.' Kathy and Terry for the moment wanted to stay behind and tried to persuade Sally not to go. She listened to his words, but like Beverly, she could not just sit there and do nothing. So, they would be quickly calling at Sally's house, to pick up her items.

Terry and Kathy said they would be so worried about her, until she was back.

'Do you want to say at my house Dad, so we both aren't on our own?' Kathy asked.

'Yes, I think I need that,' Terry replied quietly.

'Bugger that!' Our Doris said, 'You can stay here with us. Safety in numbers and all that. There will be plenty of room as over half of us are off to Friarmere. Please say you'll come?'

'Er...yes. We'll come. Okay, Kathy?' Terry's face lit up a little. Kathy nodded happily. 'Thank you Our Doris. That sounds wonderful!'

Beverly and Sally had come out this morning dressed for the weather, so there were only a few other items to pack. Our Doris said she would make a few more sandwiches for them. Beverly admitted to them that there was another reason she wanted to go. She wanted to know, what it was like over there. It intrigued her. The vampires, Norman, Kate. If there would soon be an end to it, she would have missed the opportunity.

'Just remember curiosity killed the cat!' Wee Renee said gravely. Beverly laughed.

'I'll be fine, I'm no cat.'

'Seriously though Beverly, it is not to be taken lightly. When you see them close up, well, it is hard to laugh off.' She replied.

'So, the fact that Melden has wolves and werewolf vampires, isn't enough for you?' Her mother asked.

'It mustn't be I suppose. Because I am champing at the bit to go to Friarmere. I want to see it all......and I aren't scared, not one bit.'

The group spoke for a while about their plans and where they might end up. They made a joint list of various locations, in case the others wanted to look for them. And a list of signs or secret signals they might use, that only their gang would recognise. Gary said he would lash the top of the tarpaulin down in the den, as he had done before. After they had used it, he would leave it there in case they had to make a hasty retreat, or if some of the others decided to come over. It was handy to have as a bolt hole, and it was no use keeping on carrying it forward and back.

'Er…Gary, what are you are wearing on your head?' Our Doris asked.

'Sue's pink earmuffs,' Gary said, very embarrassed.

'They're fab, them. I'd love a pair of those. I prefer a muff rather than a hat. You know, so it doesn't squash my hair.'

'You're welcome to these, if Sue doesn't mind.'

'By all means have them Our Doris. Gary's ears will get cold though,' Sue stated.

'Oooh, I think I can sort him out with one of my husband's hats. Have we got a deal?' Gary immediately pulled the earmuff's off his head, passing them to Our Doris.

'Deal,' he said.

The final group to set off from Our Doris's house were Carl, Gary, Tony, Sue, Bob, Laura, Liz, Andy, Danny, Sally and Beverly.

Haggis was staying behind with Our Doris, but Bob was very sad to be leaving him. They had a big hug on the drive and Bob said he would see him again. Haggis seemed to understand this. The little dog replied by wagging his tail happily, and giving Bob a big kiss on the hand.

Wee Renee, Pat, Terry, Kathy and Jennifer walked with the group into the village. Wee Renee had got her special meat with her. They had already put one small portion outside their house at the bottom of the drive. Our Doris did not let Haggis out on his own so he was perfectly safe. Our Doris was a little bit worried about all the other dogs or cats eating it.

'When have you last seen a cat or dog in your cul-de-sac? I personally haven't seen one out in this village since I have been here. Not loose anyway. People are keeping them in, away from the clutches of the wolves, Our Doris. Not to mention, a lot have already been got at!' Pat said. So it was settled.

Carl had everything with him so the first house they called at was Sally's. Bearing in mind that she only had a few minutes to get everything, she came out with a large backpack full of what she said was *interesting stuff*. Kathy and Terry went off to fetch their overnight belongings and would return later to Our Doris's.

The final stop was Beverly's house. Whist she went inside, Wee Renee put the bag of meat in a bowl outside her door. It was indeed quite ripe now and Jennifer covered her mouth, as she felt herself starting to heave, her stomach convulsing quickly. Wee Renee hoped, if the wolves decided to pick up the groups scent, they would stop here for a quick snack. It was after all, on the way to Friarmere.

Beverly had her bag with her soon. Wee Renee, Pat and Jennifer walked with them to the edge of Melden.

'Good luck.' Pat said to the departing friends.

'Thanks, but we don't need luck. We will be fine. I am sure of it. Don't worry.' Gary said confidently.

With those departing words, they all turned towards the snowy hill and started walking upbank to their fate

Wee Renee, Pat and Jennifer watched the group walk up the hill until they were out of sight. They hoped they would be okay and Pat said she had a good feeling about it, *in her waters*.

Jennifer had decided to stop at Our Doris's house, with Brenda and the remaining survivors for safety and company, now her daughter would not be around. This is where the three ladies called at next. She went in for some overnight clothes and toiletries.

'I am going to check the house, as I have not been there for a while. It might have been laid waste to, whilst I have been stopping at Beverly's.' Inside her house, all was well. She checked her CCTV feed and Anne could still be seen on occasion, snooping round the house. The vampire seemed very eager to see beyond Jennifer's gates.

'When I see what's been going on outside here, even though I wasn't here, I feel like I am going to be sick!' Jennifer said.

'It makes me want to do poopoo,' Pat said. 'It's her ugly face. Norman doesn't shit me up half as much as her with her twitching and her mad laughter. Actually, I'll just nip to the toilet before we set off.'

After Pat's visit, they dropped the meat into a bowl underneath the front camera, locked up and started to walk back to Our Doris's. When they got to the centre of Melden, Wee Renee paid a visit to the shops again. She picked up some more meat for the wolves and groceries as instructed. Brenda had provided her with a list and the ladies, split the bags of provisions between them. Joyfully and finally, they started back to the safety of the cul-de-sac.

Liz had felt better this morning. She thought that maybe the antibiotics had worked a little, and also she was another day further away from the initial infection. For the moment, she did not need the sledge, but the sledges were there with supplies strapped to them. If needs be, she could get on one.

This time they did not have Wee Renee to sing Christmas carols. Now they realised she had been the most necessary of their party. She got them to march to the beat, distracted them, passed the time and kept them happy. After a short while they could feel the weight of the mission on their shoulders. Of course Carl was extremely worried, now the prospect was getting closer. He was very miserable about a possible confrontation with Kate understandably, and the atmosphere around him was very dark.

Gary could feel the general mood becoming more and more oppressive with every step, so he decided to sing a few songs himself. He said he knew a particular one, from when he used to go to watch rugby. This was when he was younger. Tony said he knew another one from when he was in the army and advised that Bob closed his ears. He knew that Bob wouldn't, but instead would try to remember all the lyrics. But, after the horrors he had seen, and had yet to witness, a bit of rude singing was not certainly going to hurt him.

Gary thought that it would lighten everyone's journey and would pass away the time. His first song was *Four and Twenty Virgins Came Down from Inverness*. Laura, Bob, Tony and Sally were in absolute hysterics. They laughed so much that they couldn't walk. Laura was clutching on to Sally, so they didn't both fall into the snow.

Danny made up a few verses afterwards of his own, which they thought were great. Gary advised him he would have to write them down for posterity, so that they could sing them at another time.

The trudge up from Melden was extremely steep, but they seemed stronger than they had been when they had made this journey the first time, in reverse.

'Okay,' said Gary, 'this mission isn't going to be very nice. Is there anything that we are looking forward to, once we get back to Friarmere?'

'I am looking forward to seeing my cats,' Sue said enthusiastically. 'I can't wait to see their little faces. I am hoping that they are all well. I will hold them and hug them until they are all squashed.'

'And me Mum, I've missed them.' Bob said.

'Right, first on the agenda then is squashing cats. Anyone else?' Gary asked. No one else could think of anything, so that conversation fell flat.

It was a dull day, and with their dour moods, as soon as they stopped singing or talking, the darkness quickly returned to envelop them. It seemed to be always waiting, just a couple of steps away.

They were making good progress. Now, when they looked back they could no longer see Melden, but they weren't at the apex of the hill. Gary decided they should break for a while, as there was a good low patch of dry-stone wall to sit on. Each had a couple of sandwiches, not wanting to have too much because of feeling sluggish or getting a stitch in their sides

Again the mood went quickly downbank and Gary thought, if he didn't get them going again, they would never get to find shelter tonight. He had noticed the more miserable they were, the slower they walked.

Gary decided he was not going to stop conversation or singing until they got to the den. That was the only way. He started off by saying that he had an idea of how he could make a flamethrower. It would be a brilliant tool if he could manage it, although it could be a little bit dangerous for him to use. He would be worried about using it to rescue the kids in case one of them ran past it. What would be doubly pleasing was that he could use it to melt great swathes of snow. Danny thought this was a great idea. Tony said that he was going to tape a knife to his gun to make a bayonet and they thought that that was good too, although just being a short handgun meant it would have limited use.

They got to the highest point, which then levelled off, at about one o'clock. Walking across the brow of the Pennines, the view was enchanting. Gary knew that at this rate, they would definitely have to do some of the walk in the dark. After walking a short while he asked if anyone wanted another bit of sustenance. They all did.

'Five minutes rest. That is all, as we are sitting away the daylight,' he said, but tried to keep it cheerful.

Gary wasn't about to tell them they would have to walk a short way in the dark, and be vulnerable, very shortly. The friends sat on a wall handing out their sandwiches. Laura walked around the whole time, flapping her hands at her sides like a penguin. She didn't want to get cold. There was low cloud below them. Because of this they could not see Friarmere or Melden, only grey silvery cotton wool beneath them. They were above it and might be the only people left in the world. It was as if they were walking through a snowy heaven in the clouds. Sue noticed that Bob was not eating.

'Did you eat a lot at the last break?' she asked.

'No Mum. I haven't had anything. I don't fancy it.'

'Bob….'

'Mum, I keep thinking about Adam and how scared he must be. My stomach has kind of closed off.' Tony joined in the conversation.

'How will you help him if you are weak through hunger? Try to forget about that closed off feeling. You have used an awful lot of energy coming up here and you are still a growing lad. You will need lots of strength for what is to come,' Tony said plainly. Sue mouthed the words *thank you* to him. Although Sue just wanted her son to eat, Tony had actually spoken the truth. He needed his strength. If he was weak, they would have to drag him and Liz on sledges.

'Pat and Our Doris have gone out of their way to put your favourite stuff in there, so just think about everyone else,' Sue said to him finally.

'Yes,' Gary said, 'that it is for the best. Get something in your stomach lad.'

Five minutes were very quickly up and they set off once more. Quite tired now but glad that there was no more upbank walking. Only across a bit and at some point down, into Friarmere. Just keep putting one foot in front of the other. Don't think about being tired, or blisters. Definitely don't think about what faced them when they got to their destination.

The travellers were all warm. Their hats were off, in their bags, and their gloves too. Gary had even undone his coat to try and get a bit of cold air through to his skin. He was really sweating. When they had made the reverse journey before, he had been going into what he thought was safety. Now he knew he was walking into a hellhole again and it was affecting him.

It was definitely no warmer today than it had been just over a week ago. The sun had been out then, it had been cloudless, with twinkling snow. So the only difference to all of them, was that danger, not salvation was before them.

There was also something else on Gary's plate. He seemed to share the leading of the group, all their responsibilities, with Wee Renee and Pat. There was a big hole in the group now that they weren't here. It all was on his shoulders now.

The clouds lifted a little. As they walked over the last high ridge it was three o'clock. From this height, they could see Friarmere beneath them. Their home.

They carried on for about an hour. Walking towards their fate. The darkness rushing towards them, in more ways than one. They all knew now that they wouldn't make it to safety whilst it was still light. He would get them. He knew they would be coming over here tonight. He had insisted, hadn't he? Tick, tock. So he would get them tonight. Fear was overtaking them. Was it tiredness or the night that made their knee's tremble? It was now dark. Friarmere was closer but still way below them. They had not made any descent. Danny pointed towards Friarmere.

'What is that?'

'It's fires!' said Tony. 'I think, it is in the fields, there,' he pointed. 'But over there is a house or building on fire. There seems to be another one in a field the other side of Friarmere, as well. It's too hard to tell from here but I am guessing by the rows of streetlights……. it looks like that one is on the street, and that one is near nothing else, maybe in a field.' Whilst they watched another one sprang up, in what they thought was a street.

'What the hell is going on?' asked Gary.

'Who knows what is going on in their mind's, when they do these things,' Carl said. It was one of the first things he had said since they had left Melden. He had refused to eat anything at all. 'What is in it for them, if they burn down the whole village?'

'Whilst they are doing that though, they aren't up here. We will deal with all that in the cold light of day tomorrow. Let's forget about it tonight, get ourselves sorted and settled.' They stopped talking now, the darkness, the fires, the close proximity to The Master weighed heavily on the group. Each step was an immense effort. After a short while they nearly went past the place where the public footpath was, that would take them to the den.

'Hey!' said Bob, 'aren't we stopping?' The travellers stopped walking, and took notice of where they were. Bob was right. They had walked a few steps past the path, as their eyes had been fixed on the fires in Friarmere. Retracing their steps, then turning left, they started to walk up the path. It looked like there had been no one here since they were last here a few nights ago. No footprints. No pawprints. Bob went first, the others walking in single file. In the clearing they found the den. Sally, Beverly and Carl were quite heartened at how warm, dry and safe it was here.

The men put up the tarpaulin, lashing it quite hard to the tree's so that it would stay up and maybe take some weight from the snow if it had to.

They set up a timetable of when people would be on watch, but thought that it probably would be safe that night, at least. After all, Norman's mission was to have them back in Friarmere. It would be no use killing them up here.

They got themselves comfortable, unpacking the blankets and provisions. Taking out the remainder of their sandwiches, they rubbed at their sore feet and sore shoulders from the backpacks. Most of the group was soon asleep. The soft smell of Pine Tree's taking them to better places. In the den, warm and no longer walking, they were in better spirits than they had been when they had set off on this journey. At this point, Liz realized that she hadn't needed the sledge once. The antibiotics must be working.

'Gary, are you still awake?' Bob whispered.

'Yes, lad.'

'I have had a thought. What if it isn't the vampires setting the fires? What if its survivor's like us?' Bob said. 'If they are setting fires then there are either people or vampires after people, still about. There must be someone else alive, whichever way it is.'

'I don't get you lad.'

'Ok. If there are humans, then they are the ones setting fires. Conclusion – humans are alive. But, for some reason if the vampires are setting light to stuff, what is in for them? They aren't fireproof. It can't be solely for their benefit, or that they need the warmth. It must be to lure human's out, to put out the fires. Or to torch houses, so that the humans have to run outside into the dark, and *they* can bite them. Same Conclusion – humans are alive. Whatever is happening, there is some life left in Friarmere.'

Adam stared at the children in the school hall. He had been forbidden to eat them all. The Master brought him animals. He was to live on that for the moment. The children were more scared of him than the rest of the vampires because he never left the room ever. His eyes forever open, watching them. He had somehow become miserable as a vampire, something he never was as a human. The fact was – he was lonely. He was sick of sitting in the dark listening to kids cry and wipe snot on their coat sleeves. Was this it for him forever? He wasn't going to do this much longer. He was just waiting for what he had asked for – the only request he had made. Once he had what he wanted, he was going.

Adam, when alive had been incredibly clever. Maybe he had the potential of becoming one of the great minds of the country, but that would never come to pass. Adam waited for his friend Bob. He knew he would come. He was too good a friend, and Adam would be waiting. He knew The Master had plans for Bob and Bob's parents. Norman had promised they would not to perish. He wished to collect them very much. Adam would have his friend with him again soon. Him and Bob would be the next generation, and oh what fun they would have!

30 – Meat

That afternoon went by so slowly for the group left in Melden. Whilst Jennifer, Pat and Wee Renee had taken the travellers to the outskirts of the village, Rose and her daughter Natalie had unfortunately arrived for a visit.

In the warmth of Our Doris's house, the group filled them in about Anne's message. They had immediately noticed that there were less people in the house, when they had arrived. Rose and Natalie no longer doubted what was going on in Melden, but clearly by their demeanour, they were not hopeful of a positive outcome. The two women were fatalistic about what would happen to them.

'We are just walking carrot cake, to them lot. Not long before we are all eaten,' Rose said morosely. 'I don't know why we don't lay outside in the streets for them at night, covered in dog food. Get it over with!'

Freddie went into Brenda whilst she made tea and coffee in the kitchen.

'Do you know what Brenda,' he whispered, 'even Carl who has lost his wife does not emit such a black atmosphere as those soul suckers in there. Two women, who it hasn't affected whatsoever. Absolutely bugger all has happened to them.'

'They are just a miserable pair,' Brenda said. 'Rose has always been the same. She was always a party pooper. I can categorically say that she was born a misery. She wanted the world to revolve around her and bolster her through her turmoil's in life.'

'Well we haven't got time for it and we aren't bloody doing it.' Freddie's word was final. He helped Brenda to take in the tray of drinks.

Terry and Kathy arrived at the house with their bags, and shortly after Pat, Jennifer and Wee Renee arrived back. When Rose and Natalie found out that that Terry and Kathy were staying with the group, they said that if strangers were staying there, then they were going to as well. Freddie said under his breath, *we haven't invited you* but thought that it was mean-spirited of him so made sure they didn't hear. If he didn't watch himself, he would end up as bad as them. Our Doris however, was on point.

'What did you say, Rose?'

Rose quite clearly didn't care what anyone thought of her or her opinion, as usual.

'I said, Our Doris....that if strangers are staying then we are!'

'You cheeky rat, Rose. They aren't strangers and if you don't like it, you needn't come. Terry is my dentist and I also knew Kathy before this. They are welcome and more people together means that we are all safer. Can I also remind you that myself and Terry are infected and we need the support of each other during this difficult time. He is trying to cure me. Terry is going out of his way for me. He and his daughter are NOT strangers. So if you have a problem, or think you can't manage to be civil to them, or anyone else. Go home!'

Wee Renee watched this exchange between the two sisters. Her eyes were squinting down at Rose and she was ready to support Our Doris at a moments notice. When Rose or Natalie, didn't reply, Wee Renee gestured to Pat to go into the kitchen with her.

'Come on Pat, we have loads more meat to deal with love,' she said. Pat followed her and Wee Renee shut the door.

'Pat, I have not got time for her. We are all trying to do our best. She has just come here because she is nosy and wants Brenda to wait on her. I bet she doesn't lift a finger from go to woe. I hope she doesn't stay and that she buggers off out of my way until we have to set off for Friarmere or something.'

Pat hoisted up her leggings before replying.

'She's a bitch Rene, it's as simple as that. I am fighting the urge to clock her one up the earhole. It's not going to last forever though. If you see her tonight with a thick ear, it was me.'

'I'm not going to stop you Pat. I think, in this current situation, it wouldn't matter if you gave someone a cauliflower ear. So have at it. We are all lucky to still have our ears. It's a wonder they aren't round Anne's neck on a necklace.' Pat took this opportunity to open the door a little and look at Rose.

'I don't like her, or her spawn.' She shut the door again. 'I was thinking Rene, do you think you should tell everyone about Carol?'

'No, I don't think so. They might treat me differently. I will just deal with it in my own way. Thanks Pat. Just you knowing about it has meant it is a trouble halved, so that is fine by me.'

Our Doris and Brenda had planned a large cheese and onion pie for that evening's meal. After Wee Renee and Pat had dealt with the meat, they put it in bags. Wee Renee put one bag outside the house in an old bowl, which had been in Our Doris's garage. She banged the bowl with a screwdriver she had been using to prise the meat out of the bag with.

'Suppertime,' she screeched. 'Come and get it, you filthy critters.' Now there were two portions' full of drugged meat outside. One either side of the drive. Terry and Wee Renee did not know how this would affect the wolves. This mixture was not a drug for wolves, or any animal at all.

Even if they knew a specific measured dose of drugs for one creature, they didn't know if one wolf might eat one piece and another one might eat ten pieces. The second wolf would obviously be more affected than the first one. Even if an overdose killed them, it couldn't hurt the survivor's plight, only help it. If the drugs did not affect the wolves whatsoever, the best-case scenario would be that it might save them from biting someone else at night, if they were no longer hungry.

That afternoon Freddie put the radio on to see if there was anything about vampires mentioned, but there was only news about snow. There was going to be a lot more of it on the way.

Jennifer went upstairs and blow-dried Our Doris's hair for her. When they returned Our Doris sat next to Terry, who put his book down and turned to her.

'How are you feeling?' Terry asked.

'I don't want to jinx it, but I am actually feeling better,' Our Doris replied. 'I am feeling marvelous actually. It has made a huge difference. I mean, I am not 100% but I would say, since I have had two doses of the antibiotics, that I am 75% better.' Then she lowered her voice to say the next part. 'Do you still have the dreams? I do.'

'Yes,' he shivered. 'Positively ghoulish!' She nodded.

'They stay with you all day, don't they? Sometimes I think I have experienced it. Everything feels so real. They are living that life, the ones with her. It makes you think doesn't it?'

'It certainly does.'

'Do you want tot of whisky. I am. It helps. It's ok with the antibiotics isn't it? Do you want one?'

'You're alright Our Doris I'll pass. You can though.'

Our Doris turned to look at Rose. She was thinking things through

'You had better get some stuff from your house if you are staying for the night. It is getting on a bit now, so you need to sort yourself.'

'I am not bothering, we'll use your stuff,' Rose said with her arms folded and a challenging look at Our Doris.

'Oh you will, will you? None of my clothes will fit you and you're not stretching them. As hardly anyone else has any stuff with them, as they are basically refugee's, you will be out of luck. Serves you right for being so lazy that you can't be bothered to get your own stuff. If there was anything decent about you, you should have been lending your stuff to the ladies here. I can't believe we have the same parents!' said Our Doris. Brenda gave an audible sigh to say that she had had enough of Rose's behaviour. Our Doris looked at Brenda, her mouth tightly pursed. It was just about to kick off again, when Terry broke the atmosphere.

'What abnormalities are you still having then, Our Doris?' Our Doris had to collect herself for a moment, before replying.

'Many of the symptoms, including the tiredness and nausea have all but completely gone. Thank you so much, Terry, for thinking about this. It is the way forward for us both, especially now that we have discovered it works for other people like Liz, too.'

Brenda, who had stormed off into the kitchen, was loudly banging the ingredients down for the pie onto the table. Our Doris came in, shutting the door behind her.

'Take no notice of her, Bren. There are more important things to think about. I will keep her in check.'

'You can't Our Doris. She thinks she can say what she likes. As if we aren't under enough stress. I bet neither of them offer to help with the meal,' she said. They didn't. Brenda told Our Doris, to go and sit down because she was still recuperating and she didn't want her to do too much. Jennifer, Kathy, Pat and Wee Renee came in one by one and just got to work without being asked. The five women sat around the kitchen table, not saying anything, just listening to everyone's conversations. Natalie wandered in after about half an hour.

'I'm hungry, Auntie Brenda.'

'Biscuits,' Brenda said through tight lips, pointing at the biscuit barrel with her rolling pin.

In the living room, at one point, Haggis wandered over and put his wet nose against Rose's knee and she said *shoo*. Our Doris got up and relayed this information to the ladies in the kitchen. Our Doris was furious in the kitchen and said she wanted to get them out, but Brenda said it was too close to darkness. She agreed they would not get home in the time remaining, and thus she would be sending them to certain death.

'Reject my dog, and face death. That seems fair enough to me,' Our Doris said.

'You don't mean that,' Brenda laughed.

The pie was in the oven, and they were looking forward to eating soon. Terry had noticed that two of Our Doris's lightbulbs had gone out, so was replacing them on a small stepladder. Freddie was writing down the full list of places that his friends were visiting to find the children, and places they might stay, before he forgot what they had said. The first hints of darkness came. Shadows began to form in the corners of the living room and Freddie closed the curtains. He said he wanted a rota of people, constantly getting up and checking the cul-de-sac.

'Not just the same people looking every time. This means those who particularly haven't been pulling their weight.' As he said this, he looked over to Rose and Natalie.

It was fully dark by 4 o'clock and a grey cold night. Freddie had just sat down from checking the window when they heard a howl. They all looked at one another, knowing what this meant.

'Sounds like Anne is out for the night on a spree. I hope her wolves enjoy the supper I made for them,' Wee Renee said sarcastically. The group did not yet know, that she had six new acolytes with her. Fresh, strong and hungry for blood. There were nine people inside the house and Haggis. Only two of them were under fifty years old, and even Haggis was older than fifty in dog years. Although in a crisis most people would have rather been with Wee Renee than Natalie, who was quite useless.

Anne felt that they had had their chance at escaping and rescuing the children from Friarmere. Whatever was left was fair game and she would tell Norman that. She did not care what he thought. Her children needed feeding too. She had to deal with her own problems in the village as well. Norman would not sort those matters out for her. So tonight, was going to be her night. Now that she had more followers with her, she would definitely outnumber them in this house. She reached the bottom of the cul-de-sac and waited for the others to catch up. Anne was excited. This was the biggest army she had had since she had come to this island, and she was looking forward to this fight. She hadn't lost a fight yet and she was standing right there as large as life, to prove it.

As she walked into the entrance to the cul-de-sac, she was sniffing all the time but at the moment could only catch a brief scent. Every step it got stronger. She knew that the house contained less humans than yesterday, at least for now. Just how many there were she didn't know. She saw the curtains twitch and a woman's face look out at her shocked. The woman then closed the curtains again. She stood at the bottom of the drive. Anne tasted the air again. The information was slow coming through to her. There were several humans in the house that had not been there the previous night. She could sense that there were now two people that had drunk her blood in there. That was a bonus. Two people prepared. Another was definitely earmarked for saving and turning by her child, Carol. She would make decisions on the others on a bite by bite basis. Anne waited at the bottom of the drive for several minutes. Nothing happened.

Rose sat back down quietly, her eyes wide. She did not say a word. Rose just sat looking at Natalie, who was not looking at her. She did not know what to do. She did not want to be the one to raise the alarm, or it might be on her shoulders at some point to do something about it. Yes, best to say nothing. They would notice when someone else took a look. Let them deal with it. She was hoping that the lot outside would go away and no one would notice they had been.

Brenda said she would check the pie, as it should nearly be done. Freddie said to turn the oven out and keep it warm.

'Brenda, I got a feeling in my water, something's afoot.' He looked around at the others for a kindred spirit in his theory. He thought Rose looked strange but she generally was anyway, so he left it at that. They waited quietly for Brenda to come back again. She came in and in one deep breath addressed Freddie.

'The pie is done and I have put it on a low light, but not for long. I aren't going to miss my dinner if nothing is going on. That pie is too good to go to waste.'

Haggis started growling, his head lifted up and he faced the window.

'What is up boy?' Our Doris asked him. Haggis curled himself around her legs. Freddie looked at him and afterwards at Rose. The penny dropped.

'You didn't see anything, did you Rose, when you looked out?' Freddie asked. She did not answer him, but stared back at him, challenging him. That was answer enough. He jerked himself up and walked to the curtains, peeking through. Freddie turned quickly back to face her, his nostrils flared, he was so angry.

'They are right at the bottom of the pigging drive!' He pointed out towards the road vigorously.

'I know,' Rose said.

'Is this true? Did you see them when you looked?' Jennifer asked Rose furiously.

'Yes, so what. Nothing happened, did it? Just ignore them and they will go away.'

'So Rose, that is your plan is it? That is what we should do with all the wolves and people trying to take over our world. They are stopping us living our normal lives, preventing us from going out at night. Eating our friends. Just ignore them! It will all go away. You have just ignored them and you have put all of us in more danger, Rose. We have lost precious time, preparing ourselves for them. I suggest if you can't be any help, you sit there out of the way and don't be a detriment to me any longer!'

'Don't you talk to my mother like that!' Natalie screeched.

'Oh! It speaks. Who cares what you say anyway, you fat lump.' Freddie said. 'You were not wanted here, either of you. You've not come here to help, you came to be waited on, hand and foot, the pair of you. Now keep out of my way, I am telling you.' Freddie had a mixture of feelings. From anger, disgust and also fright because of what was now outside. He had to be sure he wasn't taking all these feelings out on Rose. He was also aggravated that the one time that he had trusted Rose to check, she had failed them. He felt a fool for ever trusting her.

'You stupid woman, didn't you understand we could have been picking up our weapons and been ready for this!' Freddie flung open the curtains gazed down at the collection standing by Our Doris's gatepost. 'Right,' he said, 'as long as we don't go outside, we'll be fine.'

'I knew we shouldn't have come here,' said Rose. 'Right into the lion's den. You are magnets for trouble. We were better off on our own. We had no problems in our own home. We aren't putting ourselves in danger, me and Natalie. Let's face it they aren't after us.'

'That's a great *I'm alright Jack* attitude,' Freddie said. He clapped his hands. 'Bravo Rose, you show what an out and out git you actually are, over and over again. I am very happy for you to go now, if you like. As you say, it's too dangerous in here. Go on.'

Rose, red faced and angry glared at him. 'No? I thought not. You paid a very expensive price for a few cups of tea and the chance of a cheese pie. Keep your mouth shut.'

Freddie took a deep breath, walked into the hall and opened the front door. The house, the street, the whole of Melden, was deathly silent. The people inside could hear every word he said, every whisper. Pat walked over to the sofa against the wall. She had had the idea of putting her favorite weapon, the lump hammer behind there. Pat took it out and looked towards the others as Freddie spoke, tapping it in the palm of her other hand. They all started to ready themselves.

'What do you want this time?' Freddie asked loudly.

Anne lifted her head upwards in her standard haughty way.

'I just thought I would let you know, before we make this visit any more intimate, that there were never any children left in Friarmere. All your old friends ate them. You see, my little brother played a trick on your friends and now they are gone. They can't save you now. Divide and conquer. Now *you* are outnumbered, not I.' She walked forward towards the door. Behind her, the wolves stood at the gate, with an older female. She seemed to look around for them for a moment but they did not follow her. Six of her followers stood with her on the drive. There were four of her henchmen standing guard at the bottom of the cul-de-sac.

'Are you going to ask me in.' she snarled as she carried on walking.

'Not on your Nellie!' Freddie shouted.

'Not to worry. I don't need an invite. I'm welcome everywhere!'

Anne started to walk up the steps to the door, two feet away from him.

31 – Chunk

Freddie moved backwards as Anne advanced towards the door. He did not have time to shut it. Besides that, they could just smash the windows and climb in, if they didn't need an invite. The rest of the party had moved closer to Freddie to hear the conversation, so now they quickly moved backwards too. Pat moved to the left, as did Freddie, into the area by the bay window. Kathy got behind one of the heavy curtains. The rest of the group moved to the right. Rose and Natalie remained seated.

Anne could indeed come into their house. They did not know how this could happen, but they had never been safe here. Haggis was barking incessantly. Pat could see through the window that most of the wolves still stood at the bottom of the drive with one of Anne's children. Pat's eyes widened to see that this was Wee Renee's friend, Carol. The dowager's hump was quite visible from this angle.

Anne pushed her way through the front door, entering immediately into the bright living room. Some of her group were close behind her, in the hall now. Three moved forward, three stayed where they were. In the house, but just to guard the exit. No escape tonight. Anne stood majestically in Our Doris's living room. She was tall, pale and dressed fully in black again. Anne looked dreadfully out of place with the décor. She smelled strongly of wet soil, sawdust and urine. She reached up a little and slapped the chandelier light fitting, sending it violently swinging. The light now made crazy patterns of the walls and ceilings. Light and dark, light and dark. *She's going to knock another bulb out*, Terry thought.

Anne made a shrill noise and dropped into an attack pose. She was almost like a velociraptor. Knees bent and set wide apart. Back slightly arched and arms up, like claws ready for the attack. She bared her teeth. They were not wolves' teeth. They were yellowing hooked vampire teeth. Her eyes darted amongst them, waiting for the first victim to come at her. She was ready to strike.

Kathy, who had studied Earth Science's about fifteen years ago, still had a small geology pickaxe that Terry had made her, to crack rocks open with. Kathy decided not to wait for Anne but to bring it on. She sprung out from behind the curtain and with all her force bought the pickaxe and down on to the person's head directly behind Anne.

There was a loud crack as she split the skull of the vampire. A central square of bone had now been pushed deep into the brain. The head fractured outwards from this in three clean lines, tearing the scalp with it as it opened. As they dropped to the floor the person was revealed to be Malcolm, who had been the conductor of Melden Silver band. Terry's brother. Kathy's own Uncle. As he fell, for a moment Kathy's stomach dropped through the floor. She had just killed her Uncle Malcolm. *Kathy had murdered him for nothing*. Just because he was in a kind of killing cult. He wasn't attacking her. *It couldn't be classed as self defence*. But as he fell and she fully saw him in the swinging light. It was quite clear, that he was what they had suspected. Anne had finally given him the precious gift he most desired. She called it an early Christmas Present. Now that his treachery had been revealed, he now had had no reason to ever hide his true nature. His shirt was unbuttoned and open. His wolf's pelt bushed out everywhere. This was so much more than a very hairy man. His mouth would remain forever in a death snarl. His long teeth were pearly white. New.

This seemed to be the signal for everyone. Terry had some quite vicious dental instruments and he held one in each hand. The scalpels were razor-sharp, sterile and glinting. He slashed away, at anything that wasn't his friend but only managed to make superficial cuts as they grabbed for him.

Their clawed hairy hands tried to close on his sweater, to grip and pull him towards their teeth. He slashed at their hands, the blackish red, tar-like blood oozed out, smearing across the cream wool of his Aran sweater. Pat was swinging her lump hammer this way and that, laughing. She caught a female on the cheekbone, which now was dented in. The skin a purple mush. As the vampire screamed, raising her hands in the air to run at Pat, Freddie lunged at her; sharpened walking stick poised. He jabbed it hard towards her torso. It entered her armpit and came out a few inches along at the back. The vampire protectively put down her arm, which trapped Freddie's stick.

'Hold her Freddie!' Pat yelled and started to wallop her again generally in the head and ear region.

Anne was currently not in battle but she shouted orders to the others. Haggis's barking seemed to annoy her. Her gaze had immediately settled on him. Once her beady eyes met his, he whined and ran into the kitchen, getting in his basket.

Another beast entered the living room from the door, stepping over the dead Malcolm. They avoided what was going on with Terry, Pat and Freddie, quite sensibly. Their red eyes looking towards Rose and Natalie who, unarmed, gaped at the dreadful scene. They took three loping steps towards the two women.

Wee Renee ran from the other end of the room, with a high *weeeeee* sound, jumping on their back. Swinging her arm round she shoved her trusty cheese knife in their eye, flipping it back out fiercely with a twist. The eye caught in the hook, thick fluid, flecked with black, shot across the face of Rose and into the open mouth of Natalie. They still did not move, like the furniture they sat on. Our Doris ran across from the kitchen door, the male, now with one eye was before her. She kicked him square in the genitalia. He crumpled to the floor. For a brief second, Wee Renee was a little shocked that it still hurt them there so much, when they were now a supernatural creature.

'Well fancy that!' She shouted to Our Doris from behind him as he knelt. She decided straight away to take out the other eye. Wee Renee brought this one out with some velocity. Eye number two flew across the room, landing in Rose's lap, who backed away from it by shoving herself further into the cushions of the chair. Unbelievably Rose still sat there, not defending herself, or her daughter. Not even bothering to get up and run away. She just watched everyone else struggling. The hero's side was two people down.

The creature was now totally blind, but still very dangerous. Our Doris picked up an ornamental brass coal scuttle from the side of her fireplace, smashing it down on to his head. He dropped from a kneeling position to a lying position.

Within five seconds he began to pull himself up again and was six inches up from the carpet, when Wee Renee ran up the length of his back and jumped on his head. His head went down, she jumped again. There was a crack that resounded through the room. His fingers still grasped handfuls of the carpet. He wasn't gone yet. She jumped again. His face seemed to slip sideways, moving away from the back of his head. Wee Renee yelled.

'Argghhh, bloody die will you.' As she jumped for the final time. The back of his head went to the right, and his face remained stuck to the carpet on the left. It wasn't easy balancing on the top of a disintegrating head and Wee Renee slipped down to the left side of his head. This sent it even further to the right, totally removing the face away from it's head. Wee Renee was now standing on top of the upside down red mask that had been the vampires' face. It was embedded into the carpet. Fibre's had been ground through the flesh.

She looked down at her feet in their pop socks. His hands twitched and grabbed at her ankle. Our Doris brought the coal scuttle down again and again on his head. The vibration of the metal hitting scalp thudded through the floor. His grip lessened and soon his head was just a pile of indescribable red, white and grey objects, all tinged with green.

'Are you intending to do that again. Because I don't have another coal scuttle and this one is bent now,' Our Doris said, laughing. A twinkle in her eye.

'I might. I enjoyed it.'

'Well, this was an antique. Try to do it round my cheap stuff. I don't really want to waste stuff on her lot. You know for future reference.'

'I'll bear it in mind,' Wee Renee replied.

Pat was still, clonking the vampire around the side of the head, and she was reeling around as if she was drunk, which she found hilarious. Freddie had managed to disengage his walking stick from her armpit and was looking through the window at the wolves. They stood at the bottom of the drive, apart from one that stood near the door. This one seemed the largest. It had it's head cocked listening calmly. From what Freddie could see, one of them was eating something and he half-smiled to himself.

Most of the wolves were behind Our Doris's garden wall so he couldn't see much. They had one vampire who had stayed with them, but she seemed distracted. *She must be the lupine wrangler*, he thought. There were another couple of vampires with the large wolf on the drive, but they stood rigid, as if they could not join in, unless ordered. Freddie really wanted to stab the wolves with his stick. Drugging them had made it so much easier. He should be able to manage a sleepy wolf, even at his age. He did not like them at all. Like Sue, he preferred cats, and these beggars ate cats.

Wee Renee looked around the room for her friend Carol but couldn't see her. Suddenly Brenda rushed past her from the kitchen, throwing a saucepan of boiling water, over Anne who started screaming. There was no doubt that this had scalded her, her ancient skin seemed melted more than blistered. It looked like several layers of the white flesh had liquefied where the boiling water had touched it. Anne curled into a ball onto the floor. She seemed to vibrate. But not attack back, at least. Brenda rushed back in, filled the saucepan again and put it back on the still burning gas ring.

Terry was flailing around with his dental instruments, being quite unproductive. He overbalanced himself and fell to the floor. His scalpel hand downwards. Terry fell half on top of Anne, as she curled in her fetal position. As he flung his arm back to get away from her and raise himself up, he managed to cut her deeply at the back of her neck. If only she had been facing the other way, he probably would have ended all this. Kathy was attacking another vile creature with her pickaxe. This one was young, male and broad. Quite advanced in their transformation and a lethal fighter.

Kathy managed to slice her weapon into his cheek, just below the eye. She pulled downwards and it seemed to open like a zip. The gash ran up from the corner of his mouth to just below his eye. It was fully open one side. A black liquid, mixed with red and white strings of mucous dribbled down his chin, dripping on to the carpet. The creature growled at Kathy, who just laughed.

'No matter what I did, I couldn't have made you look any worse.' These creatures were definitely different. They all had a broadening of the nose, discoloration of the skin. A rash on their bodies. They weren't so pale as the classic vampires in Friarmere. The hands were purple, bruised, the nails were longer. They tended to claw at their victims to grab them. The vampires in Friarmere fought with their teeth. They acted more human-like. These creatures bent at the knees slightly. Looking more like they were one of the missing links rather than a fully formed human.

Our Doris's Haggis stood with her now, he growled and his teeth were bared. There were no wolves in the house yet and he was protecting his mistress. The nasty woman no longer stared at him. She was on the floor in a ball. Our Doris had a sword on the wall that she had bought when she was on a cruise to Japan. She had been waiting to use it in for the reason that it had been made, which was killing enemies. Although, she could bet that the swordsmith would never have thought in a million years that this would be its destiny.

She took it off the wall, at that point remembering just how heavy it was. This would be a two-handed job. Our Doris had unsheathed it. Years ago, she had asked her husband to sharpen the blunt sword, which although he disagreed with, he did. Thank heavens she had had the foresight. Our Doris held the sword, the tip resting on her Axminster. The next creature that came through the door, she was having.

She saw a shape pass the crack in the door, between its hinges, where it was joined to the wall. She ran, the momentum helping to lift the sword high. It was a one shot swing. All or nothing. The force that she put in, would rotate her round, if she didn't connect with the vampire. She did connect, and how! Straight in the neck, taking the head clean off, before they had even noticed her. Our Doris was such a small lady, but she fought like a demon.

Whilst the water was on the boil, which Brenda thought was incredibly effective, she returned with the biggest meat knife that Our Doris owned. She ran forward at a female vampire not knowing whether to aim for the head, or the heart, or the neck. She decided on the heart and ran forward with it in front of her she was surprised that the knife slipped in quite easily. It disappeared into the creature although she had not hit the heart. Brenda's knife went straight through this female. Right through the left nipple, through the breast and into the rib cage. Pat had moved to the other side of the vampire, with her hammer, looking at Brenda's work.

'Ooops! I bet that smarted!' Pat said. Brenda pushed the vampire, backwards with her foot, one hand still on the knife. She plunged forward again into the right breast. Freddie who was looking over at her in awe, raised his eyebrows.

'Why Brenda? Have you got something against boobs?' he asked.

'I must have, and I never knew it,' she replied.

Our Doris came behind the creature and took off its head. The creature dropped to the floor. Our Doris and Brenda looked at one another over the dead enemy and smiled.

'Thanks, Our Doris.' Brenda said, as if she had just been given a chocolate digestive.

'I wish you had bought more of them from Japan, Our Doris,' said Freddie. 'We could all do with one of them.'

'I know. I'm proper chuffed with it,' she said.

'I meant to ask... if you go tonight, can I have the Jag in the garage?' He shouted. Our Doris shook her head, laughing

'There is no chance of it, our kid!'

They were all focusing on different things. Our Doris, Brenda and Freddie seemed to be having a brief conversation after killing the female, about her husband's car. Wee Renee was looking out of the window. Kathy was dealing with the young fierce male, with the heavily dripping cheek. No one was looking at Anne. She was no longer in the fetal position on the floor.

Terry, who was just about to help Kathy, just happened to glance backward, to see that Anne had bitten a chunk out of Natalie's neck, who still remained in the same seat, arms frantically trying to push Anne out of the way. Even scalded and slashed, she was definitely stronger than Natalie.

Kathy was just finishing off her vampire with another pickaxe strike straight through the forehead. He fell to the floor. Kathy put her foot on his neck, to remove her weapon. At this point she noticed what her father had noticed. Terry was walking over the dead bodies, scalpel in hand towards the two large women. Kathy tried to get round the others too with the pickaxe. Terry shouted *'Freddie'* and Kathy shouted *'Wee Renee'* at the same time. The whole room looked at Anne.

Anne dropped Natalie back into her seat as the young woman gave a last twitch. She grabbed Rose by a fistful of hair and began to pull. Rose still just watched everything going on. Anne pulled her head to one side so fiercely that they knew this would have been excruciatingly painful for Rose.

'You take one step and this bitch is a goner,' she said. Our Doris held her sword up but did not move. Her arms shook with the effort. Freddie had been more or less at the side of Anne, whilst this had been taking place. With his stick held high, he thought Anne could not see him. He moved one more inch towards her.

She quickly swiveled her head towards him, growling. She lifted her head back, again imperious. Looking down on the humans she felt superior to.

'You are insane!' Wee Renee shouted.

'So what,' Anne replied sarcastically. From its high and mighty position, she bought her head down and bit out Rose's throat. She chewed the chunk, blood running down her clothes, as she looked about at them. Catching each and everyone's eye.

'You are all so sad. You really thought I was not going to do it!' She laughed then shouted 'Sophia!' Freddie was just about to run at her with his stick, when the wolf that had been waiting just outside, ran through the door. It jumped, biting down on his hand between his thumb and first finger. Straight away the blood started to drip down over the carpet. They were terrified. Whilst Sophia kept Freddie at bay, Anne took this opportunity to move away from Rose and a little nearer to the front door.

'I wondered where you were Sophia,' she said, stroking the she-wolf's head whilst Sophia still held on to Freddie's hand. He lifted his other hand, which was holding the stick upwards to bring it down onto the wolf.

Anne grabbed this arm with her thin bony fingers, pinching it.

'Oh no, you don't!' It was at this point that Brenda's saucepan had boiled again and she rushed over, as Anne's mouth opened towards Freddie's neck. She threw the boiling water inside Anne's mouth some of it splashing on Freddie, most of it going on and inside the foul creature.

The noise was inhuman, not even animalistic. It seemed like something supersonic. Anne's call of pain was a clicking, howling, whining noise that was terribly loud.

'She sounds like a bat!' Wee Renee shouted. Anne ran out of the door, into the cold night. The she-wolf still had its jaws locked on Freddie's hand. Wee Renee saw Freddie flinch and knew what he wanted to do.

'Don't pull it Freddie! It will take a chunk out of your hand and then we won't be able to stop the bleeding!' She screeched. It was so tempting for Freddie to do this. He was now burnt and bitten. Weakening by the second. Our Doris sprinted over, her face set, determined. She lifted her sword high as she ran.

'Geronimo!' she shouted and brought the sword down from top to bottom taking the head off the wolf so fast, that the wolf did not have chance to pull away. Wee Renee grabbed the wolf's head, by the ears. The body fell away. She held the weight of the head whilst Terry opened the wolf's jaws forcefully. Brenda held Freddie's arm and he pulled it off the upper set of wolf's teeth. One deep hole after another.

His skin made a quiet popping noise only he could hear as each tooth was removed from its current circular home. His hand was free. The bloody punctures had gone all the way through. Freddie's hand and arm were covered with his own blood.

32 – Carol

Terry and Brenda got Freddie by either arm and helped to seat him in the armchair. There were no longer any wolves or creatures alive in the house. He was shaking with shock, blood loss and stress. Terry quickly examined the wound.

'Brenda fetch a clean tea towel,' he said. She darted away, fetching the cloth immediately. Terry bound Freddie's hand, telling him to bend his elbow up, elevating his hand, so that the hand faced upwards against his shoulder. Brenda kissed his forehead, and stroked his head.

'It will be alright, we'll be fine,' she quietly said over and over again.

Wee Renee walked to the open door. What was left of the party that had attacked them were close to the bottom of the cul-de-sac, apart from one. Anne, herself was nowhere to be seen. There were several dead creatures behind her to deal with, including a headless wolf.

The only threat remaining was Carol, who stood at the bottom of Our Doris's drive in the snow.

She had not been part of the fight. Carol was sadly looking at Wee Renee. Her eyes were mournful, lost, pleading. Wee Renee walked towards her. As more of the pavement was exposed from behind the wall, she noticed that there were four wolves lying in the snow. She did not know now whether they were drugged or dead, but at least they had not been part of the fight. Wee Renee stopped six feet away from Carol.

'I bet that this was you, wasn't it?' said Carol. Her voice was different, it had a rumbling deepness about it.

'Aye, it was.' Wee Renee said. 'What's it like Carol?'

'Horrible. I had no choice in the matter. I am what I am now. You are still what I was.' She cried out to her old friend, her arms open, pleading in distress. 'I don't know if I am alive or dead. I hurt all the time. I think I am a wolf. I walk with the wolves, I sleep in the pens with them, I eat raw dead animals. I think I am turning into something.' Then she seemed to have an inward conversation with herself. 'Are you a vampire Carol? Are you a werewolf Carol? Are you? What are you? Dead? No you can't be, you're speaking.'

Then she turned to Wee Renee and addressed her again. 'Have you seen my face? I have felt change in it, when I touch it. I can't look. Wee Renee, I am sorry that this happened to your friends, but you must understand that we cannot fight what we have been asked to do. Besides it is our nature now. To feed. To kill. I have not helped tonight and I will be punished for that. As an old friend, I ask that you help me. Can you think of a way that I can be what I was, instead of this wolf thing, this beast?'

'How much of the old Carol is left inside you?'

'Enough. Enough to ache for my old life and be shameful about my new one. But not enough to change back. Too much of that part has gone.' She began to talk to herself again. 'You can change back, of course, Carol. Don't tell her anything. Shhh!!! Silly Carol. Kill her!' Wee Renee ignored this conversation.

'Look at yourself.' said Wee Renee. 'Apart from your face. Your hands are bruised because they are trying to be paws. You have a red rash with hair growing out of it. On, your face, Carol, you are halfway to having some kind of a muzzle. A dog's face. You are well....very unusual. This does not make you a werewolf, I think. You are a vampire. You are definitely dead. Your Mistress has infected you with the vampire strain. You are a strigoi. Carol love, you can never go back. Part wolf, part vampire. Whatever you have to call yourself, Carol, you are a creature of the night and I cannot help you. You can't go back because you are dead.'

'Please help me. Who else can I turn to?' She asked.

'The only way to help you is to kill you again. A final death. I really don't want to do that, but that would be the best medicine for you, if I am honest.'

Carol looked at Wee Renee for a long time. She had listened to every word. The wind blew. Her hair untethered and full of straw blew in the arctic wind. She groaned, clutching her stomach.

'So much pain, burning unbearable pain.' Carol put her arms round herself and rocked herself for a moment. Wee Renee felt the utmost pity for her. This unnatural state had been thrust on her. Her life was gone, whichever way she looked at it.

Carol's spasms, seemed to ebb away.

'Do me the kindness, please. Take it all away for me,' she begged. Carol squared up her shoulders. Her gaze fixed on Wee Renee. She gave the briefest of nods.

Her friend acknowledged her in the same way. Carol closed her eyes. Wee Renee held her machete in one hand. She put both her hands on the handle, lifting the weapon high in the air. The streetlight gleamed off the blade for one moment, before she brought it straight across the neck of her friend Carol.

The vampire collapsed on the floor amongst the four bodies of the wolves. Wee Renee dropped the machete, which embedded into the snow. She screamed up to the sky.

'No...No....arrghh!' The noise came from the bottom of her soul, a dreadful scream. Her body was rigid, the sound raw, nearly an inhuman sound too. A scream of mourning, lost hope, desperation.

Pat, Our Doris, Brenda and Jennifer came rushing out to see Wee Renee. They all put their arms round her. The street was so silent, they had heard the conversation inside. She started to cry, great heaving sobs. With each sob, her body relaxed slightly. This had been pushed down. She let every bit out. The women still held her. A five woman island, drifting in a snowy ocean. Terry came out to see the sobbing group, then thought again about interrupting them. He put his hand on the wolves one by one.

'They are all drugged, not dead,' he said. His voice was loud in the street. 'I'll do it with my scalpel, it's fine,' he said.

'I want to do it. I've lost people tonight. I need to kill some more,' Our Doris said. She let go of the others and wandered exhausted back to the house, picking up her sword. Our Doris dragged it down the snowy drive. She methodically plunged it in to the heart of each wolf.

'Check them again,' she said to Terry. She stood over him as he checked. She was ready to stab again if required. He moved from wolf to wolf nodding over each one. All were dead now. That would form part of her revenge. Anne had lost four more of her beasts. The thought gave her strength. No time to grieve. She needed this pain to keep going. *Never give in*, Our Doris thought. *Never, or else lie next to Rose and Natalie*. She painted a smile on her faced and lifted her head. Our Doris was back.

The group went back in, still holding one another, and shut the front door. Kathy had stayed to look after Freddie. His face looked quite grey, but in good spirits.

Our Doris, forever a glass is half full lady tried to lighten things up a bit, even though she had just lost her sister and niece. She took a deep breath.

'Well, I don't think my living room could look any worse. We might as well have a wild party whilst we are at it. Who's for a Malibu?' she laughed. It was a crazy little laugh, but that could be excused in the circumstances. Apart from the smashed antiques, and upside down furniture, there were two dead humans, six dead creatures and a beheaded wolf. There was blood, fluids, brain tissue and two saucepans full of boiling water sprayed over carpets, furniture, curtains and wallpaper. Outside there was another dead vampire and four dead wolves.

Jennifer sighed, looking at the two dead family members.

'They did nothing. Nothing to defend themselves. Why?'

'Not to speak ill of the dead and all,' said Freddie from the chair, 'but that was Rose all over for you. It finally caught up with her.' He shook his head. 'I can't believe they did nothing. I mean it's a natural instinct. Fight or flight. They didn't do either one. The pair of them might as well have just stood out in the street, waiting for them, like Rose said. A steak dangling round their necks. What was the point of being in here with us?'

'What are we going to do with all these, though?' Terry said as he looked around at the bodies on the floor.

'I don't want any of them in here. I want to forget it happened,' Our Doris said.

'Do you think she'll come back tonight?' asked Jennifer.

'No. Not tonight, I think,' Pat said.

'Yes, she'll be off somewhere licking her wounds.' Our Doris said thoughtfully. 'Remember we have made a massive hole in her plans. She has lost five wolves. I don't know how many she has.'

'Not to mention, lots of lovely creatures of hers. Some that were quite well turned,' Kathy said.

'Well the thing is, they are all going to be quite heavy. Where are we going to put them, in the garage?' Our Doris asked.

'Not with the Jag!' said Freddie shaking his head. She quietly laughed.

'Alright Freddie. You can have the Jag. We won't put them in there. What about next door?'

'What do you mean?' Brenda said.

'Well the house is for sale and there is no one in there. I have a spare key that the previous owner gave me. Sometimes he sends people over without an Estate Agent and I show them round. We could put them in there, out of the way at least. Maybe, think of a better solution, another time. I think house prices will have plummeted in the street anyway, don't you?' she said and they all agreed.

'Right, let's get it over with,' Terry said, standing up stiffly from the sofa. He looked sore and tired.

'Then we will have a nice drink and a calm down,' said Brenda with a smile. With a person holding onto each leg, they all, apart from Freddie, managed to pull a vampire corpse through the living room and down Our Doris's steps into the night. Here it got easier as the person slid on the compacted snow on the drive. Off they went, down her drive, onto the pavement and up into the next person's house. After the first one there was a trail of blood and goo, going from one door to the other. Like a large blackish-red U. Our Doris wasn't bothered at all.

'No one will question this, with what's been going on,' she said. Our Doris thought that surely there must be people still alive in their cul-de-sac besides them. But not one person had come out to help them at any point. So if they were alive, well....they could all knickers.

Freddie was the only one that wasn't taking part for obvious reasons. It was easy to move the wolves. There were a couple of heads, to dispose of and Our Doris walked with one under each arm, which Freddie found hilarious. The others started nervous giggling at this too, and although feeling guilty for it, it was a tonic to them all.

When it came to moving Natalie and Rose, Wee Renee, Pat, Terry and Kathy said they would do it. Our Doris went upstairs and got two bed sheets and they wrapped them up, which was the only distinction between the vampires and the people.

Wee Renee picked up the wolf's decapitated head up, by a fistful of it's hair. She turned the face of the wolf towards her, looking at the she-wolf's dead eyes square on.

'I tell you what, if I could get in Anne's house, she would find this in her bed a la Mafia. Casa Nostra Anne!' Wee Renee said. Pat chuckled. She was currently on her knees, trying to prise the mask of skin out of the carpet with a metal kitchen spatula.

After they had finished, they were absolutely exhausted. When the room was empty of corpses, the devastation could be examined properly. It would need a full decoration, that was for sure.

'So, er.....if I give this a full clean tonight, are you happy staying here?' Our Doris asked, who was very hygienic. She thought that she would do a really thorough clean of it and it would be fine for her guests to sit in, for tonight, at least. They were shocked that she would start cleaning for them at this hour of the night, after a battle. She was still recovering from a debilitating illness too. They told her to leave it, and would just try and avoid the worst patches.

'If you are really sure, that is alright, then I will manage to leave it,' Our Doris sighed and put her hands on her hips.

'When things are back to normal, I am going to have new carpets throughout. Upstairs and down.'

'Are you sure about that?' Wee Renee asked.

'I am.'

'If you are set on it. If nobody else wants it, I would love to have your carpet that you don't want. I could fully carpet downstairs, just with your bedroom carpet!' Wee Renee asked meekly.

'You can definitely have it.'

'Thank you, Our Doris. You see I can fit it all myself, that's no problem either.'

Freddie smiled at one side of his mouth.

'I bet you could as well, Wee Renee,' he said.

Terry had another look at Freddie's hand.

'I'm happy with the way that looks. Quite clean indeed. I have those antibiotics that I have been taking, along with Our Doris. You must start on those too. Also, and lucky for you, amongst the liquids I gave to Wee Renee was a painkiller injection.' Terry went into the kitchen where the drugs were in different bags, inside a brown cardboard box. He returned with a syringe, the liquid, tablets and a glass of water.

After that Freddie seemed to be a lot more comfortable. Whilst the other group had taken Rose and Natalie round to the other house, Brenda had put the kettle on. In came several steaming cups of tea. She had cut up some fruitcake into small pieces so they could pick at it and didn't need plates. Terry told them that they must wash their hands vigorously before eating or drinking anything. For half an hour they sat in their dirty clothes amongst the blood, quietly eating the fruitcake, washing it down with tea. There was a tranquility about the moment. It fully refreshed them. They could feel themselves relaxing, the tenseness drifting away. Adrenalin draining out of their system. After that came immense tiredness, however, especially as the majority of them were no spring chickens.

'I've still got that cheese pie in the oven,' Brenda said.

'I can't face it, Bren,' Freddie said. The others agreed, so Brenda took the now cold pie, out of the oven and placed it in the fridge.

'We need to think about what to do. I think that tonight we are all too tired to make rational decisions. Or have a decent conversation about it all. I vote that we all try and get some sleep. Then we will think about our next steps in the morning. But early!' said Freddie. The survivors said that was the perfect idea and they locked the doors. Jennifer said she wouldn't sleep that night, so would stay and keep watch for them. The rest went to bed. For the first time ever, Our Doris allowed Haggis to come upstairs and stay on the duvet with her.

Excerpt from Anne's Diary.

Wednesday, 14 December
Tonight I took eleven children and five wolves, my best pack, to the house. Norman had made this plan for his own purposes, but it suits mine too. Many of the people had returned to Friarmere, so I was no longer outnumbered. My infected local was still there, and as a lovely bonus another male infected was there with her. Alarmingly his infection is somehow fading. How did that happen? The group inside were surprised that I could just walk in. I told Sarah to wait at the end of the street with three of the new children.

They were still weak and would have been useless in the fight. These three struggle with instructions, and I suppose I should have kept them inside until they were stronger, but I wanted to have a show of force. And for their own progression, they could watch and learn. I took seven strong acolytes to the house with me. Although Carol stood with the wolves at the gate, during the fight. So, the truth of it is, they have spoiled my looks. That is what I am most vexed about. The group killed six of my children tonight. Three faithful experienced ones and three, which were strong new ones. Luckily my Sarah, my best creation was safe. I managed to take two of them out however, but they were not the most useful humans that I have ever seen. I had to leave at the end but I left Carol there to bring home my wolves. They have not returned and it is nearly light now. I fear that Sophia is gone. I last saw her biting down on the old man's hand. She saved my life, but I had to flee and I left her there. I will regret that forever. I will now treat my wounds with the fresh blood of a child. I have one somewhere. I have done it before. It does not work straight away, but it will work over a matter of days. I will be beautiful once again. How dare they? Who do they think they are?

33 – The Return

The group that was staying in Bob's den woke early, had a quick sandwich and began packing their backpacks. They did not know where they were going to start in Friarmere. People were quiet and thoughtful especially Carl. It was a cool crisp morning. Although they wanted to get on, a couple of them were reluctant to move out of the relative warmth of the den.

They wandered one by one out of the trees, moved onto the footpath, and finally congregated as a whole in the middle of the lane. The group in unison walked over to the opposite dry-stone wall. They looked over towards Friarmere. It looked quiet and content in the morning light. As if nothing had ever happened.

The rescuers started to walk down the lane. Not talking, just looking at the village. Watching it come ever closer. Within a few minutes, they went from the flat of the Pennine Ridge to the descent down to Friarmere.

About half an hour after that, they came to the junction that would them straight into the centre of the village. Opposite them was the road where Christine Baker and Norman lived. Danny was the first to break the silent magical spell that they were all under. He pointed to Blackfriar's Grange.

'Down the bottom of the lane, the big house. That's where he lives. The head honcho. The Nosferatu,' Danny addressed Carl mainly with this information.

'That is probably where Kate is now. I will go there then. While it's light,' Carl said nervously.

'No,' Gary said. 'Come help us with all them kids and then we will come and help you with Kate. I think that that's sensible.'

'Yeah, Carl you have no idea,' Danny continued. 'You are going to be walking into a load of predators and she won't save *you* mate.'

Laura then pointed to Christine's house.

'There is one or two in there as well,' she said.

'Shit!' said Beverly. 'We really have walked into the lion's mouth!'

'We did warn you.' said Gary, 'Come on, let's go further down his throat.' They set off again towards Friarmere. 'The obvious place would be the school, but that really would be a trap especially the way it is situated with the long drive. Once we are up there, they could come out of the trees and surround us.'

'I have been thinking,' said Sally, 'I might be wrong though.'

'Yes?' Gary said.

'Maybe it is kind of like a trap with no cheese. They would think we will check there first, so might be waiting there, and the kids might *not* be there,' Sally said. 'So where else is there in Friarmere, you know, public buildings, large houses, I suppose. Big enough to house all the kids. I mean, I don't even know how many kids we're talking about.'

'I don't know,' Gary said, 'but a lot less than we think. So many were taken the last night we were here.'

They were moving quite quickly now as the descent was steep. One of them would slide every so often on the thick snow. Luckily it had not snowed for a few days now and the snow was becoming compact. With less to fluff it up, it was easier to walk on.

The group still had their eyes on Friarmere, but nothing was happening. It just looked its usual sleepy old self.

'I would like to call at that lady's house where we saw the Coopers,' said Sue. 'Now, before anyone says anything, I know she won't be alive. I just have a feeling I would like to sweep that area and not have it behind us.' Gary agreed with that wholeheartedly.

'Anything you like. We need to act on our gut feelings. Trust ourselves. We won't go wrong like that.' Gary thought for a few steps, quietly looking at the village. 'Going back to where the kids are. Maybe they will be in an unexpected place. Perhaps he has split them up, hiding them in lots of places, each with a vampire guarding them. There is no guarantee they are all together, or that he has them all. There could be pockets of survivors. We have a long laborious job in front of us.'

In a short while they were at the lady's house that Sue had spoken about, which was one of the first houses in Friarmere. The group put their backpacks on her drive and walked up to the house. Sue looked at the state of the curtains when she was still six feet away from the window. They were still half pulled out of their curtain hooks, in fact Gary looked up and saw that the plastic curtain rail had been bent downwards. They were exactly like they had been a couple of days ago. Obviously there was no hope that she had survived. Sue looked through the gap in the curtains and so did Gary. They couldn't see much in the half-light washing over the room, just that furniture was tipped over. It was quite dark in there. Maybe dark enough for …..what….them, to walk around in.

'Do you still want to go in?' Gary hoped that she would say no.

'I want to go in, even if Sue doesn't,' Liz said, surprising Gary.

'Ok,' he said.

They decided that Gary, Tony, Andy, Danny, Liz and Sue would go into the house. Liz wanted Sue with her, so these two and Gary were the first to go in. The other three would follow them and sweep the upstairs, which they thought was most likely to be housing a bloodsucker. They crept towards the back and the kitchen door. The door was open about six inches. They looked at one another and thought this was not a good sign. The first three walked into the kitchen and took ten slow steps inside. Gary had a bad feeling and thought he should actually take his own advice and follow his gut feeling.

'Sue, you know she's not going to be alive. What are we doing?'

'Getting used to scouting out buildings and getting jumped. If we can't defend ourselves against an old lady, how will we manage against Norman's gang. Is that a good enough reason?'

'It's a reason, Sue. I don't know if it's a good one,' he muttered unconvinced. The other three came in behind them and pushed past, to check out the upstairs.

'Wait a minute. Let me get my knife out ready,' Liz said. She took it out of a zipped compartment on her coat, grasping the handle. It led the way. She started to talk, it was more to comfort her than anything else. 'Right, okay we don't know what we are going to face. Well we do really. Something horrible and then we will have to do unspeakable things to it. Okay Liz, you will be alright.'

'Liz, do you want to go back out? You are talking to yourself now,' Sue said putting her hand gently on Liz's arm.

'No I have to do it,' she said, squeezing her mouth together tightly. They walked into the hall, listening for any noises every couple of steps as the house went quiet. Not a sound could be heard. Inching into the dark living room, Sue thought it looked darker in here than when she had just been looking through the window. Now there were more faces outside at the gap in the curtains. Beverly, Laura, Sally and Bob were crowded there. Carl just behind them, trying to see over their heads. Bob pointed to the sofa, which was tipped over against the wall. When he had caught her eye, he put his two fingers either side of his mouth pointing downwards. Sue furrowed her brow. She wondered what he meant and then the penny dropped. Sue realised that there was obviously something under there and his young eyes had spied it. She tapped Gary on the shoulder. Then began to whisper in his ear.

'Go round there. To the front, where Bob is looking. I think there is one under there.'

The three of them walked around the sofa, from the back of the room, by the door, to the front by the window. The sofa had been tipped against the wall and this had left a triangle of space behind it.

Just peeking out of the space, half in the shadows and half in the dull light was a hand. An old ladies, very white, hand.

Gary stepped closer and stooped down. He could see her long thick yellowing nails. Dried blood was under her fingernails the cuticles were caked in it. He stood up and stepped back.

'I think she's one of them,' he said quietly, 'we need to fling the sofa back. Liz moved to the front and readied herself with the knife. Sue went to the back of the sofa so that the sofa would lift easily. Liz and Gary would be at the dangerous end of the vampire.

'Wait,' said Gary, 'I have an idea.' He took the big hammer out of his belt. Alongside that was a pouch full of long nails that he had used to attach the tarpaulin onto the trees. He took about five of the nails out, put them between his teeth, all pointed outwards. He took another, walking slowly to the hand. Placing the nail above the middle of the hand, he looked at the other two.

This had to be done in one shot. With a mighty sweep of his hammer, he drove the nail straight through in one hit. The nail went well into the floorboards pinning the hand to the floor.

The scream was terrible. A piercing, vibratory, dreadful noise. Sue threw back the sofa. Gary dropped the nails out of his mouth. There she was, Mary, pinned to the floor thrashing about, trying to pull her hand out of its tether, whilst at the same time trying to grab and claw at Gary.

The men upstairs had obviously heard the scream, their footsteps thundered up above, towards the stairs. Sue backed out of the way, towards the window. She had not taken out her weapon yet as she had needed both hands to throw up the sofa. Liz was hacking away at the old woman, but Mary was still very quick and unpredictable, so Liz wasn't landing any fateful blows. Tony picked up her coffee table and smashed it across her head, which certainly damaged part of her ear and face. It also made an awful lot of wooden stakes that smashed all over the floor. Gary grabbed a big sharp chunk of it. He cocked his head at the vampire, examining its movements.

'Look how much she wants my face. Why the face, not the neck or anything else. Weird.' Mary was still thrashing. She had not noticed Andy at all. He ran to the other side of the sofa behind her. Her knees were still on the floor. He did a round kick to her head from the back and she fell forward. He walked up the length of her body until she was flat. Andy stood on her shoulder blades, which kept her down. She still wriggled even with his weight on her.

'These suckers just don't give up. Gary, nail her other hand down,' Andy said. Gary quickly picked up one of his dropped nails. Mary's hand was on the floor, as she was trying to push herself up with this one hand. He whacked his hammer down on top of the nail. This time it was so hard that the head of the nail, disappeared into Mary's hand. He picked up his chunk of wood again.

'Let's see if this works, shall we.' He plunged it down through her back. Mary's flesh gave no resistance. Just like flicking a switch, she stopped.

'Now she's properly dead!' Gary said.

'Yeah that wasn't much fuss at all,' Sue said sarcastically.

'Let's take some of this broken wood. This is invaluable.' Danny said. They picked up the larger pieces of the smashed coffee table.

'One dead vampire nailed to the floor already. Just the safe rescue of tons of kids to do today. One down, about three hundred to go,' Andy said.

'So what shall we do now?' Liz said.

'We are leaving here now,' Gary said, 'but I suppose we had better check the house for any more. Or any of the kids.' They opened the front curtains. The ones outside spread out to see the carnage. They went into each room, opening the curtains and checking every wardrobe and cupboard. The house was clear. Mary seemed to have had a meal of an owl, upstairs, which distressed Liz and Sue greatly.

As they walked out of the back door, Bob was waiting for them.

'Dad, we might have to do this a lot.'

'More than I want to, I bet,' Tony said.

'Yeah lad, we probably will, why?' Gary asked.

'I was thinking of some kind of sign on the house, so that we know which ones we have done. Just so we don't forget and have to keep coming back. Someone else might be going round, doing this as well. I think it would save them time too. They will work out, that it's our sign and know it's safe. They will also know that they are not on their own in Friarmere.'

'That's a good idea lad. What about a red cross on the door,' said Carl.

'That would be the best thing,' Gary nodded, 'but we would have to carry some red paint around. What about if we just leave the front door open and then we know that we have checked them.'

'Yes, that is a good idea.' Bob said. Gary and Tony walked again to her back door, went inside then straight out the front, leaving it wide open. He looked back that the house.

'Yes, I'm pleased with that. It is a clear sign that the house and been cleared.' Andy looked amongst Mary's rockery for a loose stone. He found a large white one, walking back to the front door, he placed the stone in front of it.

'There. Now it won't blow shut.'

They all put their backpacks back on and set off again. Within a couple of minutes they arrived at Wee Renee's house. The house had had it's back door forced open. It was obvious from all the dirty footprints in the house that it had been searched, but there was nothing sinister inside and her house was safe.

'Right let's do mine now,' said Sue. She was a little worried about not finding her cat's alive. The front looked safe but again, as they got halfway around the house they could see her back door had been forced too and the house searched. She was so angry. Sue felt violated. She ran through the lower floor of the house, returning to the kitchen. She could not find her cats and felt heartbroken.

'Oh Tony,' she said, her eyes full of tears. He put his arms around her. Then there was a small bump outside.

'Sue, quick!' Sally shouted. Sue heard a meow and her little ginger cat was there. As large as life, happy to see her.

'He must have heard your voice,' Andy said. She picked him up, cuddling him.

'I was sad. I missed you so much Basil.' He purred and nuzzled into her neck. 'Where are the others, eh?' He looked at her as if to say *how should I know.* She went into a box under her table, pulling out two bags of cat treats. Standing at the back door, she shook them. It sounded like maracas. Within one minute the other two cats had returned. They were all in hiding but knew the sound of treats from their owner. She was so happy that they were safe. What clever cats they were. They had managed to evade all the vampires and the wolves from Melden.

Sue put some fresh wet food down for them and was stroking them. They would not leave her alone.

'It's nearly twelve o'clock now. I suggest we have something to eat, if we may Sue. Then try the school while it is still light,' Gary said. Sue had loaves of bread in the freezer, beans in the cupboard and cheese in the fridge. She defrosted the bread in the microwave. Sending Tony out to the shed for a carton of longlife milk that she had there, in her Christmas Food Hamper. Sue always put a couple of items in her shopping basket every week from September, all longlife. By the time it got to Christmas, it was only fresh meat and vegetables she had to buy.

Tony had also retrieved some ammunition from the shed. He took some duct tape, laid his gun on the table, along with one of Sue's sharpest long knives. Taping them together, so that the knife did not impede the gun barrel he made a very effective bayonet. However, now it was no longer easy to carry. He would put up with that.

'Do you want to sort out those homemade flamethrowers you were talking about, Gary?' he asked.

'No, it would take too long. I would have to get to the back of my workroom for the stuff, then I have no petrol anyway. I would be roaming the streets, trying to get into every car's fuel tank with a long pipe. Sucking all that out in the street. No, Tony. It's definitely happening another day, that bugger. I need to get in my workroom for some more ammo' for my nail gun too. That's stuck at the bandroom, useless.'

Sue made them all a hot drink, then got to work on toast with beans and cheese on top. They all ate in Sue's living room. Carl still did not want to eat, but Bob had his appetite back. Now sitting in his own house, with his own stuff, he felt a lot more like himself. They sat planning for a while. They were really running into everything blind.

'Ok. Enough plotting, we can't pre-empt him. Back to reality, it is time to go,' Gary said. This time they all had weapons handy. They knew this would be an awful fight. If the vampires were at the school, they did not know what else would be waiting for them. At least it was daylight, and they were full of energy after their lunch.

The friends reluctantly shuffled out of Sue's house. Out of the warmth, comfort and the small amount of normality. Back into the cold snow. The problem so much bigger than this small group could handle.

The school was not a long journey. In summertime it could be reached in five minutes, from where they had just been. It had a very long drive. The rescuers stood at the gates, gazing towards the school in the distance. Blinking every so often as the sheer amount of glistening snow hurt their eyes. It would be pretty stupid for them to try and do this in the dark. There were so many places where vampires could hide.

Danny suggested that the vampires could even have burrowed themselves into the deep snow around the edges of playing fields. Under the hedges, it was surely dark with feet of snow, drifting up, caught in the spiky leafless bushes. They wouldn't get cold or hypothermia. As soon as it was night, they could just spring out of the snow banks, freshly refrigerated.

The friends started to walk up the drive. It was turning out to be not too bad a day at all. The sun shone weakly out at them. They were hoping for a decent outcome. There was a low hedge that ran the length of the path, that the children used. They were following this hedge as a guide. It was natural. A couple of them had taken their children there over the years. Bob happened to look over to the left. Sometimes if the teachers weren't watching, if a pupil was late, for instance, they would not follow the curve of the path, but run across the playing field. An *as the crow flies approach*. Bob had done this many times. Where he used to run, there were fresh footprints. Lots of them. Adult ones. They were here.

'Guys, er……definitely be ready,' Bob said.

'What's wrong?' Sue said immediately.

'Look, Mum,' Bob replied. Pointing to the track across the playing field. Tony walked over to the footprints. He bent over examining them closely.

'Yeah. These are fresh, very. Maybe a couple of hours old. There are even two sets of high heels in these prints. No guessing who one of those is. No kids ones though. I would say the smallest size is an adult size five or six.' He trudged back through the snow.

'Which means they are either not there, or if they are, they haven't been out of the school since it last snowed,' Danny said.

Continuing, their steps seemed to get slower and harder the closer they got to the school. It loomed over them. Larger and larger, like their fate. The closer Gary got, the more his hair stood on end. Goosebumps formed. The back of his neck tingled. He knew that they were in there. That there were surprises in store for them. His gut told him, *he would* play a crucial part in this. This was important.

The school hall had enormous windows and the curtains were shut on each and every window. They only usually used the curtains when school was showing a film. Sue remembered watching *Mamma Mia* here, years ago. They were proper blackout curtains. The rescuers could imagine why this unusual situation had occurred. The hall curtains were double blackout ones. They were used only for large film nights and the school plays. Each classroom had curtains too. Used for sunny days, to keep the heat out and for an occasional joyous educational program they watched. Every single curtain was shut. What was in every room?

Reaching the double entrance doors, they peered through the glass. It was certainly dark in there. There was not a glimmer of light a few inches past the doors. This was not a good place to be, but would be even worse at night. They had come here to do this. The time was now.

Gary pulled the door towards him, which of course was unlocked. They all started to file in. Liz caught her breath.

'Listen, what if when we are in there, Michael comes up and chains the doors together, or something. You know he can wander around out here in the day. He could be anywhere,' she said.

'That's true,' said Gary, 'what shall we do?'

'I suggest me and Andy wait out here,' she replied. 'I know it is splitting resources, but it could save us. He might have made more like Michael, that could do this for him.'

'Yes, that is right. It is a good idea for you to stay here. Hopefully we won't be long.' Gary smiled. He was kidding no one.

Liz felt strong that day. Those antibiotics certainly were doing the trick. She wanted Michael to turn up. Liz had felt like she was not pulling her weight so many times. She would like a good go at Michael. Liz needed to do something for the group.

The remaining clan walked into the entrance hall. The door swung shut behind them. Danny had put his phone on charge in Our Doris's house. He now switched the torch facility on.

They walked past Reception, the Headmaster's Office, the Staffroom. There was a gloomy light from behind them that graduated to blackness, as they got to the hall doors. These glass fire doors were shut too. They had their own black curtain the other side, which was of course closed. This was a real leap in the dark, unless they ran in and opened the curtains, the vampires would have the better of them. They became scared to move forward. Frozen to the spot. This was probably just full of vampires, in coffins, who would reanimate at their scent, once they got the other side of the door. Sue was hardly breathing. She had her fingers pressed into Bob's shoulders. Then they heard a child cough inside and knew that there were living humans in there. These poor kids would be more scared than them. Gary whispered to himself, *grow a pair Gary*. Without thinking, he flung open the doors and they all stepped into the darkness.

Danny's torch illuminated lots of little faces. They shone back at him, pale and tearstained. They were sitting cross-legged on the floor hugging one another. Lots of little children that were perfectly alive and well, squinting at Danny's light shining in their eyes. They heard a match strike and the light of a candle could now be seen coming from the stage. Sitting beside it on a high teachers chair was Adam, Bob's friend.

He gave them an enormous grin. It was obvious from his colour that he was no longer human.

'Hello mate,' he said, 'sorry to disappoint you. I aren't full of the pumping red stuff anymore. But I am strong and confident and powerful. It's nice to see you all here.' Bob didn't reply but his father did.

'Adam, nice to see you again. We are not here for a chat with you. We are here to take these kids away,' Tony said flatly.

'Hmmm….I will only talk to Bob. What about that.'

'Me?' Bob said, 'I am still normal. You know what I will do at one point. You know what I have to do. You'd do it in the same position.'

In the pale light from Danny's phone, they saw Adam scowl. Noise seemed to come from all around them and door's opened from several places at the sides of the hall, where different classrooms were situated. One or two vampires came out of each one.

'Stand up kids, we're going,' Danny said. The kids did stand up, running toward the rescuers. They backed towards the double doors behind them, to the entrance hall.

Sue opened the door, so they could quickly make their escape. She heard a creak behind her. Norman Morgan seemed to glide out of the Headmasters Office. His head was tilted downwards and his eyes looked up, he smirked.

'Back in the room, back,' she said, 'he is behind me!' They rushed forward to make room for him, to get through the door. Now he gave them a full smile. His eyes constantly moved about them, examining them.

'Fresh blood he said how lovely for me. I have three from Anne's clutches, for my delectation,' he laughed. 'She isn't having you back. Oh no. She trust's me far too much.' A thought seemed to strike him. The smile left his face and it became angry. 'Where are the others?'

'They are outside!' said Gary. 'We have two more outside, Liz and Andy. Just in case you think you are trapping us.'

'There is more of you than that!'

'Yes, not all of us have come back.'

'What!' he shouted. 'I wanted all of you to come here! What use is part of you? You have just brought the vegetable one and her protector. You can still open your mouth and spoil it all for me. Where is the one that keeps thwarting me with her efforts?'

'Who do you mean?'

'The garlic smelling one. The small one. Old and Scottish? Is she still in Melden?'

'Yes, she is still over there.'

'No! That is the one I wanted to collect the most!'

'Anne never told us, we *all* had to come. That's not our fault!' Norman looked at Gary whilst he thought. Gary could almost see the cogs whirring.

'You can have these kids, when you fetch them back over here. All of them. The small one and the very big one that make a pair. The man with the stick too.'

'We are taking these kids now!' Sue said. 'We have others outside. We will sacrifice ourselves. Shout for them to burn this place to the ground, if that is what it takes.' Norman now examined Sue for a few moments. She could do that if she had a mind too, maybe he hadn't thought this through as well as he imagined.

'What about we negotiate. I settle for something that I would like, and in exchange you take the children away for at least a few more hours of their worthless lives. Try and keep them safe from my children. What about that? What about a trade of resources?'

'What do you want for these kids?' Danny asked.

'I'll take him,' Norman said, pointing to Gary. To say that they were crestfallen was an understatement.

'I don't think so,' said Tony, 'think of something else.'

'You can have me,' Carl interrupted. 'I have a bone to pick with you anyway. You can have me instead of him. I am staying here, let the kids go.'

'How very gallant of you,' Norman said amused. 'I wonder what bone you have to pick with me. Perhaps I have stepped on your toes. Have I upset one of your family? It will be interesting to find out. I advise you though, there have been many with a bone to pick, but I end up picking theirs. In reply to your trade. No, I still want him. He is more of a threat than you. Without your two leaders, you will be running around like headless chickens. With one away in Melden, I have already won. I want the Scottish Sow and her friends.'

'Stop calling her that,' Laura said, 'it's disgusting.'

'Tell me her name then!'

'No, I am not telling you her name. You have plenty of people here from band who can do that. I bet you already know. You just prefer to call her a sow.'

'I will stay if you let every child go,' Gary said. 'That is fine. Deal done.'

'Where are the rest of the kids,' asked Sally. 'This can't be the whole school, this is more like a class.'

'This is your lot, my dear. For some are now my children. Some just got cast aside. I think there are some squirreled away with their mummies and daddies, but I will get to them don't you worry, my dear.'

'Master, I want you to keep him here too,' said Adam.

'No not yet my child, we will get to that. And his family. I have done the deal now. I want all of them, not just one. Only that will satisfy me.' Adam looked very angry at this and constantly stared at Bob. For one minute, Bob was actually thankful to The Master even though he never thought he would say that.

Liz and Andy stood at the front entrance, shivering and stamping their feet. They were constantly alert. Looking to the left, right, front and back of the school entrance. They did not speak, their eyes large with concentration. A great deal depended on their vigilance.

Out of the absolute silence of the snowy hill, they heard a car door shut. It seemed to come from the right of them and they turned in that direction. From around the corner, strode Michael Thompson. He was smiling. Rubbing his hands together against the cold. He indeed had a chain and padlock over his shoulder. After about six steps he looked up and was shocked to see Liz and Andy. He had parked the car in a way where he could see all the people coming up the drive, but could not see the entrance door.

'Oh shit!' he said.

'I knew it,' Liz said. 'I knew you would turn up. That was how you were going to trap us all in there.'

'No you didn't,' Michael said, annoyed.

'Why are we standing here then, if we didn't know that that was what you were going to do? There's only you that could be walking round doing things like that. I know what kind of bloke you are.' Michael lifted his head up, he had decided to act brave.

'You are in a lot of danger. Lets just say that,' Michael said.

'It's two against one,' Andy said. 'The thing is if we killed you then you can't make trouble for us anymore.' All the bravery drained out of Michael, like air out of a balloon. He tried another tactic.

'I will admit that a lot of things I do, I don't want to do,' he said. 'But I am stuck in this bloody situation, aren't I?'

Liz thought for a moment about how she was infected the same as Michael. She had been supported and shielded from Norman getting to her, by Andy and her friends. Michael with his lonely life had needed to feel wanted. In his position, would she have slipped easily into being used as a pawn? She thought she might. Liz started to feel a little bit sorry for him.

Andy stepped towards Michael. He had a large knife plus the sticks of wood that had broken off the sideboard in the house.

'I will have to use the knife, mate. The wood won't work for you, will it!'

In the school hall the trade was being made. Carl wanted to stay. Gary did not, but would stay for the release of the children. He thought the chance of the rest of his friends getting them away and safe was good enough for his sacrifice. Norman said he would release Gary when they bought him Wee Renee, Pat and Freddie.

'Do you really think we are going to kill them?' Norman said. 'I have better plans than that. These people excite me. They were clever when they fought. They were the best of this Village. Why would I not want them for my own children? I will waste the useless, but these people are resourceful. Brave. It is not just about them getting out, raising the alarm, so that I am eliminated. It is about me having the strongest army. You come back with those people and I will not kill this man. You will all then become members of my flock. Whatever happens, I will be after you. So you have the chance of getting him back with you or not, that is up to you. As for the other one, I don't know what he is up to. I will not guarantee he will be here when you return. If you want that guarantee, you must persuade him to come with you now. I may have to defend myself and deal with him strictly.' Carl stood proudly with his chest puffed out. His planted his legs firmly. He wasn't going anywhere. He was finally going to find out what had happened to his wife and stand up for her.

'So take these children now.' Norman said. 'They may have a few more hours of sitting in terror, waiting for one of us to get them.' The Master said this very matter-of-factly. It was already written and gospel to him.

'That is fine by me. I will take my chances. I will have them,' Sue said. 'Come on children, quickly!'

They started to get up walking towards Sue. She walked to the door and looked into the entrance hall. There were no other vampires.

'Go outside. Wait for us. We have two friends outside.' They pushed open the door hastily, walking, silently through the entrance hall, out of the door and into the bright daylight. They immediately began holding each other, crying.

Liz gathered them outside to wait for the other rescuers. Andy was around the corner near the car Michael had been sitting in. He had Michael up against the icy wall, with the knife up against his throat.

Sue waited until the last ones were gone, before herself and the other friends started to walk outside. Danny squeezed Gary's shoulder.

'We will get you back. Don't you worry.'

'Whatever happens, I have saved them. I am happy Danny. Forget about me. Think of the bigger picture. I am,' Gary said solemnly.

The group exited the building, leaving Carl and Gary in the very dark room with the other vampires.

'We are taking these kids somewhere safe now,' Sue said. 'Make sure he doesn't follow us. When you've done that, come and meet us,' Sue pulled Liz to one side and whispered their destination in her ear. Liz nodded, smiling.

They walked away with the group of children. Andy did not release Michael until Liz told him the group was out of sight. They were under no illusion that Michael would not be able to follow their tracks, or that The Master wouldn't smell them. But it would buy them a bit of time.

Liz and Andy looked at Michael. He stood against the wall with his eyes closed, rocking himself. Michael was a pathetic creature.

'What should we do?' They really didn't know what to do with him.

'Should we lock him in there with them and put a chain across the door, like he was going to with us?' Andy said.

'No,' said Liz, 'there are loads of doors, round the sides of the school. We would have been prevented from using them but what's to stop him, just running straight through from front to back, out onto the playground and being with us in five minutes.

'What shall we do?' Andy mused. He looked at his surroundings after an answer. Liz followed Andy's gaze. She knew immediately.

'What about this? We'll lock him in that car he was sitting in, with the window open so he can breathe,' Liz said. Andy grabbed Michael by his coat, walking round to the car. This car had previously belonged to the Headteacher, so was very comfortable.

'Give me the key,' Andy said. Michael reached into his pocket, the key had the BMW sign on it. He reluctantly gave it over.

Andy got in and switched the ignition on. He pressed a button with the window sign on it. The window cracked down two inches. Andy switched the ignition off, getting out of the car. 'Now get in.'

He sat himself in the driver's seat. Andy wound the chain tightly around him, through the headrest of the car seat and through the steering wheel. Liz put the padlock on. The chain was very tight. She threw the padlock key onto the back seat.

'Your mates can rescue you, when it is dark,' Andy said, putting the BMW key in his pocket. They shut the car door and followed Sue and the rest of them down into Friarmere.

Norman walked through one of the doors, out of the school hall, into the gym. In here, the former Music Teacher sat with all the little vampire children of Friarmere. They could not be trusted to be anywhere near the other children. Little vampire children were unpredictable and always uncontrollable. She was reading them all a story, which was not one that the school would have allowed generally.

'They can have the run of the place now,' Norman said. 'Let them go. Run off their excess energy, little darlings. Fly little birds.' They ran out of the room causing mayhem. A plague of deadly locusts.

34 – Cowboy Boots

It was four am in the morning and Anne was checking her kennels. Her five best trusted wolves. Her alpha pack had not returned. She had been so caught up with the fight, that she had not seen what had happened to them. Then she had returned to her house, surveying the damage to her face for a while. They had spoiled her looks. She would have to treat this with an awful lot of blood for it to repair successfully.

She doubted that they were trapped somewhere, so she had to assume that they were dead. If they were trapped, she would hear their howls from her house, wherever they were in Melden. Anne had more wolves. Lots more, but they were younger. Most of them were the children of the wolves that she had with her that night. She had young adult wolves, adolescents and even wolf cubs. Anne had been allowed five wolves as a Private Zoo. However, she had not mentioned that she had bred from this pack.

Her favourite wolf, her queen of the pack, Sophia had gone. She knew that for certain. Sophia had been protecting her mistress. Biting down on the hand of one of those people. She had surely perished. Tonight she would go back. She would keep going until she cut them out of Melden, one by one.

Wee Renee woke refreshed, even though last night had been terrible. Despite losing Rose and Natalie, she still felt like it was a victory. Anne had lost a lot more of her people, than their two. Plus a whole pack of wolves.

As she opened her eyes, blinking to the light, she noticed Pat was sitting in the armchair by the window. She had been awake for a while.

'You awake, Rene?' Pat asked.

'Yes, I am just pulling myself together,' she said. She hitched herself up, putting the pillow behind her, so she could see Pat.

'What do you think about last night?' Pat asked.

'I wish it hadn't happened. Norman and Anne had divided us.'

'I can't tell you how worried I am about the other lot.' She was hesitant as she said, 'are you ready to go back to Friarmere?'

'Just try and stop me!' Wee Renee replied enthusiastically. Pat released a breath she had been holding and nodded towards her.

'It's about bloody time I got my old Rene back. I was worried for a while.' She sniffed.

They could hear banging around in the other rooms, voices and a toilet flushing. It was time to get up.

When the few that were awake were washed and dressed, Pat and Wee Renee got themselves together and went downstairs too. It would still be dark for a couple of hours, but they needed to make plans. Working ahead of the dawn would benefit them greatly today. Jennifer was very low in mood. She sat downstairs, eyes puffy, twisting a tissue in her hands.

'I've not had much sleep. I've been thinking all night that Beverly is dead. I was stupid to let her go. Now I will never see her again.' Jennifer was lost, desperate. This was the worst she had felt since all this had begun. Wee Renee recognised the feeling that she had had from the previous day.

'Listen Jennifer, I can understand how you feel. It has been a long, dark, horrible night. You are bound to think the worst. But just for a moment stop and add it all up. We have all survived Friarmere. Just a bunch of pensioners and Beverly is a very fit young woman. Think of the people she's with. All experienced in fighting these creatures. I would know if there was a problem, and there isn't. You trust me don't you?'

'Yes I do,' Jennifer said.

'Then heed my words. Your girl is safe. Now wash your face, get your makeup back on and lets make some plans,' Wee Renee said. Jennifer hugged her and went upstairs.

Our Doris, Terry and Kathy were still asleep, but everyone else was awake.

Brenda put the kettle on. The morning routine began. Bread was put in the toaster. Pat slipped Terry's shoes on, and took Haggis half-way down the cul-de-sac for a tinkle, whilst Wee Renee stood watching at the front door, her machete ready. Brenda filled his bowl, by the time Pat returned and Haggis was soon guzzling his breakfast. There was an air of excitement in the room, but Wee Renee was still a little worried about Jennifer. They started to hear more noise upstairs. Floorboards creaked and there was the distant noise of Our Doris playing her Elvis CD whilst she got ready.

The other three were soon down. Terry and Our Doris felt amazing. The antibiotics were still working. Each day was an improvement. Our Doris had a *let me at them* attitude. Freddie was low. You could see he was in pain. His hand had an ugly look about it. The skin was pulled in round the centre of each hole, with what looked like dead tissue around it. Terry examined the area. They could tell he wasn't happy with what he saw.

'I am sure that those wolves are just plain old wolves,' Terry said. 'When did you last have a tetanus?'

'I don't know,' said Freddie. 'Brenda! When did I last have a tetanus?'

'I don't know Freddie. Did you have one when you had your prostrate done?'

'Er...no, no. I don't know, Terry.'

'I think that it is more likely, that it has given you a nasty infection, more than anything else.' The skin around each bite mark was grey and so was Freddie's face.

'Anybody would feel the same you know, if they had been bitten by an enormous dog,' Brenda said. 'I will get him right, not to worry.' Freddie realised, not for the first time, what a good wife he had.

'Me and Pat have decided to go back to Friarmere on a rescue mission for our old gang and the kids. Does anyone want to come?' Wee Renee asked.

'I do!' Our Doris unexpectedly said.

'Are you sure?' Brenda asked. 'It is an awful long way over the tops. All in the snow too.'

'I am,' Our Doris replied. 'I'll be taking my sword, rest assured. You'll come with me, won't you?' she asked Haggis. He wagged his tail, stood up and wandered over to her, putting his head in her lap.

'I won't be able to make it,' said Freddie.

'Too right you won't,' Brenda said. 'Look at the state of you!'

'We will catch you up, soon,' Freddie said. Wee Renee shook her head.

'Then we will have to stay too,' Wee Renee said.

'Why?' Freddie asked, indignant.

'Well the thing is, it really has to be all or nothing, doesn't it? Because this house now is not safe. She can get in and she knows we are here. If we leave you like this, with only Brenda to look after you, we are signing your death warrant,' She said.

'I am going to stay. I don't think I can make it. I feel very weak. What about if you came and stopped in my house. We have cameras. A big gate. We can take as many weapons as we like, keep coming back in the daytime. Everyone knows where it is if they need to come back. What about that? They won't necessarily be looking for us there,' Jennifer suggested.

'That is a good idea,' said Freddie. 'Yes, I like it.' Brenda felt happier about the whole idea of staying in Jennifer's house too. No blood all over the carpets, more security, and they would have escaped from the place Anne would come back to.

'Are you happy with that Rene?' Pat asked.

'Jennifer's house is safer than here, I'll give you that. But it does seem a little like catnip to her doesn't it, with all the camera activity.'

'I have to stay here in Melden. It can't be here, that goes without saying,' Freddie said. 'Wherever we go, she will us find in time. I would imagine Anne is bandaging her face and wondering where her wolves have gone. She will definitely be out for revenge, but we are dealing with a weaker threat. I think Jennifer's house, although stalked, is the safest place. The security it offers is without question the best in Melden. I am very happy to go there.'

'I agree, Freddie, whoever says here. It is their best bet,' Wee Renee conceded.

'What are you going to do, Terry and Kathy? You are more than welcome to stay too,' Jennifer said.

'We'll go to Friarmere.' said Terry. 'We have already spoke about it. Sally is there. We need to help with the kids.'

'I am going to do some more of that meat,' said Wee Renee. 'That was invaluable last night, wasn't it?' They all agreed.

'You've got all the wolves. There wasn't any more. We only ever saw five.' Brenda said.

'You don't know how many she's got wandering about. After all they aren't exactly distinctive are they. If she had one Dalmatian, one Red Setter, and a Chihuahua, I would say yes. But they all look the same. What if she's got a hundred, but she only takes five out at a time. Those kind of things, well…. they bloody breed like rabbits! There is also the chance that one of her human monsters will get so feral, that it will eat the raw meat too and then we are sorted. What if it drugs them and they are scattered round Melden one morning. All that it would take is one of you going round, putting them out of their misery. It all helps the cause,' Wee Renee said. They all thought this made sense. Wolves or vampires, if drugging some was an option, they should take it. 'I also thought that I would get some more meat, drug it and take it with us. You know, in case they pick up our scent. We will be very vulnerable in Bob's Den. Last night the wolves were busy with us, so didn't go after the others. But tonight, they might be on the warpath!'

Brenda made more cups of tea, setting to work on a mountain of toast. She had a look what would go off in their fridge. They would take this to Jennifer's. Wee Renee and Pat came in. Pat said she would *butter-up,* which freed up Brenda.

'Listen Brenda, do you think you could learn how to do this meat? It will be invaluable for you here in Melden,' Wee Renee asked.

'Yes. If you show me what to do and I write it down,' Brenda replied.

Wee Renee told her what to do. She gave her half the drugs, which was still a lot. Wee Renee turned to her friend.

'You know Pat, we weren't expecting all this here. We don't know what we are going back to. I'm taking the other half of the drugs to Friarmere. Maybe it will only work on someone like Michael Thompson. But if it does, it could save our lives.' She left all the injectable antibiotics and painkillers, for Freddie.

'Are you feeling better about it all?' Brenda asked Wee Renee.

'Yes I am, I feel stronger again. I had a day of weakness. But I have my faith and I think that at some point we will triumph. Nothing good is worth having unless you have to fight for it. I keep thinking about the war. They fought for a lot longer than we will fight this winter, and in worse conditions. They didn't give up, ever. Victory will be ours in time.'

'I piggin' hope so,' Our Doris said, who was now bustling around the house gathering items for the journey. She was putting them together on the kitchen work surface as she collected them. Our Doris now knelt down on the kitchen floor. A lot of banging and swearing went on as she was messing around in the bottom of one of her cupboards. She was trying to reach right at the back, and as she was rather short, with small arms, it was a struggle. In the end she bought out an industrial size flask, with a wide set neck.

She proceeded to fill it with five tins of vegetable soup. She made more sandwiches and cut up the cheese and onion pie from last night, then packed the slices back together. This crisis seemed to have infused new vigor into Our Doris. She then got changed into her travelling outfit which consisted mainly of her regular clothes. A turtle neck sweater, cardigan, skirt and tights. She laid out a union jack fleece, for under her coat and a pair of brown cowboy boots.

'Aye, I like your style Our Doris, but I think you have underestimated how bad the snow is up there, on the tops. It will soak right though the leather on those boots. I think those might be ill advised.'

'Yes, I get that, but it's the only thing I can go for miles in because of my bunions, Wee Renee. I'm going to put carrier bags inside them, to protect me from the wet.'

'Bless you. You've thought it through well. Ignore this old fool.' Wee Renee said. Our Doris kissed her on the cheek.

'I'm planning on making this trek a right laugh. Are you with me.' Our Doris said.

'I like what I hear.' Wee Renee said and gave her a hug.

'I tell you what always makes me feel like facing an obstacle. Putting some glitzy eyeshadow on,' she laughed. 'I don't know why, but it does.'

'Have you got any green?' Wee Renee asked.

'Oh yes, come up.' They left the kitchen giggling like two schoolgirls. When they returned ten minutes later, Our Doris had a shiny, blue cream eyeshadow on, which she had generously applied with her finger. Wee Renee was sporting a small amount of forest green. 'What do you think?' Our Doris asked when she was fully dressed. Cowboy boots, pink earmuffs and her iridescent eyelids.

'Dressed to kill!' Pat said.

'That's the look I'm after,' Our Doris said excitedly.

Brenda thought it quite amazing that the previous night Our Doris had lost one of her sisters, but their brains seem to be in survival mode. There had been certain errors made by Rose and Natalie that seemed to have eased their passing, unfortunately. If it made Our Doris feel better by dressing up and putting eyeshadow on, then that was fine.

Soon everyone was ready. Terry said he wanted to call quickly at the dentist and pick up various drugs that he thought might be useful, if they came across people who had been hurt or infected in Friarmere. Freddie struggled on with his coat. They had bandaged his hand very well out of Our Doris's medical kit that she had found behind the flask. Pat knew that the others were all right in Friarmere and would be until they got there. She also knew that they would find them and help them. It was a feeling she felt very strongly. If she hadn't, she would not have been able to carry on.

Our Doris had a large metal sledge in the garage. She said in bad winters she walked to the shop with it, dragging all her shopping back on it. It turned out to be very handy as they had to have quite a good amount of dog food on there and blankets. The others were leaving the tarpaulin up in Bob's Den. All they needed to take was something to keep them warm overnight. The sledge was packed full of blankets. Their own provisions they carried in backpacks. Jennifer and Brenda carried their belongings and some poisoned meat. Freddie was using his father's stick just to walk. He could just about manage that. The mystery of the missing bung, which fitted on the end of the stick was solved when Wee Renee found it in Rose's handbag. Very ominous. They dropped more meat into the two bowls either side of Our Doris's drive and set off.

'I like this weather, you know.' Our Doris said. 'It means that the boy racers aren't out causing a menace!' The others laughed. Of all the reasons to pick, it was a strange one. Wee Renee wanted to call at the kebab shop and see if the man who worked there, Nigel, was still safe. Also, for his wellbeing, she wanted to advise him of what had happened last night, and the fact that they were setting off back to Friarmere.

The kebab shop was not yet open. She knocked on the side door. After a minute they heard someone coming down the steps from the flat. She put her mouth to the letterbox opening it and shouted.

'It is alright, love. It's only Wee Renee and party from the other night. We were in the kebab shop. You might remember us.'

The man immediately opened the door after he heard her accent, as she was the only Scottish woman he had talked to for the last five years. He asked them in, but they said for the moment it was too much fuss bringing everything in, and taking their hats and boots off. Very quickly Wee Renee summarised the tale and said they were going back. He listened and nodded without saying anything, taking it all in. At the end, she looked at him with her twinkling eyes.

'What do you think of all that?' she asked.

'Would you like a *hanger-on*?' Nigel said. They were quite surprised about this but very pleased as he looked like he could handle himself in a fight. He had stood alone against the mob in Melden previously, and bested them. They all nodded in agreement and he asked if they could give him about twenty minutes to get his belongings together. They walked back to the front of the kebab shop. It was time for Jennifer and Brenda to say their goodbyes. They had to go a little further on. Jennifer who was still quite sad wanted to call at the shop for more chunks of meat, if there were any left. But they might be back before Nigel was ready and they would see them again.

Freddie sat on a wall outside the kebab shop. He looked exhausted already. He would wait with the Friarmere group, whilst they were waiting for Nigel. He would then go to Jennifer's with them.

Our Doris, Jennifer and Brenda kissed each other. Everyone else hugged. The two women set off for the shop. Nigel came out after about fifteen minutes.

'Are you sure you don't want us to wait with you, Freddie?' asked Wee Renee.

'No, I'll be fine here. They will be back soon, you need to use the daylight. Don't be daft.'

They did as he asked, looking behind them after a couple of minutes they saw the two women returning, with their groceries. All was well there.

'I hope he's ok,' Terry said. 'I didn't want to say it, but his hand is pretty badly mangled. He needs the hospital really.'

'He has antibiotics and Brenda. He will be fine,' Pat said.

'Yes, he's a fighter. Always has been. We'll see Freddie again and *he'll be well*,' Our Doris said.

Terry wanted to call at the dental surgery to pick up more drugs. The rest of the group waited outside. It seemed weird now that several of them had stopped there a couple of nights ago. They started chatting whilst they waited.

'What did you think of the kebab the other night? Did you all enjoy it?' Nigel enquired, smiling. Pat opened her mouth to speak and Wee Renee nudged her quickly.

'Aye, they were beautiful, Nigel,' Wee Renee said. 'Lovely, tender meat. Very tasty. They were a credit to you!' Pat looked at Our Doris and she winked. It was probably for the best, not to upset Nigel as their lives may depend on him at some point. Terry soon returned with a full backpack, which he lashed to Our Doris's sledge. Finally, they started their walk up the bank.

Freddie, Brenda and Jennifer watched the others go, waving sadly.

'God speed,' Brenda said. When the adventurers were out of sight, they began to make their way to Jennifer's. Freddie had to stop every couple of minutes to rest. This group, at least, had plenty of time before nightfall.

'Who did you see in the village, while we were at the shop?' Brenda asked him.

'No one. It's like the Marie Celeste here, Bren,' he replied.

After what seemed like an eternity, they arrived at their destination. An examination of the meat left the previous day showed that only a few chunks were missing. They topped it up then Jennifer used the keypad to let them in. Freddie had only been here about three times in the last five years but was always impressed at the size of Jennifer's home. There was a wall all the way around her house. He could not imagine a safer place to be in. Jennifer settled them into a bedroom. Brenda insisted that he lie down for a while. Freddie said he didn't want to lie on the bed. He really felt like he didn't want to be on his own up there, with his thoughts and worries about the others. He would just like to sit down for a while on the sofa, and pull himself together. Brenda went to put the kettle on whilst Jennifer went to have a look at the clip from last night's CCTV. There were no sightings last night of them at all. They knew where they had been for most of the night.

'You'll be okay here for a bit won't you?' Jennifer asked. 'I just need to get my head down for a while. I had no sleep last night.'

Brenda said they were fine. She asked if Jennifer could quickly show them how to use the TV. She did this, and Freddie began happily watching a Cary Grant film.

Jennifer lay on her bed. She looked at the ceiling. She thought about Beverly. That she would never see her again. About the desperation of their plight.

She took one of her sleeping tablets with a tumbler of white rum, which was her favourite. She picked up a picture of Beverly from the side of her bed, holding it to her heart. She needed rest. Her brain needed to switch off, just for a while. She needed to sort herself out, so that she could be useful. See Beverly again. Help the others.

35 – Masculine

The party of six plus Haggis sat off towards hell, their fate and Friarmere. Wee Renee and Pat were quizzing Nigel about his business in the kebab shop. Where he got all his meats from, and what were the best sellers. They found him very interesting and entertaining. He had picked up some of his skewers from the shop, which he had found quite useful previously and also some very lethal looking knives. Wee Renee told him and the others about the texture of the vampires that were in Friarmere. How they were softer than a human. She tried to paint them a picture; by saying when you poked then it was like pushing something through a hard skin of a rice pudding, with nothing underneath. Pat told them that inside was a green powder like substance. They very quickly went mouldy.

In fact they were waiting to go mouldy. Wee Renee asked both Terry and Nigel for their opinions. How quick firstly, would a dead human turn green in a refrigerated environment and secondly, how quickly would meat go green. She asked them about changing composition and whether this was just generally degradation of flesh or actually an aspect of the vampires.

'I think it is an aspect of the vampires. I did notice that the scalpel was cutting them easier in Our Doris's house. I wondered if my scalpel was unusually sharp, but now I realise that they were softer,' Terry said.

'Raw meat is still definitely firm. It's all about the vampires,' Nigel said.

'If they had not been softer, I doubt I would have been able to do what I did with the sword. Thinking about it too…. the wolf was certainly harder work than the vampires to cut through. I suppose it was because they were living flesh,' Our Doris said.

'Do you think that the Friarmere vampires and the Melden vampires were the same or slightly different textured?' Terry asked. Wee Renee thought for a moment and so did Pat. They agreed that definitely the Melden vampires had the hardest texture but agreed with Our Doris that it was not as hard a texture as living humans.

'Another thing I noticed, is they had a lot more red blood in them and less greeny-black. Don't get me wrong – it was in there. But the Friarmere vampires had no blood whatsoever. There was no doubt, when we dragged the Melden lot in the snow round to the other house, that there was certainly some red blood in them, as well as the black. The snow was stained red and black,' Pat said.

'Aye it was!' Wee Renee agreed. 'Maybe the Friarmere vampire is more, I don't know, completely dead. Perhaps there is part wolf in the Melden one, which retains the solid texture of the being, at least partly.'

Pat also told them that the vampires, whilst they looked quite ill and white, could sometimes pass as human.

'Apart from the stink.' Pat said.

'What of?' Nigel asked.

'Mould. Soil. A bit kind of shitty.'

'I'll try not to get downwind from one,' he said.

'I had to play horn next to one!' She said offended.

'Yes,' Wee Renee continued. 'You could not spot them as easily as what we have all encountered in Melden. They were changed. Some had dog ears!'

'And of course, they had the obvious?' Nigel added.

'What was so obvious about them?' Terry asked.

'The eyes.' No one said anything, but all were thinking.

'Oh my word, yes!' Wee Renee said. She felt so stupid about not seeing it herself. 'They were reflective, like a badger or something. I saw it really plain on CCTV. Of course, I never thought that we don't have them.' They all took this in.

'So be careful,' Wee Renee continued. 'There is a definite look about the ones that have been changed by Anne's blood. I never heard a vampire growl, although they made some weird noises. They did not have a stance like an animal either.'

Kathy asked if they didn't mind talking about something else for a bit as it was getting her down and making her very worried for her sister. Wee Renee suggested that they sing Christmas Carols as the others had enjoyed it on the way over. Pat was the only one that had come over the first time and she was happy to do this again.

'I shall start at the beginning of the Carol book. Everyone is to do harmonies. Only Nigel and Our Doris are exempt as they aren't bandsmen.'

'Wait. I play guitar,' Nigel said.

'Our Doris is the only one exempt now.' This was the way they charged up the bank on their way out of Melden. Haggis, occasionally barking at the raucousness of it all, in his little tartan coat.

They sang all morning, following the footprints of the others that had gone the previous day. It made them feel like they were all together, in a small way. At one point they could see that they had stopped and there were a few footprints against the drystone wall. They imagined that this was where they had stopped for lunch. Pat decided that they would stop and have a break too. Our Doris put out a thick pad, which Haggis got on straight away. She wanted him to have a rest from the snow. Our Doris said dog's paws weren't meant to be on snow continuously and he would end up ill and unless anyone knew better, there were no vets to treat him. For his own part, Haggis was happy for a sit down too. She made a fuss of him, hand-feeding him some dog treats.

As Nigel had rushed out, he had not been as prepared as the rest of the group. They shared their food with him, there was an enormous amount anyway. He was really pleased to have a packed lunch and a cup of hot coffee. Our Doris told him that she had a flask of soup that they would share later. But for the moment even their warm coffee with sugar was a help.

'We are making good time,' Terry said. He looked out into snowy moors. His mind drifted off. He was miles away in thought. He hoped Sally was alright and wondered what the others had encountered as they would have been in Friarmere a few hours now.

'I'm worried about Sally,' Terry blurted out. Then he completely changed the subject. 'The others will be shocked that we had to battle Anne and her many creatures right inside Our Doris's house.'

'I don't think they would be shocked at all,' Pat said. 'They have seen Anne, she's one crazy bitch.'

'No,' Terry said, shaking his head, he was adamant. 'I don't think they would have gone if they thought *that* was going to happen.'

'I don't think that they were thinking about anything only rescuing those kids. Obviously some people felt they had to do it. It is no use thinking about what *they* were thinking, or what *we* were thinking, because this mess is down to Norman and Anne exclusively,' Pat commented.

'It's bloody terrible isn't it, when you just can't be in your own home, minding your own business without having this shit!' Our Doris said. 'My husband would have been going berserk now, after this home invasion. His home was his castle.'

'Let's set off again,' Wee Renee said.

'Wait a sec,' Our Doris said, fishing in one of her bags. She produced a full bottle of whisky. 'Let's all have a swig of this.' They started passing it round.

'You know, strictly we shouldn't be having this along with antibiotics,' Terry said, giving her a stern look.

'Get it down your neck,' Pat said. He took the bottle off her and had a swig. They got themselves back together and continued their journey. Pat thought that the mood had gone down-bank after Terry had been thinking about Sally. She thought about Our Doris telling them what her husband would think if he was still alive and this made her think of tale to tell them.

'Would anyone like to hear something about my husband?' Everyone muttered their consent. It was as good a subject as anything else.

'I don't miss much about him. He was a miserable selfish sod. But I do miss how he used to wake me up every morning. Every morning without fail! He was comical really.'

'How did he used to wake you up, Pat?' Kathy asked.

'He used to wake me up by banging something on my head and passing me a lit Capstan Full Strength every morning,' Pat said. Wee Renee laughed.

'Oh yes, you told me about that. It's a wonder you haven't got a dented forehead,' Wee Renee said.

'I miss it. I really do. He had an anchor tattoo. Very masculine. And a lovely bushy moustache.'

'Am I right in thinking that he used to bang your forehead with his er...' Our Doris asked.

'Yes!'

'It sounds like a film I saw in the seventies. X-rated.'

'That's probably where he got the idea, Our Doris.'

'Was he like Errol Flynn. I loved him,' Our Doris asked, a dreamy look on her face.

'No. Think Burt Reynolds with bad skin and you are on the right path.'

Kathy had a big soppy smile on her face, although she had only heard part of the story.

'That was a lovely story, Pat. What a romantic husband you had. What was his name?' Kathy asked. They walked for about two minutes, Pat furrowing her brow. Wee Renee looked amusingly at her. Pat burst out in huge guffaws.

'Do you know Kathy, I can't bloody remember.'

'She must be having a senior moment,' Wee Renee chimed in. 'He was named Dennis, and it is funny that you remember what he woke you up with, but not his name.'

Nigel found this amusing. Even Terry had a wry smile on his face.

Sue tried to rush all the children as quickly as she could, away from the school. She knew they did not have an enormous amount of time before it went dark. When she was talking to Norman, she knew she had to find them some kind of sanctuary. And that word exactly had given her an idea.

She wondered if there was anyone in the church. She hoped if they could get in there, that none of the undead could get to them. Obviously there would still be Michael Thompson, but they hopefully could deal with that one person.

There were a few churches in the village, but there was one in particular, St. Dominic's, that had grounds all the way around it. There was a graveyard on four sides of the church. Even though this was not nice to go through at night, she thought that this must all be consecrated ground. That would be like having a castle with a moat against the creatures. She realised that this was one of the farthest points of Friarmere and these children were scared and small, but this was their last chance of a safe place. She, and some of the others would just have to carry some along, if they couldn't make it. She hoped that Liz and Andy could get to them before it was dark too. They rushed through the village, which was silent. There looked to have been struggles in various houses. Some houses had been burnt out inside. They could not imagine the horrors that had taken place in the last few days. Whilst they were, in some respects, living in safety at Our Doris's house in Melden.

Adam realised that The Master had lied to him. He had made a deal and The Master was not keeping up his end of it. Adam had been assured that he could have Bob straight away. Now he had let them escape. Who knew if he could ever get Bob in a situation where he could turn him again.

Adam didn't like being on his own. The Master would pay for this. He would be a long time holding this grudge.

Keith and Stuart had taken Carl and Gary to a classroom on the left of the hall. They roughly grabbed them both by the arms, throwing them inside the room.

'I hope you aren't going to leave us here with no food or water,' Carl shouted.

'We will bring something later. Just be thankful you are still alive. That could change quite easily.' The vampires locked the door behind them.

They looked around the classroom. The blackout curtains were shut. Carl walked up to them and flung each one open, revealing a dying light outside. Now that they had a bit of light, Gary looked around for anything that they could use as a weapon. He thought there must be scissors for cutting paper, as there were plenty of cut flowers and shapes on the wall that the children had made.

He tried to open the teachers desk, finding it locked. That was probably where the scissors were. Carl discovered round one corner, that there were two little toilets. A boys and a girls. Strangely enough, he was quite desperate to use this. He hadn't eaten much, but had been drinking.

'I'm just using the loo, Gary,' he said.

Carl shut the door in the cubicle. It was now quite dark in there. He undid his trousers, and began to sit down. His bottom didn't hit anything. He went further and further down, surprised at just how low these tiny toilets were. When he finally reached it, he stretched his legs out, closing his eyes. He thought about the fact that him and Kate had wanted children at one point. Now that would never happen. Why was that too much to ask for? Now he just wanted to see her again whatever she was like. He needed some form of closure.

Gary was still looking around the classroom, opening up the children's trays that contained their work. Each one had their little name on it. Gary wondered how many of them were still alive. If they would ever use these trays again.

The chairs and tables were made of plastic. No chance of them being hacked up for stakes. He checked out the windows. They were very strong double glazed, from what he could see. They even had the words, safety glass stuck on them. So, probably not much chance of breaking out quickly, without the vampires hearing them and rushing in. It was a pity he didn't have Pat's lump hammer.

Gary's eyes frantically searched the classroom, from top to bottom. There must be something. There is always a way out. He wasn't going to give up.

The group from Melden had finally reached the peak of the hill. They began walking along the flat ridge, looking forward so much to being able to stop soon. They knew the worst part of this journey was over. Just flat walking, and down-bank tomorrow. Melden was far behind them now.

'You stupid woman!' Wee Renee shouted suddenly.

'Who?' Pat asked.

'Me. I haven't been using my secret weapon. I forgot!' They stopped for a brief moment whilst she rooted around in her bag. She got out some of the pieces of raw poisoned meat and scattered them about. 'When or if they come looking for us in Melden and can't find us, they will know where we have gone. If they get this far, we can hopefully stop them in their tracks.' Every so often she scattered a few pieces of the meat behind them.

Soon they could see Friarmere. It looked perfect and quaint. They could almost forget why they were here. In the arctic landscape, free, they tricked themselves into thinking that they hadn't got a care in the world. Pat and Wee Renee glanced at each other and smiled.

They were glad to be home, whatever hell they might encounter. They were so grateful for Our Doris's hospitality, but it was nothing like being in your own place with everything you knew, the shops, the pub, the bandroom. They would extend the same hospitality to Our Doris party, as they had received, naturally.

It was now mid afternoon, only a couple of hours of daylight left. Wee Renee said she was concerned about finding Bob's den again, but Terry reminded her to just follow the footprints.

'Oh heavens, my brain today. I don't know where it is. Of course,' Wee Renee said.

'We had better get a wriggle on actually Rene, because all bets will be off as soon as it gets dark,' Pat commented. Her friend nodded and reached in her bag for the poisoned meat. There were about ten pieces left. She considered the bag.

'Do you think I should scatter some meat near to the den? To protect us. Should I save what I have left for that?'

'Ooh, no. It will be more like a trail to us and by the time the drug has worked on them, if the meat is that close, they will have a chance at killing us. I think just putting it here will be the best thing to do. I've just had another thought too. We don't want it too near to where we are staying in case Haggis wanders out and eats some,' Terry said thoughtfully. They all looked horrified and realised that this was a dreadful thing to happen.

Wee Renee emptied out the contents of her meat bag. The last few red lumps plopped out onto the pristine snow. She estimated they were just over a mile away from Bob's den.

Sue's group got to the church. The gate was shut but they opened it with the latch. She led all the children through the graveyard, up the path and towards the church door. Tony took up the rear, shutting the gate behind them. She tentatively walked up to the churches big doors. Sue hoped it was open, or that someone was inside. There was no way they would be able to break in there. They still had a short amount of daylight left but if they could not get in here, she did not know where else to try.

The door did not open as they got close to it, even though there was quite a lot of children and nine adults chattering and stomping up the path. Maybe there was no one there. She knocked on the door. Using the big knocker, she banged again. She tried the latch, nothing. Then she thought she heard a slight noise from the other side.

'Shh!!' she said to everyone outside. She listened again. Nothing. She was sure someone was standing six inches away from her. Just the door between them.

'Please,' she said, 'is someone there. I have a lot of children here that need a safe place to stay, and it is going to be dark soon. If you are there please open up.' There was no answer. Laura came beside her to help. This was now an urgent situation.

'This is not a trick or anything. Do you think we would be out in the daytime, if we were one of them? Please, there are lots of children here. We need your help,' Laura said.

'Shout kids!' Sue said, and they did. *Help! Help us! Hello!* The kids shouted.

They all heard the large door unlock. The hasp opened and inside were about six people including the vicar.

'Come in, come in.' They all said. The group all filed in very quickly out of the cold. A lady in a nice tweed skirt and twinset addressed them.

'We were so worried, that you were one of those things. Tricking us.'

'We are the ones trying to fight them. We have rescued all of these children out of his clutches and couldn't' think of a better place to stay. Thank you for letting us in,' Sue said.

One of the ladies locked the door and another went to a pew against the window. She stood on it, looking through the stained glass.

'We usually start looking through the windows at this point in the evening,' the Vicar said. 'We would have seen you if you had been fifteen minutes later.'

'If we were fifteen minutes later, we probably wouldn't have got here,' Sally said.

'Have you been followed?' The lady asked at the window.

'I don't think so. But there are two more of our party to come here. Then I will tell you our story,' Sue said.

'I'll be glad to get out of the triangle, tomorrow morning, I can tell you. We've been lucky. But I've been blessing us and surrounding us in a bubble of glittery light. It's worked, as you can see,' Wee Renee said.

'What triangle?' Nigel asked.

'Rene's tinsel triangle,' Pat giggled.

'Eh!' Nigel said.

'Take no notice of Pat, cheeky devil. You will see my tinsel triangle, in time. And I think you will be shocked at it. When you see it in the flesh, well…. it's hard to ignore.'

'I'm still none the wiser. Worried but intrigued, I think I would call myself,' Nigel said, desperate to know more.

'I am on about the Melden triangle. We are in it now. It cuts off the top of Friarmere. This hill, Melden and Moorston are included.'

'Surely a triangle has three points but you are only mentioning two villages.' Terry said.

'Aye, I'll give you that one. You will see it. Think of it more, in technical terms, that you have a scalene triangle, not an equilateral. Does that help you?'

'A bit. But what's the third point?'

'Bloody hell, Terry.' Pat said loudly. 'The triangle is not the important part. It's what is inside it. If it makes you feel better, the other point is the reservoir!'

'Alright!' Terry replied, a little embarrassed.

'Well we've sorted out that bit, and I realize we aren't talking about Wee Renee's private parts now. Can we get to the important bit? What is in the triangle?' Nigel asked. Wee Renee laughed. Pat elbowed her in the side.

'I told you it sounded rude, all along Rene.'

'Ok, I believe you. But it is what it is. It *is* my tinsel triangle.'

'I thought you were on about your tuppence as well!' Our Doris said. All the women thought it was hilarious but the two men had red, angry faces.

'The Melden Triangle is like the Bermuda Triangle but worse! That's it, in it's simplest terms,' Wee Renee said.

'Worse than the Bermuda Triangle? Where ships and planes have gone missing?' Terry asked.

'Oh yes.'

'Go on. I'll buy it. Why?' Nigel asked.

'People go missing all the time. Never to be seen again. Weird lights can be seen overhead. Armies of ancient ghosts walk through it. Wee faeries dance in the day and wraith's drift at night. Black magic rituals are performed, there are ancient monoliths, secret caves containing lost creatures and great black beasts hunt at night. There are evil mermaids in the reservoir. That is just a small part.'

'Shit!' Nigel said. 'That's is worse.'

'How do you know all that is not a load of hokum?' Terry asked.

'I have witnessed most of it. Apart from the missing people.'

'Are you calling Rene a liar?' Pat asked. She looked at Terry out of one eye. He didn't reply.

'You aren't the first to laugh at my triangle,' Wee Renee said. 'But now, consider this. Who lives in a house, in this part of the triangle, Norman. Who is over there, Anne. I wouldn't be surprised if one has moved into Moorston!'

'Oh, don't say that, Wee Renee. It gives me the willies. We can't even cope with two of them,' Kathy said.

'I am sorry Kathy. Don't die of ignorance. Everything comes in three's in my experience and there are two of them and one part of the triangle left we don't know about. I am sure of it. Mark my words.' It was a sobering thought, mostly for Pat. She knew her friends track record in these matters. She was always 100% right. The atmosphere was back however.

'It's so cold isn't it?' Kathy said.

'And bleak here. We are vulnerable. What if a really dark cloud comes over us. A snow cloud and it is dark enough for them all to get us,' Terry said.

'You are a little ray of sunshine today, aren't you,' Pat said. Our Doris looked sideways at Pat and Wee Renee. Something had better get done and quick. The *ray of sunshine* comment had given her an idea.

'What are you talking about, Kathy. Cold? It's boiling,' Our Doris shouted. Everyone stared at Our Doris, was she having a senior moment now, and didn't know where she was. She winked at Nigel. 'The sun is cracking the blasted pavement between our feet. The sky is blue, the sand is warm between our toes and we can hear the sea. Can you hear that? A song.' She lifted one of the flaps up on her earmuff's. She started to hum the song, badly and tunelessly. As was not a musician, none of them could recognise it.

'What are you talking about Our Doris?' Terry said, a little agitated. She ignored him.

'It's so tropical. Get your bikini's on, guess where we are going?' Then she started to sing and they knew what she was up to.

Oh, this year
We're off to cause some pain

'Come on everyone!' She raised her arms in the air, wafting them this way and that, in the imaginary hot sunshine. Now they knew the tune was *Y Viva España.* They began to sing.

Oh, this year
We're off to cause some pain
In the tinsel triangle
Off to decapitate
And maim
In the tinsel triangle
If you'd like to
Walk across the moor
Have a deep snowy ramble
Then find and kill
A carnivore
Blood and guts galore!

'Again!' she shouted. They sang it again and again. Even Terry. It was hard to stay sad and cold when you sang that. Our Doris had a big smile on her face, her eyes were closed. She sang as loud as she was able. The song rang out through the Saddleworth Moors. Only the snow heard it. It was silly, but so beautiful.

'Are you warmer now, Kathy?' Our Doris asked. Kathy was rosy and content, everything was going to be ok. She would get on a plane one day again. They would win. She knew it now.

'I feel wonderful, Our Doris. Thank you.'

'Just a warning. If anyone says they are cold again, we all have to sing that five times! It's the law!' Our Doris said.

The dying embers of the day were close and they realised that soon they had to find shelter. Friarmere was becoming ever nearer. They couldn't' have missed it surely. Then Wee Renee saw the sign for Lazy Farm and knew it was basically opposite the entrance.

'We are close,' she said, 'keep your eyes peeled.' Our Doris was extremely relieved about this. Even though the antibiotics had been working, she was starting to flag. After all, she had retired a long time ago now and all this had been one hell of a hike in the snow. They saw the place where the footprints had gone. They followed quickly, getting off the road onto the path. The snow was still too thick for normal vehicles. Norman's snowmobiles however, would be able to pass up the road, although they could see no tracks. He must have cut across the moors and come out just above Melden. The path off the road was too narrow for even a snowmobile, so they were happy that Norman wouldn't come across them by chance.

'I am pooped, I can tell you that, for nowt,' Kathy said.

'We will be settled within five minutes, you just wait and see,' Wee Renee reassured her. When they got over the dry-stone wall, the others could not see where Pat was leading them too. All of a sudden they saw a flap of blue tarpaulin. The wanderers had arrived. They were surprised at how warm, dry and cosy it was underneath the tarpaulin. Unpacking commenced.

Our Doris put down the dog's thick pad so he could lie down next to her. She fed him first with items out of her backpack and gave him a drink of water. He seemed to want to lie under her blanket with her, which made them both warm. She got out her flask of soup. With six in the party, there was nearly a full tin each, but they would have to take turns with the cup. The friends each ate their sandwiches, waiting for their turn with the cup of soup. There was a small amount of coffee left and Our Doris said it would be cold by the morning, so they might as well have it now. She said she was having a nip of whisky in hers and that was up to them. Without exception everyone had a nip as well. Our Doris had given the other group the parkin but she had decided to venture into her Christmas cake that she had made a month ago. She had been feeding it Brandy on a daily basis. Our Doris always made a large one. She liked a piece of Christmas cake nearly every day with a drink at eleven o'clock. It was a deep twelve-inch fruitcake, which would remain forever un-iced. She had sliced it up at home and then packed it back into a circle. They all took some, even Terry, who wasn't fond of anything containing dried fruit. Their bodies absorbed the sugar, butter and alcohol. It was tasty and rich, doing them the world of good.

After they had finished their meal they felt extremely content and happy. Wee Renee remembered the night that she stayed here. In the cold blackness, herself and Gary had heard the wolves. She hoped they would not hear them tonight, but feared she might. Tonight would be far more dangerous. Now they were being hunted. Before they would have found them by chance. She voiced this opinion to the others, advising them that they should sleep with their weapons out. The group then made a schedule of people for the watch. Our Doris's eyes were closing even before it was made. She fell asleep almost instantly, they gave her the last watch. Terry didn't feel too bad at all, so he took the first one and hoped he would feel tired after two hours watch. The rest fell asleep within ten minutes, apart from Wee Renee. She started to talk to thin air. Terry watched her with his mouth open. She focused on an area twelve inches from her nose. Every so often she would say a few words. 'Aye...I see. I know. Thankyou. Aye Bless you.' Then she laughed and said 'Farewell, I hope to see you again.'

'What's going on?' Terry asked.

'I have just had a conversation which was very informative. I am content about what is in Friarmere now, and our future.'

'Who told you?'

'A wee faerie. Didn't you see him?'

'No.'

'Ah yes. You aren't open enough. You will see him as something else.

'What?'

'A single midge.'

'Do you mean, like when midges are in a swarm, in the summer?'

'Aye, that is them. But there was only one of him.'

'I didn't even see a single midge!'

'Well Terry, you are sitting ten feet away after all. That's not his fault is it?'

'I suppose not. What did he say exactly!'

'That all signs are good. We will have obstacles and bring disruption to The Beast's plans. In time we will be victorious. Good night, Terry,' she said.

'Good night,' he replied. Terry was alone with his thoughts. About the midge, Sally and unfortunately Pat's husband. He sighed, watching Haggis cuddled against Our Doris. Cosy and warm together.

Anne rose as soon as it was dark and walked out to her other wolves in the pens. Her alpha pack had definitely not returned. She spoke to the wolves in another language, which they seemed to understand. She told them what had happened and that they were going to have to find some meat tonight. Anne spoke to her remaining children and said that they were going to go back to the house and get those people. If they had escaped, she would find them. Even if it meant running all the way to Friarmere. It started to snow and she knew this was not good for the wolves scent but nevertheless, she was determined to find them tonight.

Maurice went out on one of his jaunts. He liked to do this only because he might pick up information about his friends from the band. He didn't feel the cold and he was also not worried about attacking anyone, because there was never anyone about these days. The supply of liver had dried up, as the shops were empty now. Nearly two weeks had gone by since a delivery. Maurice knew that as long as his electricity remained, he would have a supply for months, tucked away in his chest freezer.

He was standing outside the pub looking through the window when who should he see wandering around looking for victims, but Stephen Thompson.

'Hello Steve,' Maurice said. 'What are you up to, as if I don't know?'

'Just after a bite to eat, Maurice. Although The Master has plenty tucked away, but they don't keep forever, so we might as well get some before they expire in their houses.'

'I see, good thinking. Any goings-on up there?'

'There is as a matter of fact. You know we had all them kids up at the school.'

'Er...no I didn't actually.' He was quite shocked that he had not heard this snippet or maybe they had kept it away from him. Stephen was and always had been an open book, so he would tell him everything.

'Yeah, yeah. We had quite a lot of kids up there, that we had rounded up. The Master was using them for bait, to get the others back. They were over in Melden, you know. There is some of us over there, our cousins. So Norman's sister, Anne went and told them that we had all these kids. Some of them, not all of them, came back. The Master did an exchange for some of the kids. But now he has a special prize in there and they have to get the oldies back over here, or he won't get released. I don't know what they think will happen after that. If they think they are going scot, free they aren't.'

'What oldies?'

'Pat, Wee Renee and Freddie. They are still in Melden.'

'Where are the kids now?' asked Maurice.

'Beats me. But we'll find them. Don't you worry. We'll find where they are, sniff them out and get them back. Probably better not to do it though until the oldies are here, or else we will be showing our hand.'

'So who have they got? What is the big prize?'

'They've got Gary as a hostage. Until they fetch the others. They have also got this guy from Melden. He wanted to go as an exchange, so there's two of them up there. They should last with the gang up there for a bit, until the others get back, at least.'

'That all very interesting. How's your brother?'

'Still down, because The Master won't turn him. But you can see his point. He needs someone that can wander around in the day. Michael will get it at some point. I have told him not to worry, but he does. The Master shouts at him a lot too. I said he is just a bit moody sometimes. But don't tell The Master that. He's pretty decent really,' Stephen laughed. 'Michael wasn't happy today though. The Master told him to trap all the lot from Melden in the school with a chain and padlock. Instead Andy and Liz got *him* and chained him up inside a car. We all stood outside and laughed for ages at him before The Master would unchain him. He was livid Maurice, especially with me for some reason.'

'Alright I had better get on, Steve. See you around.' Maurice walked off, deep in thought.

'Do you want to come out with me, hunting?' Stephen shouted after him.

'No, no lad.' Maurice had a lot to think about.

Excerpt from Anne's Diary.

Thursday 15th of December
I wanted to get them tonight. I wanted to kill all of them in revenge. I had to take a younger pack of wolves out. They have not been out with me over the past week. They do not have this groups scent. I went back to the house that we had fought in. Tonight it was empty. I could smell that. They seemed to have dragged my two victims, my children and my sweet Sophia, plus her sisters, into the house next door.

I will wait, go take what is mine. The door was locked but later we will go there. My new pack can't smell the Friarmere lot. (I don't know why) The pack managed to follow a brief scent of some of them into the village and then they seemed to split up. But, what do you think? One of them is bleeding, bitten by my sweet Sophia. I think I can smell the man very slightly. Guess where? The other house with the walls. Of all the places! Now I can't get to them until they make a mistake. And they will. I may have to involve my brother Len in this matter. (sigh) I am again outnumbered.

At one am, Wee Renee was on duty. She looked out of the tarpaulin, to the path and saw that it was snowing. That this was great to cover their tracks but it would also cover up the meat for the wolves. She hoped that one would cancel out the other. If they couldn't smell the meat then they couldn't smell them either. Wee Renee thought about everything the faerie had said. Help would come from an unexpected source. From three of *them* in Moorston. Did he mean three vampires? He said this was the only way. She hoped to see him again, but would have to steer this group to their fate. Well this winter wasn't proving to be boring. She could say that in all honesty. Wee Renee settled down to do the job she was there for and listened until her ears hurt for the sound of the howls.

36 – Tracks

Norman was out that night. He did not want to eat the children, but he did want to know where they were. He could then quickly pick them up after the trade with Gary was made. Children were precious to him and he would make sure that he enjoyed every last one of them, one way or another.

It hadn't taken them long to find out where the bandsmen had taken the children. Bit of a hitch really. They could not just go in and get them, when they wanted to. The one named Sue had been a clever bitch.

'What are we going to do about this Master? They have got all the children tucked away in an impossible place for us.' Keith, Stuart and Stephen whined. Kate was very upset as this was her favourite thing of all to eat.

'Why did you let them take my food. They are on consecrated ground now. We cannot get them Master,' Kate said.

'Don't worry, we will burn them out. We can easily throw some Molotov cocktails in there. Burn it all. There are ways for us to make consecrated ground, unconsecrated. I haven't been around all this time and not learned a few things.'

'Michael could go and set fires outside. He could walk right up to the door,' Kate said. 'He could smoke them out. But if we burn them inside, they won't be nice to eat. We need them to come to us, alive.'

'It won't be a problem. It is just a little hiccup. Turn your frown upside down. Let's go raiding some houses. We might find some more little cherubs for your tummy,' Norman said

'You are a good Master.'

'You know, I have been lonely all day at the school without my trusted sentries. You at Christine's house. I have missed having you at my side. You did miss the fuss, when they came back and brought some other people with them. I reckon you will get round to conversing with them all at some point, won't you?' Norman said. Kate smiled and they set off walking, to *pillage the village* once again.

Mark was watching them from afar. Taking it all in. He enjoyed watching everything from a distance, never close up. Mark thought he might have a wander through the streets himself and see if he could find some mischief.

He was not hungry tonight, but still might be able to enjoy himself. As he turned into one street, there was a man standing under the lamplight. The man in the street noticed the vampire, turning towards him. Mark started to walk up to him thinking that this was his lucky night for a bit of tea, he might get his appetite back. When he got closer he noticed that it was one of his old friends from band. Maurice looked up at him.

'I thought you might come past. Can I have a word?'

The group in the den, woke up refreshed the following morning. They were ready to get on with the job. After having a small breakfast consisting of fruitcake and sandwiches, they packed up and set off. Their arrival in Friarmere was not expected. They did not know where to aim for. The snow that had fallen last night was powdery, lying on top of compacted glacial layers. It was chilly and the sun kept trying to come out for them. As they walked down the road, past The Grange, they looked for movement of any kind. Wee Renee wanted to check on a lady called Mary, who she feared might have been attacked. She took Pat up the drive to investigate.

The door was ajar, propped open with a rock and all the curtains were open. They looked into the front room. Wee Renee gasped from the shock of the scene. Mary, now a vampire, was nailed to the floor at the hands. She didn't have to think for long to imagine the scene.

'Come on everyone,' Pat said. The two Friarmere ladies, didn't tell the others what they had seen. It was just a scene from a horror movie. That was all over with now. Nothing to see here. Move along. They were even more vigilant now. Their eyes darting from windows to gardens and further into the village. They hoped to find the group quite quickly, as they really had no idea where they would be. Wee Renee walked to her house. She encouraged everyone to come in and look at her tinsel triangle, and they started to walk up her drive. The back door was open and items were strewn about. But other than that it was fine. She had hoped that yesterday's group would have left a note. She found nothing. Wee Renee introduced them to her CSI board and local map, enhanced by three pieces of red tinsel. They were amazed that so much had happened in such a small area and no one had picked it up previously. Especially the police. Wee Renee had wanted to check on something and searched on her walls for a particular piece of paper. She read it quietly to herself, muttering, so no one could hear her.

'Well, I knew there was something, but well, what do you think about that? Especially now, in the season. How lucky are we?'

'What's up?' asked Pat.

'Nothing, just a teeny chance of something wonderful. Ignore me.' She looked very contented.

They next visited Sue and Tony's house, which was only a couple of houses down from hers, on the other side of the road. It was quite clear that the group had been there yesterday. They had picked up supplies and had a meal. *Would they have maybe tried the school?* That could have been a bit too obvious. It had only lightly snowed in the night. They were still able to see the faint footprints in the snow. The group discovered that they did lead up to the school. They were uncertain as to whether to go up, as this could be where the trap was. There were lots of footprints coming in and out of the school. There were footprints that were quite clearly made after the snow had fallen last night. These were probably vampires footprints. Wee Renee didn't think the others were stupid enough to be running around at night.

There was also a faint group of footprints that led away down to the village. Mostly these were quite small, mixed in with big ones.

'Do you know what?' said Wee Renee, 'I think they did it. I think they got the kids away.' The looked at the evidence and could only come up with the same conclusion. Walking down towards the village, following the footprints, Wee Renee said that she would be calling at the shops to try and get some food for the kiddies. 'Those nightwalkers won't have fed them. Who knows how long they have gone without. Kids still like bread and jam don't they? I know I did.' She spoke to the others, but just as much she was talking to herself.

When they got into the centre of Friarmere, the main food shop had the shutters down. They walked round to the side and were startled to see the door was open inside.

Wee Renee looked at the others as if to say *what she what should we do?* They had no answers so she shrugged, beckoning them to come with her to the rear door.

Just around the corner, in the dark, there were two vampires lying on the floor. It was hard to decide whether vampires are dead or alive in the daytime, because they were always dead really. Terry, Kathy, Nigel and Our Doris took a good look at their first pure vampires. They were quite surprised at how perfect they looked. They were very unlike the creatures in Melden.

'What shall we do? Drag them out into the light?' Our Doris asked.

'Yes. But we have to drag them through some of the dark before that. They might wake up.'

'So what's to be done?'

'Hmmm, why are they here? They don't eat our food,' Pat said.

Our Doris and Wee Renee looked at each other. They could work this out. They both said it together.

'Because they are guarding *our* food, so we can't eat it. It's a trap!'

'What about if we come here,' Our Doris said and moved to the other side of the vampire. 'Whack them both at the same time.'

'Yes,' Wee Renee said, stepping over the vampire. 'Get ready, you lot. You are our back up if we fail.' Our Doris raised her sword, Wee Renee her machete.

'Are you sure you want to do this, ladies? I am sure me and Terry can do this for you,' Nigel said. Terry cleared his throat.

'Er..yes. I'm willing,' he said.

'Not on your Nellie!' said Our Doris. They brought their weapons down in unison.

There was a strange smell, like mould but also a whiff of the dead, like spoiled meat. The two vampires slightly screamed in their sleep, as they departed. The party looked closely at their faces. Wee Renee and Pat did not recognise the corpses. The two vampires were obviously guarding the food store and for all intents and purposes, it looked well stocked.

'Wait a minute, they were lying in front of that door, rather than the open archway into the shop,' Pat said. 'What are they really guarding? What is so important in that room?' She was worried that there was something more sinister in this shop. Maybe Norman had been out on a jolly and forgot what time it was. Maybe he was lying in there, looking at the ceiling with his dead eyes. Waiting for them.

Before they embarked on a mission that they might quickly run away from they decided to check the shop. Terry and Nigel dragged the two vampires outside by their feet one by one. They put them in a pile in an alley.

The shop had a few empty shelves especially items like bakery and fresh milk. However, there was plenty of other food available for the children.

'Lets see this room then.' Pat said. The little army all got their weapons out.

'I will open the door after a countdown of three,' Nigel said. He grasped the storeroom door handle. He got a feeling like there was another hand on the other side of the handle, ready to turn it faster than him. He took a big breath mouthing the words *three, two, one*. Nigel flung the storeroom door open. Surprisingly it was quite empty apart from three large wholesale boxes of Weetabix and a plastic, waist high, white barrel with a fitted lid. Wee Renee walked into the room and over to the barrel. She could see that there was a label on the back.

'Mayonnaise!' She raised her eyebrows at them. 'What do they need with a load of Weetabix and a vat of mayonnaise?'

'The mind boggles with them bastards,' Pat grunted. Wee Renee had the idea that she would have a look inside the catering vat of mayonnaise as she noticed the seal was broken. *Was it still fresh?* She pulled the lid up carefully which made a cracking sound as she opened it. She saw what was inside and quickly banged the lid back down, shaking her head.

'I think we'll leave that there!' she said.

'What is it?' Kathy asked.

'Not mayonnaise.'

'What the hell is in there?' Our Doris asked.

'From what I could see, human eyes. Complete with long tendrils. Floating in a thick clear fluid!' she said matter-of-factly.

'Are you kidding?' Pat exclaimed.

'I can assure you Pat, I aren't.'

'They might have been sheep's eyes,' Pat said.

'They are not. I had a wee lamb as a pet when I was a bairn. They have yellow and brown eyes, and their pupils are crossways. I saw blue and brown and hazel eyes in there. Round human adult eyes. All mixed up in the blood and goo. Do you want to check?' She asked.

'No you're all right. I'll take your word for it?'

'I will never un-see that sight,' Wee Renee said and shivered.

'I don't think there's much food in here for the kids,' Our Doris stated.

'No, I think we'll leave it,' Wee Renee said flatly. They were just about to walk out of the door when Terry had a thought.

'I wonder if that really is boxes of Weetabix.'

'I'll do this one,' Nigel said.

'Thanks,' Wee Renee said, 'I don't think I could face what's in a big box after what I have just seen in that barrel.' Nigel walked over to the boxes and went to pick one up. He picked it up easily shook it, then opened the cardboard flap to look inside.

'That's Weetabix mate.' He said, walking back out into the shop.

'Wasn't I just the lucky one?' Wee Renee said.

'What shall we get?' Kathy asked.

'Some biscuits. Kids like them. Chocolate ones. Some skimmed longlife milk and a few of them little boxes of cereal. They can have what they want then.' Our Doris said helpfully. There were only the little boxes of cereal left. All the other boxes had been taken. They did not know how many children they would find. They might get a chance for another trip to the shop today, if they found them in time. Now that these two had been dispatched they couldn't see any more coming before tonight. They lashed the food that they had taken to Our Doris's sledge and off they went. Our Doris had wiped all the vampire blood off her sword on the snow outside.

'You know, I might want to put this back up one time, in the same place on my wall. As a memory of how brave I have been,' she said.

'When this is all over, you could probably sell it for hundreds of pounds on Ebay,' Pat commented.

'Try thousands,' Nigel said. They followed the steps as best they could, hoping that they were still on the right track. A few children's steps had been trampled over from the previous night's vampire activity. As they made their way through the village, on occasion they would see an area of scorched earth in the snow. Pat wondered what had been going on. Wee Renee thought she might see a very different Friarmere at night than she had previously, when it was her old sleepy village.

'I am a bit worried,' said Kathy. 'These prints seem to be going the length of Friarmere. You have told me how they trick people. After all they tricked us to come here. I wondered if the vampires are trying to trick us using little shoeprints.'

'I don't think so,' said Wee Renee. 'But you never know. He didn't know we would be coming today. We have a few hours anyway before dark. We will sort it.' When they turned the corner and saw what was in front of them, a massive grin spread across Wee Renee's face. She knew exactly where they had taken the kids and she couldn't think of a better place. It had big doors and was surrounded by a huge impenetrable holy moat.

'They are safe,' she said. 'They are all safe.'

Michael was standing fifty feet behind Wee Renee and her group. The Master had sent him on an errand to the shop. He was to bring a scoop of the imported Eastern European eyes from the guarded tub in the storeroom. The Master didn't let anyone else touch them only Michael. Apparently they were much too tempting for a vampire to pick up. Even the guards didn't know what was in there. He had a plastic food bag in his pocket and the ladle from Bonfire Night. He was going to pick up a couple of things up for himself, out of the main shop too. Ten minutes earlier and he would have been trapped. Grabbed again by his old band mates. Now he felt wonderful. What a chance sighting. He would be in The Master's favour now. Definitely no sign of Freddie, but Wee Renee and Pat were back in Friarmere, with a few new people. The Master would be pleased. Michael kept his distance. He walked from doorway to doorway until he saw them go in – He would deliver them to The Master on a plate.

THE END

Until Book 3

37303396R00242

Printed in Poland
by Amazon Fulfillment
Poland Sp. z o.o., Wrocław